NOTHING NEW FOR
SOPHIE DREW

KATEY LOVELL

BLOODHOUND
— BOOKS —

Print ISBN 978-1-913942-50-2

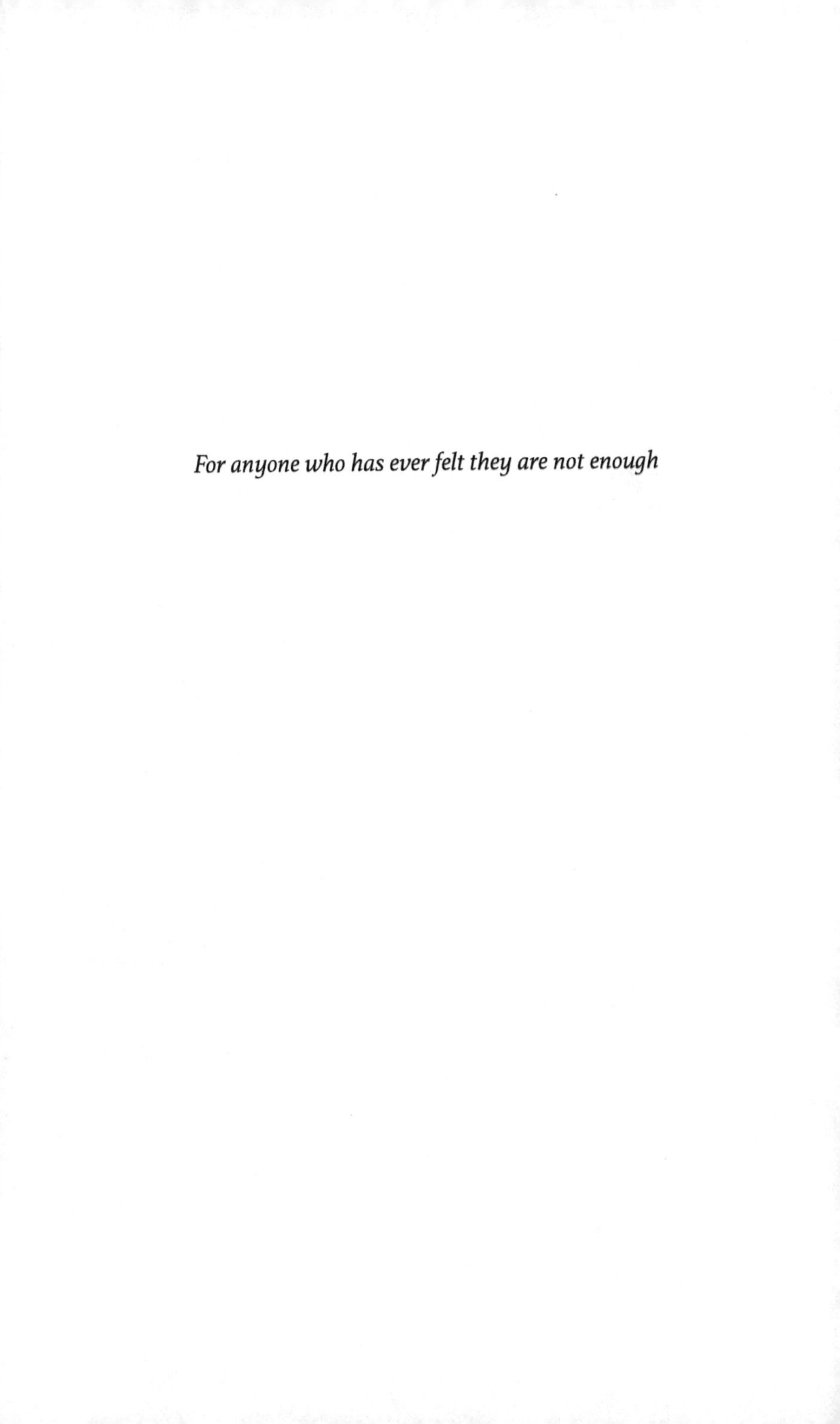

For anyone who has ever felt they are not enough

FEBRUARY

CHAPTER 1

"Show me again," Eve demanded, wrapping her hand around the door handle. "You're supposed to look surprised, remember."

My jaw dropped, my eyes widened and my hands flew to my cheeks, the way I'd seen actors in films behave when unexpectedly delighted. It might work in Hollywood, but I, quite frankly, felt ridiculous.

My best friend's lips curled, her expression somewhere between disappointment and disapproval and she shook her head at my efforts, her perfectly coiffured chocolate-brown bob swaying from side to side. That, along with the two deep-grooved vertical lines that appeared between her eyebrows, was enough to tell me my acting abilities were well below par.

I don't know why Eve expected me to be able to conjure up an on-the-spot Oscar-worthy performance. We'd been in the same GCSE Drama class at comprehensive school, both of us scraping passes. Neither of us excelled when it came to treading the boards. Eve was the brainbox who loved any scientific geekery and I was creative, but textiles and crafting were my mediums of choice, not performing. Our friend, Tawna, the third point of our friendship triangle, hadn't been much good at anything at school, other than snogging boys around the back of the sports hall.

"No, Sophie, just no! It's meant to be a surprise. Don't over-egg it or they'll think I've told you."

"But you did tell me," I reminded her. "If you were better at keeping secrets in the first place we wouldn't be in this position and I wouldn't need to act surprised because I would actually *be* surprised."

"I wish Tawna hadn't trusted me with getting you here," Eve grumbled. "She knows I'm rubbish at keeping my mouth shut."

Eve had always been the same. Back when we were at school, cocky teenagers with our skirts rolled up at the waistband to show off our pale, skinny legs, Tawna and I never shared who we were crushing on with Eve unless we wanted her to put the feelers out with the clichéd "my friend fancies you" line. She'd never been able to engage her brain before opening her mouth. For someone so clever she spent a lot of time in a dreamworld, and one which didn't align with real-life in Newcastle. The phrase 'away with the fairies' could have been coined about Eve.

I picked a speck of fluff from the sleeve of my black velvet dress – bought especially for what Tawna had dubbed my birthday night out, although Eve had already told me it was a party – ready to make my grand entrance. If all eyes were going to be on me, I needed to look my best. That had been my thought process when I'd teamed the dress with a pair of sky-high sequin-coated silver heels and a thick diamond choker. I'd had it a year but never worn it, but I'd come to the conclusion that when it comes to partywear there's no such thing as too much sparkle. I'd also stopped at the salon for a spray tan on the way home from the office, splashing out on a manicure and pedicure as well, seeing as I was there.

My credit card had taken quite a hammering and I hoped people would shout me a drink or two to celebrate the upcoming milestone birthday, because my card had to be edging closer to its limit. The bank had taken to sending me daily texts about my current account too, informing me I was well over my agreed overdraft limit. But I didn't have time to waste worrying about my finances. A bar full of people were waiting for me to make an entrance.

"I won't tell her you mentioned the party," I promised, "although she must've known you'd not be able to keep something as huge as this to yourself. Come on, let's get it over and done with. I could do with a drink. Pretending to be in the dark is stressing me out."

A raucous cheer of "Surprise" rang out as Eve pushed the door open.

I pulled my best "I really had no idea this was going to happen" face, as Jane from work offered me a hug and Tawna, wearing a little black dress so skintight that I suspected she may have had to have be sewn into it, pressed a glass of something fizzy into my hand. The bubbles tingled pleasantly against the roof of my mouth as I took a large, grateful gulp. The alcohol hit the right spot – the spot that would get me through facing up to Tawna.

"I know she told you." A flash of annoyance appeared on Tawna's face despite the thick make-up she was wearing. Primer, foundation, concealer, blusher. Eyeshadow, eyeliner, mascara. Eyebrows pencilled into bow-shaped arches. Lips carefully lined and coloured in with a neutrally shaded lipstick. It was all part of the daily routine for Tawna.

"I didn't mean to," Eve fumbled, genuinely apologetic. "But she guessed and I couldn't lie."

"It doesn't matter," Tawna said, with a sigh that suggested disappointment. "The most important thing is that everyone has a good night, especially you, Soph. After all, it's not every day you turn thirty!"

I groaned, resisting the urge to remind her I had another two full days of my twenties left to revel in. Birthdays are a good excuse to get drunk, and of course, I like the presents (who doesn't like presents?), but I didn't relish the thought of edging ever-closer to middle age. Not purely through vanity, although that did amplify my concerns. A solitary grey hair had recently made an appearance, and I had promptly plucked it out, wrapped it in a tissue and flushed it down the loo so I wouldn't have to see it again. The first small creases were becoming visible at the corners of my eyes too – not prominent enough to class as wrinkles, but very definitely there. But it wasn't only my changing looks making me twitchy. When I was young, I'd assumed that by the time I hit the big three-oh my life would be sorted. A successful career, a nice husband, a couple of kids...

It hadn't happened like that though. Substitute the career for a dead-end admin job at a law firm in town, the husband for an ex-boyfriend who I missed more than I let on and the kids for next door's cat (who kept sneaking in through the kitchen window to piss on the floor) and you'd be closer to my reality.

"I'm going to need more alcohol," I said, having finished my first glass in record speed.

As I placed the empty glass on the table I noticed the cake – a full-on multi-tiered centrepiece like you'd see in the celebrity wedding spreads in *OK!* magazine. How I'd managed to miss it before, I don't know. It was enormous.

"What's that?" I gestured towards the showstopping cake. "It's a birthday party, not a bloody wedding reception." I realised how ungrateful my comment sounded after it had left my mouth.

As Tawna tightened her grip on the stem of her glass and bit down on her lip I felt bad for being such a grump, but I hadn't wanted any of this fuss. When the girls asked how I wanted to celebrate my birthday I'd been perfectly clear – a night out on the lash, just the three of us. We'd bump into people we knew when we got into town, because that's what Newcastle's like. Even if you don't plan to meet up with people, you end up in the same bars as friends, colleagues, acquaintances, exes... that's what happens. There's a good reason the city has a reputation as a party town and draws stag and hen dos from all over the country every weekend, and the lively welcoming atmosphere is part of that. It's just irritating at times, because everyone knows everyone else's business.

"We had it made especially at that cute place that does the cupcakes you like." My friend looked stung.

"I bet it tastes delicious," I said kindly, desperately trying to make up for my snappiness.

Despite its ridiculous size, the cake did look amazing. The frosting was thick and swirling, and piped pink buttercream roses decorated with edible metallic silver balls that looked as though they'd chip your teeth when you bit into them lined the cake base. Pale pink petals were scattered across the silver board. It couldn't have been cheap. Even the cupcakes at that shop were pricey, so a gigantic cake must have been extortionate. Not that money was a worry for Tawna. Nothing was.

"I asked for the pink especially," she said, admiring my freshly painted nails (baby pink except for the index fingers which were a glittery hot pink. My toes matched too, I couldn't resist). "I know it's your favourite colour."

Her words softened me. The extravagant gesture was typical of Tawna – she could be so thoughtful. It was just one reason why although we frequently had our differences I could never stay mad at her for long.

"It's incredible."

I wrapped her in a hug, inhaling her familiar scent. Tawna

had worn the same perfume forever – DKNY, the green one that came in a bottle shaped like an apple. It was my go-to present for her at birthdays or Christmas, whereas her gifts for me were always original, even if not necessarily what I'd choose for myself. The cake took the biscuit, pardon the pun.

"You should mingle," Eve suggested, swaying her hips in time to the thumping chart music blasting out from the speakers. "Everyone's here for you."

The thought of being sociable after a long week at work exhausted me. That's why I'd suggested a night out for just us three. I turn into a cowbag when I'm cream-crackered, only wanting to surround myself with people I like. Not that I didn't like the people at the party. I should've been flattered they'd given up their precious Friday night to celebrate with me – but with the party being in my honour the pressure to be the hostess with the mostest landed on me.

The work posse – Jane and Kath and Marcie – were drinking like fish. Kath was the same age as my mum (fifty-six) but had become something of a party animal since her divorce. Maybe more of a party cougar, actually, spending her weekends on the prowl in town, eyeing up men half her age because she swore the males from her own generation couldn't keep up with her. Jane and Marcie were more traditional, but they too loved a drink. Our Christmas staff night out had been an alarmingly messy affair which had shown me a different side to their personalities. Marcie's in particular. At work she was a stickler for the rules, continuously reminding us that as head of the admin team she had to be. After four flaming sambucas the rules had gone out of the window. She'd been the life and soul.

My relatives were gathered around a circular table at the end of the room. Mum and Dad smooched like a couple of randy teenagers, which would've been quite sweet if they were anyone other than my parents. Even after thirty-four years they still can't keep their hands off each other. They were the model couple, flanked on one side by my stunningly beautiful younger sister, Anna (who'd flown in from Austria for the event with her husband, Jakob), and on the other by my brother, Nick, and his wife, Chantel, who were playing hidey-boo with my gorgeous chunk of a nephew. Ten-month-old Noah was the apple of all of our eyes. I dreaded to think what he'd be like when he was older. We'd probably have ruined him by spoiling him rotten.

I'm the least settled of the Drew siblings, despite being the eldest. I hadn't take the university route like Anna and Nick had. I hadn't secured a regular job with a good wage either, instead moving from one temp job in an airless box of an office to another before settling at my current workplace when they'd offered me a permanent contract. Three years on the work itself remained mind-numbing, but at least the people were nice. Being that bit older they were like additional mums to me; always probing to see if there were any men on the scene and keen to offer words of wisdom off the back of their own life experiences.

A couple of former colleagues from one of the more long-term temp stints were throwing shapes on the dance floor, and the old gang from school swooped in early to hit the mini quiches and bite-size onion bhajis from the buffet. I'm not sure why Tawna thought them worthy of an invite, because although we got along fine, other than a quick hello or clicking a polite "like" on their Facebook posts once in a while, we didn't mix socially. Maybe they were invited to bump up the numbers, because the private room she'd hired at the back of one of Newcastle's most exclusive bars was gigantic.

The football posse were laughing in a corner. They'd been sitting near each other in the Gallowgate end at St James' Park since I was a kid, back when we were in the Champions League and had a team worth shouting about. Dad took me to my first match – on Boxing Day, when I was five – and I'd only missed a handful of home games over the years that followed. People were surprised to hear that, because they hold on to this stupid idea that only a certain type of person goes to the football, and I don't fit the stereotype of "pot-bellied middle-aged man in an ill-fitting replica shirt, knocking back pints for fun". There are people like that at the football – I know, because I've seen them myself on a match day – but our friends smash that theory apart. There was Fred and Norma – spritely, despite being in their eighties – and Joel and Finley, who were the sweetest couple you could ever hope to meet. Burly Bez, who was a local legend after getting the club crest tattooed on his forehead as a dare, looked like a numbskull but was a total sweetheart once you got to know him. They were a motley crew, but I was glad Tawna had invited them. Dad kept me updated with what was going on, both on the pitch and in our friends' lives, and even though the matches I went to were few and far between they were people I cared about. I knew they genuinely cared about me too.

"Thanks for coming," I said, sidling up to Joel.

He put an arm around my shoulder and squeezed. "Good surprise, eh? Didn't know we were planning this for you, did ya?"

His delight was evident in his enormous smile, matched only by Finley's toothy grin. They looked like a pair of gurning Cheshire cats, and although I'd wanted to tell them I'd rather be out on the Quayside, I clamped my mouth shut and shook my head.

"We nearly missed out on an invite," Finley said, flamboyantly framing his face with his hands in mock horror. "I don't usually answer unknown numbers, see, and I didn't have Tawna's number in my phone. I'm sick of those nuisance calls trying to flog insurance. Or telling me I'm due compensation for the road traffic accident I was involved in, even though I can't drive."

He tutted in annoyance, rolling his dazzling blue eyes in an over-exaggerated fashion. I should have gone to him for acting advice. Where I failed, Finley excelled.

"I'm glad you decided to answer. It's good to see you," I said, before crouching down to chat to Norma.

"Thanks for coming, Norma." I raised my voice to a shout. She's going deaf. "Make sure you get a piece of cake later. Have you seen it?"

I waved my arm towards the cake, knowing she'd approve. Norma never attended a match without being armed with sweets from the market. Midget gems, liquorice torpedoes, mint imperials... she wasn't fussy, as long as she had something to ward off her sweet tooth. Dad jokingly threatened to send Norma his dentistry bill, saying she was the sole reason he needed a filling every time he went to the dentist.

"Smashing, isn't it?" She flashed her false teeth. "And isn't this place posh these days? We used to come here when we were dating in the sixties and it was nothing like this back then. It was a hovel, actually."

I took in the detail of the room for the first time. It was similar to a lot of the other upmarket bars in town, with black drapes covering the walls and a multitude of twinkling white lights set against them. Supposed to look swanky, I think, but it reminded me of the fairy light displays at the out-of-town garden centres in the run up to Christmas, the type of place couples go on a Sunday afternoon.

That's when it hit me. Almost everyone at the party was one half of a couple. Finley and Joel, Norma and Fred, Mum and Dad, my siblings and their significant others. Tawna had buggered off back to her fiancé Johnny's side too, leaving Eve – one of the few genuinely happy single people I knew – picking at the buffet table of "nibbles". Even the women from work had their husbands with them, with the exception of Kath who was making eyes at the muscle-clad youth serving behind the bar. He only looked about twenty. Kath would eat him alive.

I smiled at Norma as she continued reminiscing about days gone by but, after noticing all the twosomes, I couldn't rid myself of the niggling feeling that I was missing out. For the first time in four years I was single on my birthday.

My choker was choking me and I briefly wondered if Darius might be hiding in the shadows. Tawna appeared to have invited every other person I'd met in my three decades on the planet, so it wouldn't be beyond the realms of possibility that she'd extended the invitation to my ex, especially as he was in business with Johnny. My eyes passed restlessly over people from all areas of my life, but even in the darkest corner there was no sign of Darius Welch.

Norma reached into her large tan leather handbag and pulled out a small rectangular envelope.

"It's not much, pet, but we couldn't let the day go by without giving you a little something. Fred saw a pile of cards on the table as we came in, but the silly sod didn't tell me until we were already sat down. Are you all right adding it to the pile yourself?" she asked, handing me the envelope.

"Of course." Norma's spidery script, written with an old-fashioned black-inked fountain pen rather than a biro, was a blemish against the delicate lilac of the envelope. "And there was no need, honestly."

"We wanted to," Norma insisted, "but don't open it until your actual birthday."

She took a slug of her port and lemon, which seemed a funny choice of drink for February. Surely it was more suited to Christmas than the weekend before Valentine's Day? (Yes, my birthday fell on the patron saint day of couples. Oh, the irony...)

"Thank you. I'll make sure it gets put with the others." I planted a kiss on the crepe-paper-thin skin of her cheek. All four of my grandparents had died long ago, so Norma had become my substitute granny.

I headed to the table Norma had referred to, next to the cake. A heap of birthday cards were strewn messily alongside a small pile of presents and an inordinate number of bottle bags. My friends knew me well.

Looking for writing I recognised as I rifled through the cards, I noticed something unusual. Most of the envelopes were inscribed simply, either with "Soph", "Sophie" or "Sophie Drew" (with the exception of one pale pink envelope addressed in Nick's spiky handwriting, inscribed with the delightful nickname "Bumface"). But nestled amongst the cards from well-wishers was something that grabbed my attention, and not in a good way. My parents' address screamed out at me from behind the drab manila envelope's cellophane window. Letters packaged like that were never good news. They were always appointments or mailshots or bills, and in this case it was the worst of the lot. The only post that still got delivered to my parents' house was my credit card bill. I'd never got around to giving the company my updated address and deliberately avoided their ploy to get me to go paperless. That would have meant facing up to my expenditure, whereas ignorance was bliss.

Why Mum and Dad brought an official-looking letter to my party, I don't know. They probably thought they were doing me a favour, because they had no idea how much I'd grown to rely on my flexible friend. If they'd had any clue I was struggling they surely wouldn't have brought it with them when we were supposed to be celebrating my promotion to the next stage of adulthood.

I considered opening the envelope, but only briefly. It

wouldn't tell me anything I didn't already know – I was spending too much and earning a pittance. So instead, I tore the whole thing in half, then into quarters before placing the shredded remains in the bin with the flurry of frosting-smothered napkins.

And then I headed to the toilets, shut myself in a cubicle and cried, wondering how I could be knocking on the door of my thirtieth birthday and still be completely clueless with both love and money.

CHAPTER 2

"So, thirty tomorrow, eh? How does it feel to be ancient?" Nick teased, as Noah chomped on a teething ring. I swear my nephew is made up as much of saliva as anything else. It's a good job he's mighty cute.

I pulled a face. "Ha bloody ha."

"Wait until you're my age, then you'll know about ancient," Dad quipped, sucking in his breath through his teeth as he rubbed his knees. "My joints are killing me. It's all that getting up and down at the match, leaves me in agony."

"Nothing to do with the limboing you were doing at Sophie's party, Mr Drew?" Jakob winked. "I was surprised by how supple you were."

"There's lots you've yet to learn about me." Dad's voice was solemn, but his eyes twinkled. "But it's too late to back out now, you're part of the family."

"That's why we moved to Austria," Anna joked, "so no one knows we're related."

Dad clucked his tongue. "And there was I believing you when you told me it was because of work. To think how proud I was telling everyone about my daughter who'd been headhunted."

"You know I'm only messing," Anna said, wrapping her arms around Dad and snuggling into his chest. "I can't believe we fly back tonight. I wish we could stay longer, but we're on the brink of closing a major deal and I don't trust anyone else in the office enough to leave it in their hands. We'll be back again soon though, promise."

"I hope so," Mum said, entering the room carrying a plate of sandwiches. "I do wish you didn't live so far away."

Lunch consisted of leftovers from the buffet at the party, so besides the curled-edged sarnies we had mini sausage rolls, onion bhajis and two tubes of Pringles that Mum had sent me to the corner shop to fetch. There was half a layer of the ginormous cake for afters, because although everyone had said it was delicious, it was so sweet a small slice was enough.

"We'll be back in the summer," Anna promised, disentangling herself from Dad's protective embrace. "And then we'll be over in October too, naturally." She smiled at Nick, who proudly, and somewhat possessively, wrapped his arm around Chantel.

"What's happening in October?" I asked with a frown. The inane grins on the faces of my family members gave me the distinct impression I was out of the loop.

"Nick and I have got some news," Chantel said. "We told the others at your party last night, but didn't want to steal your moment so decided to wait until today to fill you in."

"We're having another baby!" Nick announced, placing his hand on Chantel's stomach to fully drum the point home. "Due at the start of October. It's still early days – we only just found out – but we wanted to tell Anna and Jakob in person. It's not the same sharing big news over Skype, is it?"

"Congratulations," I said, forcing a smile, forcing so hard it hurt my cheeks. "That's lovely news!"

A dull ache of rejection pulled in the pit of my stomach. I couldn't believe Nick and Chantel had shared their news with the rest of the family before they shared it with me. Although actually, I could. Nick and Anna had always been the closest of the three of us. There was only eighteen months between them.

As though reading my mind, Anna said, "Isn't it fabulous? There will be the same age gap between Noah and the new baby as there is between me and Nick."

I gave a half-hearted nod, before turning my attention to the buffet spread. The first prickle of tears stung my eyes, and I didn't want anyone to see me cry. I shoved a ham sandwich in my mouth. Although the bread was claggy, I swallowed it whole.

"Who'd have thought we'd be getting our second grandchild so soon after the first?" Mum gushed, affectionately patting Chantel on the shoulder. "I can't wait to meet him or her. I bet they'll be the image of our Noah."

"Babies all look the same at first though, don't they?" The frosty look Mum gave me made me realise I sounded bitter, so I added, "Although Noah is the cutest."

Anna scooped our nephew into her hands and lifted him high over her head, so high I feared his head might scrape the ceiling. Noah giggled with delight, drool escaping the corners of his lips. A globule landed on Anna's cheek but she didn't look fazed, instead laughing along as she returned him back onto solid ground and graciously accepted Jakob's offer of a tissue.

"You two will be next." Dad nodded knowingly in the direction of my sister and her husband.

"Not just yet," Jakob replied. "But one day, hopefully, when Anna's more established in the firm."

My sister beamed joyfully in her husband's direction. I averted my eyes because I felt like an imposter in the family home. They were all so settled, so together, and then there was me, Sophie Eliza Drew, single and hapless and on the outside looking in.

"I'll have to head off soon," I lied. "I brought some work home from the office to do over the weekend."

"But it's your birthday weekend!" Mum exclaimed. "Surely they don't expect you to do extra work, especially when you're working on your actual birthday." My mum, an Avon lady for over twenty-five years, had no concept of a standard working week. Her job entailed a cuppa with Beryl across the road as she waxed lyrical about the latest skin buffs and moisturisers.

"You know what Marcie's like. She's a workaholic."

"Can't you at least stay until Anna and Jakob leave for the airport? It's rare I have all my children together these days. Don't spoil it for me." Mum's expression was so full of hope that I couldn't bring myself to be the daughter of disappointment striking again. "I suppose another half hour won't hurt," I managed, reaching for a sausage roll. "It is my birthday, after all."

For the thirty minutes that followed, my parents raised toasts for Nick and Chantel's news, fussed over Anna and how thin she was looking (forcing her to eat the largest wedge of pink birthday cake) and mopped up Noah's drool from the sitting room rug. I may as well have been invisible for all the attention they showed me.

When the clock struck two and Anna made a point of saying they really had to leave for the airport if her and Jakob were going to make their flight, I also made my excuses. Mum blubbed as she said her goodbyes to Anna, instructing her to call as soon as she touched down in Austria. Even Dad looked a bit emotional, his bottom lip visibly wibbling, as my sister clambered into Nick and Chantel's seven-seater car to be chauffeur driven to the airport.

As I was leaving, Mum thrust two A5 envelopes into my hand. My stomach lurched at their familiar ditchwater brown shade.

"I thought I'd brought all your post to the party, but we were in such a rush that I must have left these on the dining room table. Never mind though, eh? They can't be that important if they're still coming here after all this time."

"Thanks, Mum," I mumbled, shoving the envelopes deep into my bag. "And try not to be too upset about Anna returning to Austria. She'll be back in a few months' time."

"I know, love. But it still pains me to have to say goodbye. You'll understand if you ever have children yourself. Children are always babies to their parents."

"I'm almost thirty," I reminded her glumly.

"This time thirty years ago I was in labour and it was agony. Two weeks overdue and I was the size of a house! I was so fed up by that point. It was such a relief when Anna arrived a week early. I couldn't have gone through that waiting a second time. It was awful."

So even my arrival had been a disappointment...

"I'd better get going. That work won't do itself," I said, as chirpily as I could.

"Don't work too hard. And don't forget the finale of the drama we've been watching is on tomorrow. I'll call you when it finishes."

"Okay, Mum. Chat then."

My shoulders were quaking with nerves at the thought of the letters in my bag, no doubt more of the same from the credit card company. I was being hounded. The question was, now they were on my tail, how much longer could I hide from my debts?

CHAPTER 3

A day, that's how much longer.

I should never have answered the phone, because like Finley, I rarely answer calls from numbers I don't know. But for some reason I'd allowed myself to accept both the call and the onslaught from the woman from the credit card company which followed. Who knew a phone conversation with someone you'd never met could make you feel so utterly deflated?

She'd caught me off guard, because what kind of reputable company rings at eight o'clock on a Sunday night? I'd assumed it was Mum ringing to remind me the drama we'd been glued to for the past month was about to start on BBC One. Didn't these people know that weekends were sacred?

I'd opened the envelopes they'd sent to Mum and Dad's house when I'd got back the previous night; two statements with payment demands in an angry red typeface, as though by typing in colour rather than monochrome I'd be able to magic up the money I owed.

It was enough to make me wish I'd switched to online statements when the credit card company had prompted me to. Maybe my debts wouldn't have spiralled out of control if I had.

Perhaps I'd have been one of those people who regularly checked their balance online and curbed their spending appropriately. I knew the reality of that was unlikely; "Spend first, worry later" had been my motto for so long that I rarely even looked at the price of anything before heading to the checkout. If I wanted it, I bought it, simple as that.

Even so, the letters hadn't prepared me for the phone call. The woman who'd rung had been snarky, her southern accent clipped as she informed me my cards were being cancelled until I brought my debts back into my agreed credit limit. I doubt she'd ever lived beyond her means, because if she had she wouldn't have been so rude and devoid of basic sympathy. She'd made me cry, tears streaming down my cheeks and snot bubbles hanging from my nostrils, as I'd tried to explain that it wouldn't be possible for me to make the payment she was demanding immediately – there simply weren't the funds in my current account.

In the end, after more remarks that made me feel like something unpleasant that she'd trodden in, she'd put me through to a softly spoken man – Guy, he'd said his name was – who'd gently questioned me on my spending habits, my income and asked would I like some guidance to help learn to manage my outgoings? I'd liked Guy. Guy actually listened, and although my out-of-control blubbering probably made him uncomfortable, he'd seemed to realise I was a human being who was in financial bother, unlike Snarkster Woman who'd made out I belonged on a Most Wanted poster.

I'd told him everything, all the things I'd been too embarrassed to admit to anyone else, even those closest to me. How I'd never budgeted in my life, but that it had been okay until Tawna, Eve and I had met Johnny and Darius on a night out and two of our trio fell madly in love with these slightly older, sophisticated businessmen. Johnny and Darius spent money without a thought, flashing the cash at fancy restaurants and exclusive bars in the Savile Row suits they'd buy on business trips to the capital. And of course, the women in these high-end venues were groomed to within an inch of their lives.

I'd taken to dressing in designer clothes rather than my old favourite H&M to head to the latest hotspots in the city, and being regularly primped and preened, and by regularly, I mean multiple times a week. My savings had soon run out, keeping up with the Joneses being an expensive business, so I'd applied for a credit card and upped the limit whenever I'd needed to. The company had let me do it, time and time again. Only when my debt nudged into five figures did they stamp down on my spending habit.

By the time I put the phone down it felt as though I'd been stamped on too. When Guy asked how much I could afford to pay back each month I'd been embarrassed, the amount I'd agreed to pitiful in comparison with what I owed, but he'd made a note on the system that the initial payment would be made on the first of March.

He'd put a bar on my account so I couldn't use the card, and encouraged me to cut it up once and for all so I wouldn't have to go through this again in the future. Through my tears I'd done it, furiously snipping the plastic into tiny pieces and throwing what remained into the depths of the kitchen bin, so it could fester with the scooped-out avocado skins and half a punnet of organic strawberries that had gone mouldy because I'd forgotten they needed eating.

I knew lifestyle changes would have to be made. Nights on the town followed by a taxi home had to stop, as did the habit of buying something new to wear every time we went out. It had become almost competitive between Tawna and me over the years, but the time had come for me to bow out. I couldn't compete anymore. Tawna and Johnny shared a bank account, and Johnny's business had really taken off, even winning him the prestigious title of "North East Businessperson of the Year" two years on the bounce. He bought her anything she wanted knowing that having nice things made her happy. Money wasn't a problem for them, but it was for me. It was a bloody massive problem for me.

I pulled my diary out of my everyday bag and flicked to a blank page. Other people managed to live on my wage, so it had to be possible. It'd just take a bit of planning, that's all, a few little cutbacks to get out of the red and into the black.

I picked up the pen, and started to budget.

MARCH

"Are you sure I can't twist your arm? You're not doing that thing where you hide away again, are you?"

I'd made excuses not to go out with Tawna and Eve for two Saturdays in a row. The first week had been easy. I'd told them I had one of my migraines and needed an early night, and they'd left me alone to recuperate. By the time nine o'clock had rolled around I'd climbed into bed with my laptop, logged into Netflix and settled down to watch *Gilmore Girls* for the millionth time. Lorelai and Rory always cheered me up, not least because their lives were as messed up as my own.

"Honestly, I'm fine, and I promise I'm not hiding away with my glue gun like I did when I split up with Darius. I'm just tired."

It wasn't an out-and-out lie, I was tired, but I also wasn't ready to share my financial struggles with my friends. They wouldn't understand. At best they'd smile sympathetically, at worst they'd offer me pity-loans. Either way, I wasn't up to it, but Eve continued to try to persuade me to join them, which was why I shared the other reason I'd rather stay home. "And as much as I love her, I can't face listening to Tawna talking about colour schemes and whether roses or peonies are the more timeless choice when it comes to wedding flowers. Since Johnny popped the question the only thing she talks about is the wedding."

"She's happy," Eve replied, and I swore I could hear her shrugging.

"I know, and I'm happy for her too, truly. But sometimes it feels like we're having the same conversations over and over again, and the wedding's not until August bank holiday! She's still nagging me about getting a date in the diary to try on bridesmaids dresses too."

"You'll be exactly the same when your time comes. Every bride wants their wedding day to be flawless."

"I don't think my day's ever going to come."

I clamped the phone awkwardly between my shoulder and my ear as I opened the kitchen cupboard to see what delights awaited me for tea. There had been baked beans galore since the phone call with the credit card company, and a fair bit of pasta. Whatever was cheap, basically.

I craved pizza loaded with mushrooms, sweetcorn and red onion, but the freezer was empty and no way was I going to cave and spend on takeaway. My credit card payment on the first of March had been made (and was well over the agreed minimum repayment, because my knee-jerk reaction to sell a nearly-new pair of Louboutins on Depop had paid off) and I liked to think of nice-guy Guy sticking a celebratory sticker on a wall chart to mark my achievement (and I stuck my middle finger up to the woman who had made me cry, as though making the payment was a 1:0 victory to me). Saving money was a test, but watching the amount I owed decrease, albeit slowly, was already satisfying. I'd even converted to an online account so I could log in and check my balance. It was helping me stay focused.

"Your day will come," Eve promised, "but first you need to meet Mr Right."

"I used to think Darius was my Mr Right."

Eve snorted.

"I know he wasn't perfect…"

"He was far from perfect, Soph."

"…but we did have a lot of good times together."

And oh, had the good times been good. The lazy Sunday mornings, where he'd nuzzled his nose into the back of my neck before kissing the spot behind my ear that turned me on so much I'd thought I was going to explode. The quickies on the sofa. The things he could do with that magic tongue of his …

"Are you sure I can't persuade you to come out? Just one little drink? I don't like to think of you home alone, especially if you're brooding over that twat Darius."

"I'm sure," I said, closing the cupboard door and deciding to have a bowl of cereal rather than a hot meal. Nothing in the cupboard appealed and anyway, I couldn't be bothered messing about with the oven. "I have a bowl of Coco Pops and a hot date with Milo Ventimiglia planned."

"Cereal and *Gilmore Girls* on a Friday night? That's such a singleton cliché."

"I think you're confusing singleton cliché for happiness," I countered, reaching for the bright yellow box and a bowl. "Say hi to Tawna for me and have a good night."

"I'll have a drink for you," Eve promised. "I'm certainly in need of one."

"Everything okay?" I asked cautiously. "Is it your mum?"

For the past few years Eve's mum had been struggling with forgetfulness. Initially everyone put it down to her taking on too much – Lucille McAndrew was one of life's do-ers and she worked long hours as a carer at a nursing home. The residents had loved her for her warm heart and good humour. It had come as a shock to us all when she had been diagnosed with early-onset dementia.

As her mum's condition deteriorated, leaving her incapable of looking after herself let alone the vulnerable elderly people at the nursing home, Eve had had to accept she wasn't able to hold down her job as a research chemist and care for her mum. She'd made the difficult decision to move Mrs McAndrew into a care home the previous autumn.

"You know how it is," Eve replied bravely. "Good days and bad days, and today's been trying. Anyway," she added, with a bravery I was convinced was just for show, "I'd better get ready, I'm meeting Tawna in an hour. Have fun with Milo."

"Oh, I will."

After we said our goodbyes, I poured the chocolate puffs of cereal into the bowl, drowned them in milk, grabbed a clean spoon from the draining board and dug in. It wasn't the healthiest tea and I knew it wouldn't fill me up, but that didn't matter. It tasted of childhood. Innocent times. Easier times.

When I finished the bowl I refilled it, wolfing down the second helping too, not feeling remotely guilty about my greed because the Coco Pops had been a bargain price (due to the box being dented. The inner wrapper had been intact though, I'd made sure of that. I had my limits).

After both bowls, the waistband of my work trousers was cutting into my stuffed stomach. It was a relief to change into my loose-fitting paisley pyjamas, wipe my make-up from my face and pull my hair into a rather severe and unflattering ponytail. Not that it mattered, no one was going to see.

Once I'd settled into full relaxation mode, I climbed under the duvet, flipped open my laptop and checked my online credit card statement one more time. It reassured me that I was doing the right thing by staying in.

I clicked on my chosen entertainment icon, and the familiar

Gilmore Girls theme filled the room. I sank back into my pile of pillows and allowed myself to escape to Stars Hollow. It felt comforting and comfortable, and I was glad not to be heading out into the meat market that doubled as Newcastle city centre on a Saturday evening. Eve and Tawna could keep their nights on the town. I was saving money, avoiding hangovers and drooling, uninterruptedly, over my fave celebrity.

What could be better than that?

APRIL

CHAPTER 5

Seven weeks and two payments had passed since the initial phone call which set my money-saving actions into motion, and other than going to work (which I'd have got out of if I hadn't needed the money it brought in), I'd barely left the house.

Painting my nails and binge-watching Netflix were losing their appeal. It didn't help that I'd reached series five of *Gilmore Girls* – the lack of Milo definitely lessening my viewing pleasure. I'd even tried defecting to *Party of Five* to drool over Scott Wolf instead, but it hadn't helped. Truth be told, I was bored, and I knew I'd have to brave going out sooner or later.

My excuses were wearing thin and Tawna and Eve were continually haranguing me – we'd not seen each other in over a month, the longest we'd ever gone without all being together. It was easier to avoid temptation from within the safety of my own four walls, but Tawna declared my suggestion of a girls' night in as "boring" and my resolve had come close to cracking. So far I'd managed to stay focused, clinging tightly to the warm glimmer of pride that swelled within me whenever I checked my online statement, something I'd never have expected to get from being frugal, but it didn't stop me feeling guilty for being a flaky friend.

Sunlight streamed into my bedroom heralding a glorious Saturday morning and, after a week of cloudy gloom, with no hangover keeping me bedridden I pulled back the covers to face the day. My next-door neighbour, dressed in an ill-fitting vest and shorts, both an unflattering shade of grey that reminded me of over-masticated bubble-gum, was washing his car for the third time this week. He looked like he'd stepped out in his oldest, saggiest underwear.

The glorious spring weather propelled me, pushing me towards leaving the house. I decided I'd head to the shops, something I'd deliberately been avoiding because it had the potential to be dangerous to my bank balance. Internet shopping was a temptation, but I was a tactile person by nature. It was easier to resist an on-screen image than an actual object that I could physically smell and touch.

I couldn't hide away forever. There were things I needed to buy. Toothpaste for one, and shampoo for another. Necessities not luxuries, although I needed to look at cheaper brands. I'd used the same shampoo for years, since giving in to my hairdresser's hard-sell. Whenever I went back to the salon she'd compliment me on my hair's condition and put another bottle behind the counter for me to collect when it was time to pay for my cut and colour. I'd find myself thanking her, as though she was doing me a favour, not adding twenty-five quid to the cost of my haircut.

My honey-blonde hair was lying just below my shoulders rather than neatly on them as it did when I kept up with my appointments. My fringe was long too; long enough that I'd taken to sweeping it to one side and holding it in place with a grip so it didn't flop about irritatingly in front of my eyes. However, my hair didn't look hideous even though I'd missed my usual monthly appointment. It just looked longer. The ends weren't splitting and, although my roots were peeping through, my natural shade was only a fraction darker than the colour I'd adopted back in the Darius days. The truth is, since stopping the spray tans (another former habit which had become a necessary cutback) my colouring had changed. Everything was that bit more muted, my skin more biscuit than orange (along with my scent, from smothering myself head to toe with an award-winning own-brand self-tanning lotion Kath had recommended). The natural hair colour I'd previously thought of as dull complimented my new-found skin tone.

Once I'd chosen my outfit, eventually settling on a favourite designer ditsy-print dress, I ran a brush through my tousled hair and liberally spritzed myself with perfume. After wolfing down a yoghurt, brushing my teeth (using the very last of the toothpaste) and grabbing my over-the-shoulder bag from the peg next to the door, I was ready.

As I'd skipped down the sun-drenched street, the heady scent of honeysuckle assaulting my nostrils, I'd instinctively known it was going to be a good day. With sunshine and flowers, how could it be anything else?

I inhaled until I was dizzy, high on floral fumes.

I'd grossly underestimated the dangers of popping into town for a few essentials. There was the lipstick and blusher that had all but jumped into my basket in Boots, and a sale at my favourite high-street clothing shop which had sucked me into the store. I'd tried on a teal-green jumpsuit – gorgeous, with a deep V-neck which made the most of my God-given assets – but even with the generous discount the price on the tag was well beyond my newly-tightened means. I'd reluctantly told the sales assistant it had been too short in the leg, even though it had fitted like a dream.

The next hurdle had been bumping into Kath outside Ann Summers (I hadn't wanted to dwell on what might be in the bulging carrier bag she was clutching).

"Come for a coffee," she'd urged. "We never see each other out of work these days."

She'd pointed to a coffee shop, one of the major chains you find on every high street, that sells the most delicious chocolate layer cake. Rich and moist and melt-in-the-mouth.

My stomach had betrayed my will by grumbling. Loudly. Loud enough that Kath had taken it as an affirmative and guided me helplessly towards the overpriced latte and cake that yes, I'd badly wanted, but wouldn't have caved and bought without her encouragement.

Every guilt-ridden sip of my coffee had burned my throat as I'd listened to Kath share the gory details of her latest conquest. A postgrad student from Colorado apparently, who was into role play, she'd added with a cheeky nod towards the Ann Summers bag. After that I'd quickly made my excuses, scared she might whip out a French maid's outfit or naughty nurse's uniform.

I'd breathed a sigh of relief as I'd set foot inside the pound shop. Admittedly, I'd looked furtively at the passers-by to make sure no one I knew saw me going in, but once inside I was amazed. It smelled a bit funny, like the cleaner had gone overboard with the bleach. In fact, the smell wasn't dissimilar to the toilets at some of the less salubrious bars in town on a weekend.

Some of what they were selling was tat, but I'd also spotted my usual brand of toothpaste, for half the usual price, and a four pack of my favourite chocolate bar. Ooh, and the branded teabags Jane favoured that I could take to work, and some of those nice chocolate-coated oat biscuits. When I checked my basket it was pretty full, especially as I'd also thrown in a variety of cleaning products (all the while knowing that despite my good intentions they'd most likely end up, unused, under the sink).

I left the shop laden with bargains and, although it was money I probably could have saved, my body was abuzz with the rush that shopping brings. Granted, buying disinfectant and scourers wasn't as exciting as buying a new outfit, but just being in town was a step up from the supermarket, which had been the limit of my shopping experience since the day of the dreaded call.

A willowy mannequin in one of the windows was dressed in a beautiful silk maxi-dress I knew would look amazing on me, and I wondered how much longer I'd be able to resist buying new clothes. My wardrobe was fit to bursting, so it wasn't as though I was short of things to wear, but I've always had a passion for fashion. I don't *want* to wear the same clothes day in, day out. I like variety, having a choice, but sadly the days of buying top-brand names are in my past. Maybe when I'd made a dent in my debts it'd be different, but what was I going to do until then?

A sadness washed over me, and although I knew it was a first-world problem, I pulsed with anger too. I worked bloody hard. Didn't I deserve nice things?

I gazed longingly at the shop windows as I dodged the shoppers coming toward me, weaving in and out of groups of teenage girls heading to the cinema, grumpy men who looked like they'd rather be anywhere but the town centre on a Saturday lunchtime, grey-haired women juggling carrier bags stuffed with purchases.

That's when I saw it. It wasn't identical to the jumpsuit I'd tried on earlier in the day – the colour a dark cobalt blue, the neckline more demure – but the cut looked equally as flattering.

I stopped abruptly to look in more detail, my brows furrowing as I tried to make sense of why this gorgeous jumpsuit was sharing a window display with a baby walker, a stack of dog-eared paperbacks and a set of golf clubs.

Peering up, I took in the sign above the shop, and all became clear. I was looking into the window of a charity shop. I noticed overflowing plastic crates piled high with books on the pavement outside, so close to my feet that I could easily have tripped over them. I bent down to look, sifting past a bestselling bonk-buster Kath had raved about earlier in the year. I filtered past the Dan Browns and Jilly Coopers, surprised to find a stack of football programmes buried near the bottom of the box. Some gave me a sense of déjà vu, Newcastle United programmes I'd bought myself as a kid, with images of Shearer and Speed and Gillespie plastered on their covers, but then I came to an older programme behind them. It was from the early seventies, and I recognised Malcolm McDonald, one of Dad's heroes of yesteryear, all sideburns and shaggy hair, gracing the cover. Dad insists he's a legend, far superior to any of the current crop wearing the black and white stripes of our hometown club. Dad would probably already have the programme in his stash, but I found myself taking it into the shop anyway. It'd make a nice gift, and give him an excuse to reminisce of bygone days.

"Hello," said the man behind the counter. "Found something you like the look of?"

It took all my willpower not to reply, "Yes, you," because the man was undeniably attractive. His fair hair was swept over to one side. His T-shirt was just a touch too tight around his biceps, showing off well-defined tanned arms which were free from the tattoos that normally got me swooning. And he was wearing glasses with unapologetically thick-rimmed black frames that looked ridiculously geeky and made me think of Brains from

Thunderbirds. He wasn't my usual type, but something about him was insanely hot.

"My dad will love this." I placed the programme on the counter before tentatively adding, "And I wondered how much the jumpsuit in the window was?"

He stood up from the stool he'd been perching on and headed towards the display. He found a label and named his price, significantly less than the teal version I'd fallen in love with in the high-end department store.

"I bet it'd suit you. Bring out the blue of your eyes."

My cheeks felt hot, and I knew they were reddening at the compliment. From most men I'd have thought it was a line, but from this man – Max, or so his name badge told me – it didn't feel like a come-on, although he was probably a master salesman, full of charm and patter.

"Maybe I could try it on?" My voice wobbled and only partly because I was well out of my comfort zone in a shop cluttered with people's unloved and unwanted objects. "If it's not too much bother taking it out of the window?"

"No trouble at all."

I studied him more closely as he clambered into the window display. As well as the deliciously-curved biceps, there was a rather biteable peach of an arse beneath his jet-black fitted jeans. A sprinkling of stubble peppered his chiselled jawline, and there was an endearing look of concentration on his face as he carefully chose where to place his feet.

"The changing room's just over there." Max pointed to the far end of the shop with one hand as he passed me the jumpsuit with the other.

It turned out the changing room was a metre-square corner of the shop with a pulled-back curtain, a battered pine dining chair crammed into a corner and a full-length mirror attached to the wall. It was barely big enough to stand upright in, let alone allow me to wrestle myself into a jumpsuit (why are they such a bugger to get into? So fiddly).

Drawing the curtain behind me, I began to undress. There was a sliver of a gap where the swath of material didn't quite meet the wall, and through the space I saw Max, sitting on his stool, engrossed in a book. As I stripped down to my underwear with just the flimsy curtain between us, an irrational vulnerability came over me. There was no way he could see me (and even if he could he was totally lost in whatever he was reading), but I was still glad I'd decided to wear one of my nicest underwear sets – a mint-green bra and pants set with white lace trim. It gave me confidence as I slipped my legs into the jumpsuit and hitched the straps up over my shoulders. Fastening the zip was awkward, but there was no way I was asking Max for help so I struggled on, my elbows bashing against the wall as I tugged at the small metal pulley.

When I was finally dressed I swizzled to view myself in the mirror. The neckline of the jumpsuit seemed lower once on, my cleavage difficult to avoid. The nipped in waist made the most of my curves and the fabric clung to my bum. Thankfully the flattering cut made it appear pert and perky, even though I'd all but given up on my formerly regimented squatting routine. They might be the answer to a beautiful butt, but they're the devil's work. The burn. THE BURN.

"How are you getting on?" Max asked from the other side of the curtain.

I jumped, startled.

"Okay, I think. It fits. It's hard to see what it looks like from this close to the mirror though."

"Come out and you'll get a better view," he suggested. "It's a tight squeeze in there, I know."

Pulling back the curtain, I stepped into the shop.

Max raised his eyebrows in response.

His scrutiny made me aware of how little the jumpsuit left to the imagination. It was a snug fit, and low-cut, and way too dressy for a charity shop in the middle of an ordinary Saturday afternoon.

Exposed. That's how I felt. I felt exposed.

"Wow," he said finally. His gaze followed me up and down and he pushed his glasses up his nose with his index finger.

My heart quickened in delight at the one-word comment, causing me to become hyper-aware of the rise and fall of my breasts within the low-cut outfit. I felt like a superhero – Catwoman or Batgirl, or some other half-naked heroine – and although the feminist in me hated myself for it, I pushed my shoulders back until the fabric strained against my chest. For a moment I wasn't sure what was going to pop out first, Max's eyes or my perky nipples.

"Do you think I should get it?" I asked, although I'd already decided it was coming home with me. It was too much of a bargain to leave behind. Surely even Guy would allow me a little treat for my recent good behaviour (although as I set my sights on the jumpsuit I conveniently blanked out the make-up and the biscuits and the overpriced coffee and cake Kath had coerced me into).

"Absolutely." Max swallowed, his Adam's apple bobbing at the base of his neck.

"Looks like I have no choice then." I smiled.

Back in the confines of the changing room the smile became a full-on beam. The jumpsuit was just the confidence boost I needed, and Max's reaction to it the icing on the cake.

I unzipped the zipper, which was a million times easier than doing the bloody thing up had been, and allowed the outfit to slip off, pooling around my feet. As I slid into my old favourite dress, which I'd been so confident in before, I noticed how plain

– how demure – it seemed in comparison to the glamour of the jumpsuit.

Scooping up my belongings, I peeped through the gap in the curtains once more, expecting to find Max still gripped by his book. Instead he was looking in my direction. There was no way he could see more than an inch of me through the crack in the curtain, but that didn't stop my heart from racing.

As I emerged into the shop, he grinned, and nodding towards the jumpsuit in my hand said, "New outfit for town tonight?"

It didn't sound like an invitation, but his interest was flattering nonetheless. It had been a while since someone of the opposite sex cared what I was doing on a Saturday night, let alone someone as gorgeous as Max.

"No plans tonight, sadly. I'll probably stay in and wash my hair with just next door's cat for company."

"That's tragic," he replied, mock solemnly, "although my night isn't much more exciting."

"Oh?"

"I'm going for a drink with my brother but only to the local. He can't meet until late because my nephew Isaac's a devil for going to sleep and he won't let anyone but Grant put him to bed. I'll be lucky if he gets in much before last orders."

"Hardly worth going at that time," I mused. "Unless you can find someone else to join you."

He cocked his head, a flicker of a smirk playing out on his lips. "Is that an offer?"

"Maybe," I said coyly, as he rang the programme and the jumpsuit into the till. I searched for my purse in the depths of my bag, and when I found it pulled out a note. "If you're asking."

"It's nothing special, the local," he said, naming a pub I'd been to before. It's near one of Tawna's ex-boyfriend's houses, although given the amount of exes Tawna has, most pubs in the North East are. "But a band I know are playing there tonight. Don't decide now, I know I've sprung it on you. But I'll be there from seven."

"O-kay." I was surprised to find I was contemplating taking him up on his offer. Then again, I'd not had this instantaneous an attraction to anyone in a long time. Not since Darius, in fact. "Thanks, Max."

"Perhaps I'll see you later…"

His voice trailed off, and from the expectant look in his eyes I knew he was waiting for me to tell him my name. "Sophie. Sophie Drew."

CHAPTER 6

From the outside, the pub was exactly as I remembered, one of those large cube-like buildings surrounded by a car park. The lack of empty parking bays suggested it was a busy night.

I'd not been to a local pub on a weekend evening for a long time and as I stepped into the baking-hot building the noise hit me like a slap.

People were crammed in and all hope I had of finding Max sat quietly nursing a pint quickly vanished. I'd made the right choice plumping for flat knee-high boots rather than the pair of heels that had also been contenders – I had the feeling we'd be doing a lot of standing, going by the sheer volume of people.

I navigated my way to the bar, apologising every few steps for bumping into someone.

When I reached the polished mahogany counter, debating whether to order a gin and tonic or a glass of white wine, the reason for the crowds became apparent. An ear-piercing wail of an electric guitar caused me to jump back in alarm, a rhythmic drumbeat kicking in behind it as a female vocalist drawled lyrics full of cynicisms. The band was in full swing.

The bartender raised his eyebrows at me, which I took as an invite to place my order. I opted for the house white in the end, thinking it would be the cheaper option. Spirits got expensive when miniature mixtures were involved, and I'd set myself a strict budget. I'd chosen to take the fifty-minute walk from my house to save on bus fare, and although it had been a beautiful day there was a chilly nip in the evening air. After being in the cold for so long the cranked-up heating of the heaving pub caused my nose to run, so I was sniffing in a very unattractive manner when Max tapped me on the shoulder.

"Sophie! You came."

"I did."

The bartender placed my drink on a cardboard beer mat, but as I offered him the money, Max interjected.

"And a pint of Guinness please." He turned to face me, the lenses of his glasses steamy from the humidity in the room and added, "My treat. You wouldn't be out if it wasn't for me suggesting it. You'd be at home, washing your hair."

It made me smile that he'd remembered my comment, and I gladly accepted his generosity.

When he'd de-steamed his glasses and the bartender had handed over our drinks, Max gestured to a doorway at the other end of the pub.

"My friends' band aren't due on for a while, so let's go out the back." His voice was loud. It needed to be to be heard over the band. "We'll be able to talk then."

I don't know much about music, but I could tell the band were half decent – the lead singer had a good voice. The music wasn't what I'd choose to listen to, but the crowd were behind them, enthusiastically singing along to the cover version of a well-known indie song. I feared for my eardrums. It was as though they were playing at Wembley Stadium rather than a local pub.

It was much quieter in the snug and luckily we found a free table. The space was small though, and equally as stifling as the main room. The window dripped with condensation, the droplets of water slithering down the inside of the pane and pooling on the window ledge. It was like stepping inside a furnace, and if I hadn't taken my cardigan off right away I might have collapsed from overheating.

"Aren't you hot?" I asked in disbelief, eyeing Max's thick cream sweater. It was chunky knit – the sort of thing a fisherman would wear for a long day working on the choppy North Sea – and looked like it weighed a ton.

"A bit," he admitted, smiling sheepishly, "but I've not got a T-shirt on underneath."

I laughed nervously at the thought of his naked skin beneath the wool, and recalled his muscular arms from earlier in the day. I wondered if his abs and pecs were equally as toned. The image left my mouth dry, and I took a desperate swig from my wine to try to push all thoughts of an undressed Max to the back of my mind. *Pull yourself together, Sophie. You barely know the guy.*

"I'm glad you decided to come," he said, sliding his sleeves up to once more reveal those gorgeous arms. The golden-brown hairs that covered them were ever-so-slightly visible against his skin, and I found it hard to pull my eyes away. "I wasn't sure if you would."

"What made you think that?"

"I thought you'd be wary of being invited out by someone you haven't met before. It's not how people meet these days, is it? It's all about swiping right on a dating app."

"You don't strike me as the kind of person who needs a dating app," I replied, swilling my wine around the glass, "and it's not like you've been hit by the ugly stick. I'd have thought you'd have women queuing around the block."

My cheeks heated up as Max raised his eyebrows at me.

"Not quite, but thanks. I've got friends who use dating apps. One met his fiancée on Tinder."

"Really?"

My only experience of the app had been one very sad rebound date soon after Darius and I had split up. I'd arrived early at the coffee shop we'd agreed to meet at, the hit of strong mocha not as emboldening as a bottle of wine would have been, but far more acceptable for ten o'clock on a Sunday morning. When my date had finally arrived – late – he hadn't even bought a drink, just walked up to me, asked if I was Sophie and told me he lived in the flat upstairs if I was "up for it". I hadn't been up for it. I'd been looking for someone to pay me a few compliments and boost my self-esteem, not a quick shag.

"It's the modern way, I suppose, but I'm not sure it's for me. I've never been good at selling myself."

"You work in a shop! Surely selling should come naturally."

"That's different. It's easy to help someone find what they're looking for on the rails."

"Not so easy to big yourself up?"

"Not without coming across like a bit of a dick." His tone was serious, but I could tell he was joking through the hint of a smile.

"You seem so confident," I mused.

"Things aren't always what they seem," he said, before taking a sip of his Guinness. The creamy froth sat on his upper lip for just a second before with one quick flick of the tongue it was gone, as though it had never been there in the first place. "I learned that the hard way."

I gave a quizzical look, but Max didn't offer anything further, instead saying, "Let's talk about something else. Tell me about you, how you spend your free time when you're not washing your hair..."

Smoky eyes peered out at me from behind his glasses, the

most unusual shade of greeny-grey, like the opaque wisps in the glass marbles I'd find in the bottom of my stocking each Christmas Day as a kid. And those forearms, which I had an overwhelming desire to have wrapped around me, were a distraction too. I'd bet Max gave good hugs, especially in that stupidly cuddly sweater. He'd be like a human teddy bear.

"What do you want to know?" The question was a stalling tactic as I wondered how I could make my humdrum life sound more exciting than it really was. "I grew up here and now rent a place in Northumberland Park, where my neighbour's ginger moggie Scrat Cat is forever climbing in through my kitchen window. I spend my free time either binge-watching a TV series or making stuff." When he looked at me questioningly I added, "Sewing, origami, crochet... anything crafty really. I find it relaxing." And I did, although I'd not made anything other than origami flowers for months. "I'd love to be able to make a living from selling the things I make, that'd be the dream, but I wouldn't know where to start. I work at a law firm in town."

"Oh, you're a solicitor?"

"Legal secretary." I grimaced, thinking of the pile of work that'd no doubt be waiting for me when I returned to the office on Monday morning.

"But you don't like your job?"

"What makes you think that?" I said with a laugh of resignation.

"The dejected tone of voice gave me a clue, but it was the look of sheer frustration that gave it away. I know how you feel. I hated my last job, answering the phones at one of the big utility companies' call centres."

I shuddered.

"Yeah, it wasn't exactly a laugh a minute. Customers complaining about the rate they were on, wanting to know why the engineer they were expecting to arrive three hours ago to fix their boiler hadn't arrived... all that kind of fun stuff. I should have known what it was going to be like. People don't ring up to say 'Everything's working with my gas and electric, so I thought I'd phone to let you know what a great job you're doing', do they?"

The voice he put on made me laugh. I think it was supposed to be a Scottish accent, or maybe Welsh. Either way, it was laughably terrible.

"You're right. It's like that in my job too. Don't get me wrong, the people I work with are great. It doesn't give me a sense of satisfaction though."

"Just what you do to pay the bills, huh?" He smiled, and I made myself smile back, not wanting to dwell on my tangled financial situation. "Luckily I love my current job. I've worked in retail on and off since I was sixteen. The shop relies on volunteers to help out, because obviously if they paid for staff there'd be less money raised for the cause, so as the manager I'm the only person who gets a wage."

"What sort of people shop there? I always imagine charity shops to be full of old grannies."

Max rolled his eyes, and I worried I'd offended him until that playful grin reappeared. "People always say that, but the truth is all kinds of people shop there. Mums looking for cheap toys to entertain their kids, record collectors hoping to find a rare LP they've been looking for, students who're into vintage clothing... honestly, normal people. You were there yourself earlier, don't forget."

A giggle escaped my lips. I hadn't thought of it that way.

"If you really don't like your job," he continued, "you should change it. We spend a lot of our lives working. You don't want to waste it doing something you don't enjoy."

"Creative industries are hard to get into though. There aren't even any factory jobs where I could spend the day at a sewing machine, I looked into it a while back. Most of the big clothing companies outsource to other countries because they can get the work done for a fraction of the price."

Max screwed up his nose in distaste. "Sweatshops."

"Yeah. I've resigned myself to the fact that craft will only ever be a hobby. There's no way to make a living from it, not for someone like me."

"Never say never," Max said optimistically, knocking back the last of his pint. He looked down at his watch, and I panicked, taking it as a sign that he wanted me to leave. I prepared to make my excuses, but he said, "Shall we go through to the other room for a bit? My friends' band is due on at eight and I should probably be supportive and show my face."

I picked up my wine glass, drank it dry and pushed myself up off the stool. "Sounds good. And I'll get us another drink in too, shall I?"

"Another Guinness would be lovely, thanks."

We left the saunaesque room and headed into the raucous melee of the pub itself, Max leading the way. As he reached his hand out behind him to ensure we didn't get separated by the sea of people, I placed my hand in his. The soft hairs of his forearm tickled my skin. The sensation thrilled me.

CHAPTER 7

The wine I'd been necking the previous night should have done a good job of knocking me out, but I'd struggled to sleep. Instead of being out like a light when I got home, I'd laid on my back, staring up at the ceiling through the darkness, trying to make sense of my blossoming feelings for Max. As well as making me laugh by telling daft jokes he'd been generous, even insisting on paying for my taxi home when his brother had shown up and I'd left them to enjoy the rest of the band's set. His kindness had meant my self-imposed budget had remained intact.

The lack of sleep meant I was swallowing down yawns as me and the girls dissected the night as we sat in the park.

"I never thought I'd see the day you went out with someone other than Darius," Tawna said. She sounded as though I was letting her down, not trying to move on. "Me and Johnny have been waiting for you two to get back together. You know he'd take you back in a heartbeat, don't you?"

"Do you think?"

"Definitely. We saw him when we were out last night and he asked after you."

My heart plummeted to my feet, but I shouldn't have been surprised at Tawna mentioning my ex – he regularly cropped up in our conversations. She and Johnny saw plenty of Darius, both socially and through the business.

In the past our double dates had been legendary. Sophie and Darius, Tawna and Johnny. Newcastle had been ours for the taking. We'd drunk ourselves stupid at the poshest bars in town, living the high life, and I'd been head over heels in love.

Eve's spidey-senses must've tingled, because she said, "You're not thinking of giving him another chance, are you? You deserve much better than that creep."

I grabbed a handful of grass, pulling it out of the ground, roots and all.

"Darius and I have a history. But there's a spark between me and Max too, I think."

"We've heard all about your sparks before," Tawna said with a bawdy wink. "All those stories about you and Darius. You don't find sexual compatibility like that every day you know, Soph. I really think you should consider giving him a second chance. There's a lot to be said for having a connection with someone."

"She just said she had a connection with Max too," Eve pointed out.

"She hardly knows the guy," Tawna said with a dismissive scoff.

The way they were talking about me as though I wasn't there irritated me.

"I really like Max," I admitted. "He's easy to be with, easy to talk to... But you know how it is with Darius. He's hard to get over."

Eve looked up at the sky, studying the clouds. I had the distinct impression I was disappointing her.

"I loved him for so long. We shared so much. And I can't even begin to put into words how much I miss Summer."

Just mentioning Darius's daughter caused my heart to swell. Summer might not have been mine, but I couldn't have loved her any more, even if she had been.

Eve nodded sadly. "I get that. She's a gorgeous kid."

"She really is. I wish I could see her."

"If you got in touch with Darius, I'm sure he'd love for you to see Summer when she's next up here," Tawna said. "We went bowling with them the other Sunday. You'd hardly recognise her now, Soph. She's really growing up."

"Stop putting ideas in her head," Eve snapped. "You're only interfering because you want her and Darius back together."

She looked like she'd been sucking on an especially sour lemon, but then Eve had never been a fan of Darius. Tawna thought she'd been envious of the two of us being in pairs as she tagged along solo, but I didn't think that was the case. Eve had always insisted she'd got a bad vibe from Darius, right from the off. She'd actually whooped with joy when I'd finally deleted his number from my phone.

Tawna ignored Eve's retort, reaching out and patting my arm affectionately. "I knew you weren't over him. I could tell. You should talk to him. I know he'd get back with you if you asked him to."

"She's over him! She misses Summer, not him."

"You never liked him," Tawna folded her arms defensively across her chest, "but he was good for Sophie. Look at how she's been lately. She's practically a recluse! That's not a healthy way to live."

"Changing yourself to keep a man isn't a healthy way to live either," Eve fired back, "nor is competing with his power-tripper of an ex."

Her words dug into me like a knife sliding between my ribs. Eve was right – I'd been desperate to get one over on Summer's mum, Nadia. But however hard I'd tried, however much I spent on top-of-the-range cosmetics and cutting-edge beauty treatments, I'd never been able to shrug off the thought that I was a poor substitute for the woman who'd given Darius the beautiful daughter who was the light of his world.

"I wasn't competing," I said faintly, "but it's hard when your partner has to spend time with their ex."

Inwardly, I could admit that I'd been jealous. I'd only met Nadia a handful of times, avoiding her as much as possible in an act of self-preservation, but she'd made it clear she wasn't happy with me spending time with her daughter, making snide comments and telling me to "take care". She'd insinuated mine and Darius's relationship wouldn't last, and that it would be confusing for Summer to form a bond with me when I'd "probably not be on the scene for long".

Actually, Summer and I had got on really well. With her large chocolate-brown eyes and mahogany hair she'd been a miniature Darius, and that had made her entirely lovable in my eyes. She had her father's genes, and I was so besotted with him that it would have been impossible not to love Summer too.

"You'd have to get used to Nadia if you got back with Darius," Eve said. "She'll still be clicking her fingers for him to come running at her beck and call."

"He runs because he's a brilliant dad who cares about his daughter," Tawna argued back.

My hackles were rising. I'd known he was a father right from the start. Summer was part of the package and I'd willingly accepted that, building a solid, loving relationship with her over time. But I'd not given much thought to the fact Nadia would always be lurking in the background, bitter and twisted, and waiting for things between me and Darius to go tits up.

"I don't like the man," Eve confirmed. "Never have, never will."

"We know," Tawna retorted, seeming even more put out than

I was by Eve's tirade against Darius. "But there's an explosive chemistry between them, even you can see that. Animal attraction like that should be acted on."

"Explosive chemistry? More like nuclear warfare," Eve said with a sarcastic eye-roll. "I can't believe we're even having this conversation. They gave it a go, it didn't work out. Why should Sophie go back? Especially when there's a hot new man waiting in the wings."

"Why take a risk on someone who's been around for five minutes when a man who knows her inside out still loves her?"

My heart panged at that. Since Darius and I had split up I'd had many a lonely night. The comfort that came with being in a steady relationship was appealing, and although things with Darius hadn't always been easy, I knew him inside out too.

"Well, you know what I think." Eve looked directly at me as she pinched the stem of a daisy between her thumb and forefinger and plucked it out of the ground. "It's been ages since you've been this excited about meeting a man. You know what you'd be getting if you took Darius back. Max is all new, you should give him a chance. You'll only end up regretting it if you don't."

She handed me the daisy and I plucked the fragile white petals away one by one.

He loves me.

Pluck.

He loves me not.

Pluck.

He loves me.

Pluck.

He loves me not.

Pluck.

He loves me.

Although it was nothing more than a silly childish superstition, a warmth radiated from my core when only the bobbly middle of the flower remained.

He loves me. But who is "he"?

CHAPTER 8

"Is it awful to be glad that my other half's got a fever?" Finley asked cheekily, as we climbed the steps leading to our gate into St James' Park. "I'm glad you could use Joel's season ticket. I always think of you as a bit of a lucky charm."

The comment made me chortle. We'd lost the previous match I'd attended at the back end of last season five-nil.

"It's the scarf that's the lucky charm," Dad insisted, fondling the fronds of the black and white knitted accessory that was hanging around my neck. "Three generations of the Drew family have worn that scarf when watching the Toon. It's forty years old."

"It can't be that lucky, we've not had forty years of non-stop glory," Norma huffed, pulling herself up on the metal handrail. "If only!"

"There have been some great nights though," Fred reminded her. "More than some supporters ever get. Think of those poor sods stuck watching non-league week in week out, they'd love to be here in the pouring rain at a big match like this."

A man barged past Norma, almost sending her flying on the slippery steps. "Watch it," I shouted, firing him a dirty look.

Norma was a tough cookie, but she was still an elderly lady and it annoyed me when people didn't show the older generation respect. "Are you all right, Norma?"

"I'm out of puff." She exhaled as she reached the top of the concourse, her body almost bent double as she clutched at the wall. "It's those steps that'll be the death of me, not some idiot with no manners. I'll be fine once I've got my breath back."

"Take your time, it's slippy." Dad hooked his arm and offered it to Norma. "And there's no reason to rush, there's still ten minutes until kick-off."

The familiar strains of one of Newcastle United's most famous anthems played out. Mark Knopfler's "Going Home", the theme from *Local Hero*, had become synonymous with watching our beloved Magpies. Being at the ground warmed my soul, bringing back memories of some of my happiest times. Coming to the match with Dad had been as much about bonding as it had been about football, and being back on this patch made me wish I came more regularly. Maybe one day I'd get a season ticket again, if I could afford it.

We filed through the turnstiles, the sounds of match day all around us, and I drank in the atmosphere as we made our way to our seats. It felt like coming home. Even though the ground had changed over the years, nothing was unfamiliar. The same smell of Bovril coming from steamy plastic cups clutched in the hands of monochrome-clad fans, the same roar of the crowd as the team took to the pitch, the "Blaydon Races" song accompanying the eleven chosen ones. Most importantly, there were the same people around me, with the exception of Joel, whose seat I was filling.

"Werther's Original?" Norma offered me a paper bag brimming with the butter mints, and although they weren't my favourite I took one. I noticed Dad craftily sneak three, popping one in his mouth and the other two into his pocket for later.

"Get stuck in!" Finley yelled, face creased in annoyance as the midfielder who'd given the ball away three times in as many minutes shirked a tackle. "I could do better than that and I've not put on a pair of boots in twenty years."

Two minutes later everyone rose to their feet – some more quickly than others – as our star forward (as much as we had star forwards, not being in a position to compete with the Real Madrids of this world) surged into the box. There was a collective intake of breath as his foot connected with the ball, everything seemingly in slow motion as we waited to see if it found its way into the back of the net...

It didn't. The ball bounced back off the post, to the chagrin of the crowd.

Fred was apoplectic as he lowered himself back onto the plastic flip seat, furiously rubbing his hand against the contours of his hairless head. "Players these days don't know they're born. They need to take lessons from the greats. Watch videos of Alan Shearer or Malcolm McDonald and see how it's done." Fred blew out a puff of air in exasperation as he replaced his flat cap, covering the liver spots that speckled the skin on top of his head.

"Sophie surprised me with an old programme," Dad told him. "Supermac was on the front cover and I was telling her what a joy it was watching him play the beautiful game."

"Where did you find that?" Finley asked me.

"Second-hand shop," I mumbled, not wanting him to ask what I was doing rifling through a box of mildew-damaged programmes.

He raised his eyebrows quizzically, but didn't have chance to ask any further questions because we were on our feet again, the ball having crossed the halfway line. Two passes later, it was skied over the bar, to much derision from the crowd.

Swearing and chuntering (not just from Dad) echoed around the stadium as we sat back down, fifty thousand people lowering themselves into their seats in a reverse Mexican wave. That's when I noticed Norma wasn't hurling abuse, she was calling for help as she whacked the heel of her hand into the groove between Fred's shoulder blades.

"He's choking on a Werther's!" she screamed, her eyes wide in terror. "Do something, someone!"

Finley, who was sat directly behind Fred, immediately intervened, instructing Fred, whose face was turning the colour of an overripe blueberry, to lean forward and cough as hard as he could. I didn't think Fred had a cough in him as he helplessly gasped, but he somehow managed to release a loud bark, dislodging the sweet and firing it out of his mouth and into the hood of an unfortunate child in the row in front.

"Thanks, Finley." Fred sat down as though he hadn't just scared us all half to death.

"Always good to have a nurse on hand." Finley pretended to brush dust off his shoulder, proud at the success of his first aid, and Norma offered him another sweet as a reward. He refused. "No other medics around to save me if I choke," he whispered.

The remainder of the match was uneventful, both on and off the pitch – a nil-nil draw devoid of any drama other than the choking incident which we were still talking about as we walked away from the ground.

"Coming to the pub, Finley? I'll buy you a drink as a thank you for saving my life." Fred laughed, seeming oblivious to the worry he'd caused his wife. Poor Norma. She'd looked petrified when she'd thought her husband was going to snuff it. They'd been together so long I couldn't imagine them ever being apart. They were the partnership to end all partnerships. Norma without Fred would be like Ant without Dec – unthinkable.

"I'd best get back to Joel," Finley said, although his gaze lingered longingly on the pub door. "He'll be ready for a bit of TLC by now."

"Chicken soup and a cold flannel," Norma advised, as though Finley's nursing registration counted for nothing. "Makes any illness better."

"I'll bear it in mind." He winked in my direction, showing he was only humouring her. "Good to see you, Sophie, even if we didn't win."

"Can't win them all." I shrugged.

"Can't win any of them at the moment," Dad complained. "At least there's only one more home match to get through and then the season will be over. I'll be glad of the break."

I knew that wasn't true. He'd be bored stiff on a weekend without football. Mum would have to drag him around Homebase or Ikea and get him started on a project around the house to keep him busy until August rolled back around.

"Want to go for a quick drink, Soph?" Dad asked.

"Come on," Norma encouraged. "Live a little. We need some young blood for company or we'll only end up talking about how much better everything was in the good old days."

"All right," I conceded, and I swore my Dad perked up at my response.

"I knew I could rely on you." Norma placed her hand on my arm. "You're a good girl, Sophie." Then she turned to my dad, saying, "You did something right with this one. Kind-hearted and would bleed black and white if you cut her open."

"Indoctrination," I quipped.

"Maybe," Dad agreed good-naturedly. "Although it never worked with Nick or Anna. Even as kids they weren't fussed about football. Tried all the usual tricks – bribing them with hot dogs from the burger vans and taking them to matches under the floodlights so they'd associate the football with staying up late. None of it worked. Although I used to love our Saturdays together, just me and my biggest girl."

A rush of happiness took over my body at his words. It was

as though a blanket had been thrown around my shoulders. I'd loved those Saturdays too.

"I'm glad you came today, Soph," he continued, wrapping an arm around me. "It's been like old times. Just a shame the lucky scarf didn't work its magic." He sighed.

"Maybe it brought another kind of luck," I suggested. "Fred could have been in serious trouble with that sweet, if it wasn't for Finley knowing what to do."

"That certainly was lucky," Dad agreed. "And I feel lucky to have spent time with you. We should do this more often, get together, just the two of us."

"I'd like that."

"Me too," Dad said, planting a kiss on my head. My heart gushed with love.

In that moment I was a little girl again, and when he handed me a packet of dry roasted peanuts to go along with my drink, the same way he had so many times in the past, I was full of contentment.

CHAPTER 9

"You knock."

"No, you."

Eve and I had been standing on the doorstep of Tawna and Johnny's house for five minutes already, debating who was going to take the initiative and let them know we'd arrived. Bridesmaid dress hunting had been scheduled for a month, but with Tawna still insisting I should give Darius another chance I wasn't particularly looking forward to what should be a special day. Neither was Eve, who was firmly in the opposite camp.

"Do we have to do this? Can't we turn around and go back to my place instead?"

"No. Tawna's expecting us. We should have been here quarter of an hour ago."

"I wish she'd stop pushing me towards Darius," I moaned. "My head's in a right mess."

He'd been on my mind even more often than usual lately, and I'd even caved and pored over photos of the two of us with Summer, looking every inch the happy little family. Sadness knotted within me at what I'd lost. *You know he'd take you back in a heartbeat...*

"We'll have to see her sooner or later, so let's get on with it. At least by the end of the day we'll have the bridesmaids dresses sorted and it'll be one less thing for her to be fussing over."

Tawna's continual eulogising over Darius was annoying, but combined with her bridezilla behaviour over the last few months she'd driven me completely around the bend. But despite everything, she was still one of my best friends. Misguided? Yes. But she'd be devastated if she knew her comments had given me a run of sleepless nights as I mused over the pros and cons of Darius and Max. My current frugal lifestyle meant the newness of Max appealed, but I couldn't rid myself of the sense that Darius and I had unfinished business.

"Go on then," I said. "You knock."

Eve played out a tune on the solid brass knocker, a rat-tat-a-tat-tat that sounded unnaturally loud. It probably had to be loud so Johnny and Tawna could hear visitors arriving from the far end of the house. It was a bit different to my place, where any knock on my neighbour's door caused my walls to shake.

Tawna swung the door open with a flourish and a squeal, before throwing her arms first around me and then around Eve. She clearly didn't share our qualms, excitement bubbling out of her every pore.

"You're here! It's great to see you. I've been so looking forward to today, we'll have so much fun."

I cringed with guilt as I disentangled myself from her lithe limbs. She was right, the dress shopping would be fun, and the three of us hadn't spent nearly enough time together since my birthday.

"Me too," I said. "And I'm glad we're all choosing dresses together."

"It wouldn't be fair to choose bridesmaids dresses without your input, would it? Although you know I wouldn't choose anything hideous. I'm not into lavender puffball dresses anymore." She laughed, referring to the time she won the May Queen competition (of course she won – teenage Tawna had been equally as beautiful as present-day Tawna, and had aspired to be Miss World one day). She'd worn a satin dress that made her look like a china doll and had slept in plaits for a week to give her poker-straight hair zigzagged waves.

"Yeah, lavender's never been my colour," Eve joked, as we entered the house.

Although Tawna and Johnny had lived in it since their engagement, I still couldn't get used to this being her house. It was in Gosforth for one thing (which meant it was bloody massive – almost a mansion) and was immaculate for another. That was down to the cleaner who came twice a week rather than my friend, who wouldn't dream of doing anything that might damage her nail extensions, but nevertheless everything about the house screamed upmarket. Not only was it posh, but everything was sparkly-new; like a show home, right down to the vase of fresh red roses on the hallway table and the overflowing fruit bowl at the centre of the kitchen island. The vivid colours of nature contrasted starkly with the starched white of the cabinets and work surfaces, illuminated by strategically placed spotlights that showed the room to its best advantage.

"Come on through. Johnny's at the gym so we can spread out in the conservatory. I've got a stack of magazines for us to look through before we hit the wedding dress shops, to give us an idea of what we're after."

My ballet pumps padded along the tiled hallway, through the kitchen diner (which was probably twice as large as the whole downstairs of my house) and into the conservatory, although that made it sound like a small sunroom rather than the full-on extension it was. It had one of those roofs with a central point, so the room looked like a big top from a travelling circus, minus the bright coloured canvas. All the colour was outside, in the landscaped gardens. Rhododendrons and rose bushes, fuchsias and ferns, and a whole host of other botanical beauties I couldn't hazard a guess at naming were kept perfectly pruned by one of Johnny's gardener friends. I pushed down my envy as I compared Tawna's garden to the collection of half-dead potted plants that littered my kitchen windowsill. But there was no competition, it was the Chelsea flower show versus the reduced section at B&Q.

"Make yourselves comfy, and I'll fetch us some drinks." She waved her hand in the direction of an expensive-looking teal three-piece suite I'm sure wasn't there last time I'd visited. "I got some fizz in especially, and none of that cheap rubbish. Only the best for my girls." She beamed.

Eve and I did as we were instructed, our bottoms bouncing as they connected with the firm cushions of the settee, confirming its newness.

The coffee table was piled high with bridal magazines, all boasting the absolute must-haves for the picture-perfect big day. Headlines screamed "Silk or lace?" and "Twenty unique table favours" from the covers, but the publications had one thing in common – the dresses the beaming "brides" on the covers were wearing all cost more than my monthly pay cheque. When we'd gone shopping for Tawna's dress at the tail-end of the previous year the prices hadn't shocked me. Since I'd started counting every last penny the thought of paying hundreds, or even thousands, of pounds for a dress that'd be worn once now horrified me.

"I've folded down the pages of the bridesmaids dresses I like best," Tawna called from the kitchen. "To give you an idea of what I've been thinking."

Eve and I exchanged another loaded look. Tawna wasn't sticking to a strict colour scheme, instead going for a rural theme to match the village church her and Johnny had chosen for the wedding itself and the luxury country house reception, which meant we had no expectations. Other than the absence of lavender puffballs we'd not been given so much as an inkling of style or colour palette.

I picked a magazine from the top of the pile, immediately taking a dislike to the couple on the cover. A dark-haired "groom" modelling a well-cut navy suit looked lovingly at his "bride", a slender woman with caramel curls wearing an ivory dress with a voluminous layered tulle skirt. Even though I knew it wasn't real – it was two attractive people who'd been paid to pretend to be wildly in love with each other – my stomach spasmed. It wasn't the dress that my body was anguishing over, it wasn't a longing for a day in the spotlight. No, the pit of my stomach was writhing over what it represented – what every stupidly expensive, ostentatious wedding day represented. That one person loved another enough to *want* all that fuss, all that show.

Eve craned her neck to see as I flicked to the first marked page. I knew it must be a favourite of Tawna's, because as well as the corner of the page being folded down, it was labelled with a luminous green Post-it note.

The dress wasn't what I'd choose for myself – a slash-necked lace peach tea-length dress with a thick silky ribbon a few shades darker tied around the waist. It was pretty, but not suited to my colouring. On a pure English rose like Eve it'd probably be perfect, accentuating flushed cheeks and bud-red lips.

I flipped to the next marked page, hoping it would be more suitable. I was faced with a full-length strappy dress in a sickly lemon shade.

"We'd look like walking bananas in those," Eve whispered. I was glad she didn't like them either.

"Seen anything you like yet?" Tawna asked, entering the

room with a champagne bottle in one hand and three glasses clutched at the stems in the other.

"I'm not sure about the yellow," Eve said diplomatically, "but we're just getting started."

"How about the sage green? They're beautiful and would fit perfectly with our country theme."

Tawna placed the bubbly and the glasses on the coffee table, taking care to move the magazines safely out of the way in case of spillages. She peeled back the gold foil that covered the neck of the bottle and, twisting the bottle one way and the bulbous cork the other, opened it with a satisfying pop.

"You'll have a glass won't you, Eve? I know you're driving, but a small one won't hurt. It is a celebration."

"As long as it really is a small one," Eve warned. "You know it doesn't take much of that stuff to get me drunk."

Tawna poured a trickle into one of the glasses, probably no more than two mouthfuls' worth of champagne altogether, and handed it to Eve.

"You'll have a proper glass though, won't you, Soph?" She'd already decanted the fizz into the glass, a frothy cloud of bubbles spilling over the rim and dribbling down the outside. "I can always rely on you to be my drinking partner." She smiled.

"I'm probably turning into a lightweight," I admitted. "I've not been drinking as much lately."

I sipped at the drink, the sharp tang of the champagne coating my throat as I swallowed.

"You're not pregnant, are you?" Tawna peered judgementally down her long slender nose.

"What? No! Don't be ridiculous."

"I wasn't being ridiculous. Besides last week I've not seen you in ages. I don't know what's been going on in your love life." Tawna harrumphed, as though she was the one being insulted, and her eyes skimmed over my stomach looking for any sign of a bump. There was a bump, but that was down to the bag of reduced Sainsbury's doughnuts I'd eaten the previous night rather than a new life growing within me. It would have had to have been an immaculate conception anyway, because the innocent hand-hold with Max at the pub was as intimate as I'd got lately. It would be hard to take things further anyway, without a phone number. A particularly raunchy dream about the two of us had left me hot and bothered and in need of a cold shower, and wishing I'd been brazen enough to ask for his number. "I think I've got every right to know if one of my best friends, not to mention one of my bridesmaids, is going to be pregnant on my big day."

It was so like Tawna to expect everyone else to put their life on hold because of her wedding day. "I assure you my womb will remain uninhabited for your special day. The only new babies in my family this year will be Nick and Chantel's."

"I can't believe they're having twins, especially so soon after Noah," Eve exclaimed, lowering the magazine she'd been browsing onto the table.

It had shocked me too. Mum had called to share the news; typically as I was on my way home from the supermarket, two weighty Tesco bags for life hanging from the hook of each arm. Lifting my phone close enough to my ear to hear what she'd had to say had been a struggle, with the thick plastic of the handles sliding down the fleshy part of my forearm. The friction stung.

"I didn't realise you were going out. I thought you'd be in bed with a sore head on a Saturday morning." She'd laughed as she said it, but yet again I'd felt like a failure of a daughter. She'd never say something like that to Anna or Nick, instead she'd be praising them on their work ethic and perfect home lives.

"I'm reining in my partying," I'd said defensively, jiggling my arm so the bags hung at my elbow.

"Are you heading into town for some retail therapy?" she'd

asked, and once again I bristled. She was obviously convinced I was a raging shopaholic.

If only.

"I'm on my way back from the supermarket." I'd reached my front door by this point, relieved to be able to drop the weighty bags to the floor.

"Good, good," Mum had replied, in a way that made me think she'd not been listening. "I didn't ring for small talk, actually."

There'd been a pregnant pause as she waited for me to beg for details. "Oh?" I'd managed, rummaging distractedly in my pocket for my key.

"Chantel had her twelve-week scan yesterday."

Again Mum had stopped, dragging it out for dramatic effect. "Come on, Mum. What's going on?"

"It's twins!" Her squeal was so high-pitched that it wouldn't surprise me if every dog within a ten-mile radius pricked back its ears. "Isn't that wonderful news?"

Nick and his perfect life yet again. As if one beautiful son wasn't enough, he had to go and get Chantel pregnant again, this time with double the reward.

"Wonderful," I'd replied duly and dully. I knew I'd be happy about it once it sunk in, I'd felt the same when they announced they were expecting Noah. But all I wanted to do in that moment was wallow in self-pity.

"I can't believe it," Mum had answered, her words coming thick and fast, "and they're identical!"

"I can't believe it," I'd echoed, breathing a sigh of relief as I'd retrieved my key. "It's lovely news, pass on my congratulations."

"You should call Nick yourself, he'd be glad to hear from you," Mum said, and I'd humoured her with a non-committal "hmmm" before ending the call, going into my house and sobbing. I felt like the most selfish sister in the world for being jealous of my brother and his perfect family, and even more than that, being jealous of how happy he'd made my mum. I'd never done anything that had filled her with such obvious pride.

Tawna prodded the magazine in her hand, annoyed the attention had shifted away from her and the wedding. "Can we get back to looking at dresses please?" She pushed a handful of the glossy brochures towards me and directed me to the pages showing her favourite dresses. Most were much of a muchness – floaty fabrics in one ice-cream shade or another. The selection ranged from knee-length to floor-skimming, and I was quietly hoping Tawna would pick the shorter style. My body wasn't as svelte as the women's in these glorified catalogues, but walking everywhere to save money ensured my legs had become one of my best features.

"I like that one." Eve pointed to a simple dusky lilac dress with a classic cut. Rounded neck, capped sleeves and falling just below the knee, the only detail was in the ruched folds of fabric around the bust. "The colour is subtle. It looks classier than the bright dresses."

"That's what I thought." Tawna beamed at Eve for the vote of confidence, before looking warily my way. "Do you like them, Soph? It's you two who need to be happy; it won't be me wearing it."

"Sure."

I took the magazine from Eve, scrutinising the detail of the dress. It was pretty, and I tried to imagine me and Eve wearing them as we followed Tawna and her mum down the aisle. That in itself was enough to make my emotions brim over. Tawna had been incredibly close to her dad and it had hit her hard when he'd died a few years earlier. A lump rose in my throat and I clamped my lips together to stop the tears welling in my eyes from falling. We'd been through so much together, all three of us.

"Oh, Soph, you old softie." As Tawna folded me into a hug, the tears started flowing good and proper. "I thought it was the bride who was supposed to get emotional. If you're like this now, what will you be like on the day?"

"I'm sorry," I snivelled. "It's just strange to think of you getting married. It doesn't seem long since we were sat at the back of history class, making fun of Mr Maloney's comb-over."

I sniffed and laughed at the same time. What would those cocksure young girls make of the three of us now? Eve would be proud of her academic achievements, I'm sure. Tawna would be happy too, marrying a good-looking self-made businessman and living the dream in her glamorous pad. But me? My dream as a fifteen-year-old had been simple – marry Milo V and live happily ever after. Somewhere along the line I'd realised that wasn't going to happen and that had been the end of my dreaming. Why hadn't I replaced my ambitions to marry the delectable star with something else, something more achievable that I had control over? I couldn't say. Instead I'd chosen to float through life, watching, as everyone else moved towards their goals.

"A lot's happened since school," Eve said, joining the hug.

"It has," Tawna agreed, "and I know how fortunate I am to have friends like you two. Having one best friend is lucky, but having two – I'm blessed by the friendship fairies. So what do you think? Shall I call the bridal shop and ask if they have this dress in stock?"

Tawna clapped her hands together excitably as Eve and I nodded. "You're both going to look gorgeous!" Tawna stated gleefully. I wouldn't have been surprised if she'd started jumping up and down. "Totally stunning."

"I'm sure we'll look lovely, but you're going to be the star of the show," I said. "The most beautiful bride in the whole wide world."

Then Tawna welled up too, frantically flapping her hands in front of her tear-filled eyes so it was hard to believe it was the same opinionated person we knew and loved (and, in all honesty, often got frustrated by). She was suddenly softer, in need of reassurance that she could fit the criteria for "perfect bride".

"Sometimes I can't believe it's really going to happen. Me and Johnny getting married." Her eyes sparkled with tears. "He could have anyone he wanted."

"But he loves you," Eve pointed out rationally. "Anyone can see you're his absolute world. When the two of you are together he goes from one of the lads to a gooey-eyed mess. He's crazy for you."

"Good," Tawna replied, taking a deep breath to regain her composure. She blinked, then shook the tension out of her shoulders. "Because I'm crazy for him too."

As she retreated to the kitchen to call the bridal shop, my chest heaved. Had anyone ever loved me like that? Darius might have, once. Maybe, if what Tawna said was right, he still did. Could Max, maybe, with time?

CHAPTER 10

A bell tinkled melodically as we entered the shop – correction, "bridal boutique" – to search for the perfect bridesmaids dresses. Tawna had tried the shop she'd ordered her wedding dress from first, but they didn't stock the design we'd all admired. Another two bridal stores had said the same. That's how we'd ended up in Sunderland, in a tiny shop as white as Tawna's kitchen but for one rainbow-coloured rack of bridesmaids dresses. The glare of the lights reflecting off the shimmering fabric of hundreds of bridal gowns caused me to squint. It was like stepping into a scene in a film where a dying person gravitates towards a bright light. Death by wedding dresses.

"Hello," said a glamorous yet hard-faced brunette, rearranging a display of glistening tiaras. The gems that adorned the headwear had more sparkle than either her eyes or her voice. "How can I help?"

"I'm Tawna, I phoned earlier about the mauve bridesmaids dresses?" Tawna presented the piece of paper, on which she'd written down the details, to the assistant.

"Ah, yes. We have it in stock, if you're sure that's what you want." Her lips twitched first to the left and then to the right as she looked me and Eve up and down disparagingly, before saying, "Some people find detail on the bust draws attention to the chest area. Of course, if that doesn't bother you then it's not a problem." I couldn't tell who she was directing that comment towards – me with my ample bosom, or Eve with her bee-stings. It was hardly complimentary, however you looked at it. "Feel free to browse the stock, see if there's anything more... *suitable*."

That was all the encouragement Tawna needed to start pulling at the dresses on the racks, immediately dismissing anything too garish.

"I like this," she said, pulling out a silky floor-length sheath in a pale pink shade.

"That's gorgeous." I stroked the delicate fabric with the tips of my fingers. "So elegant. And it's pink, my favourite."

"And look at the tie around the waist." Eve pointed to the sage green ribbon, tied into a feature bow to one side of the dress. "It's the same colour as that other dress you liked, Tawna."

"We don't have every size in that style available at the moment," the assistant said through pinched lips, "although you're welcome to try on as many dresses as you like."

Soon we were posing in all styles. The one we'd originally come to look at was gorgeous, but I had to begrudgingly admit that the assistant knew her stuff – I'd looked like a pair of tits on legs. A silver shift dress looked stunning on Eve with her Twiggy-like figure but left me looking like a chicken drumstick wrapped in tin foil. A classy sky-blue dress was flattering for us both, but Tawna's mutterings about halter-necks not complimenting her own dress had vetoed it.

"And you're sure you don't want to try the yellow?" Tawna cajoled, to resounding "no"s from me and Eve.

"We all know the pink one's the winner," Eve said, looking back towards the dress that had caught Tawna's eye on the rail.

"It's grown up, simple, flattering, and won't date in the photographs. It's a timeless classic."

When Eve had tried the smaller of the shop samples earlier, Tawna and I had gasped at the vision of Eve, whose dark hair contrasted with the subtle tones of the dress. She really had looked breathtaking.

Despite my best efforts I'd not been able to fit into the largest dress they had in stock. The zip went so far and then refused to budge no matter how hard I'd tried to make my frame smaller. My chest was the problem, being two sizes bigger than my waist. In the end I'd resorted to putting the dress back on the hanger and looping it over my head, to at least see if the colour suited my skin tone (which was paler than ever, since stopping using even the cheap fake tan).

"You're going to look amazing in that," Tawna confirmed. "You'll need a good bra though, Miss Boobalicious."

"Maybe I'll make a move on the best man," I joked, reaching out to touch the smooth cool material of the dress. It slid through my fingers, fluid. "Isn't that the tradition? The bridesmaid and the best man get it on?"

Eve laughed. "Why do you get first dibs? It might be someone I take a shine to."

"Ah." Tawna's lips formed a pained smile, her eyes flitting nervously between the two of us. She clucked her tongue, then inhaled her breath sharply through her teeth. "I wanted to talk to you about that. Johnny's asked Darius to be his best man."

Eve's eyes widened at the revelation and I struggled to find the right words, making sounds that could pass for gibberish, before finally managing, "I thought Johnny was going to ask Paul." Paul was Johnny's brother, near identical to him in looks, but not in business nous or work ethic, which was why Paul's barber's shop was struggling to survive (which is what happens when you turn up three hours later than the advertised opening hours, because you were out on the lash the night before), whereas Johnny's company was expanding every year.

"He did, but Paul turned him down. He doesn't think he's reliable enough to handle all that responsibility, and you've got to agree he's right. Can you imagine trusting him with the rings?" She laughed as though it was ridiculous. "That's why Darius is stepping up to the role. It's not exactly out of the blue, he is Johnny's best friend. He's still been asking after you, Sophie, and I don't want the two of you at loggerheads on my wedding day. Why don't you meet up with him? Talk things through and clear the air?"

"Woah, woah, woah," Eve interjected, rearing like a startled horse. "Don't push Sophie into spending time with that jerk."

Tawna frowned, her usually beautiful face hard. "I don't believe she's over him and I don't want her to have any regrets. And from the things he's been saying to Johnny, Darius is still in love with her."

Why was it that every time Tawna made a declaration of love on Darius's behalf I found myself catching my breath?

"But she's not in love with him," Eve replied, exasperated.

"Because she's in love with this Max, is that what you're saying?" Tawna laughed sceptically, and I wished they'd stop making out they knew what was best for me. I felt invisible. "After one date, if you can even call it that?"

"I never mentioned love, but I like him. What's wrong with that?" The sales assistant glanced up cautiously, my loud voice leading her to believe a full-blown cat fight was about to kick off. That wouldn't be good in a bridal boutique. Too many delicate materials.

"Darius never got over you. He says splitting up with you was the worst mistake of his life."

"Maybe we'd still be together if he'd spent less time chatting up other women."

Talking about it brought the painful memories of rejection to the fore. It had got to the point where I hadn't wanted to go into town with him. I'd only end up crushed by the lack of attention he'd pay me, but despite knowing his eyes would wander towards other women, I'd get dolled up and go with him regardless. After a day at work I was more than happy to have a long soak in a bubble bath, change into my PJs and read or sew in front of the telly, but Darius called me a boring old fart if I suggested a night in.

Even the trips we'd shared to the club capitals of Europe – Ayia Napa, Faliraki, Magaluf – had required not just stamina to last the all-nighters but a thick skin to turn a blind eye to his antics. I'd paid for the last holiday we'd had together, because of a cash-flow problem at the company, even though the trip had been his idea. He'd made me promise not to let on to Tawna, because "it would only worry her if she knew things weren't as good for Johnny's business in reality as they were on paper", and of course I couldn't tell Eve because she'd have blabbed. Darius assured me he'd pay me back when he could, because a fortnight at an all-inclusive top hotel right in the heart of the action had been costly. He'd finished with me a week after we got back without offering to reimburse me, and I was too ashamed to ask for the money. I hadn't mentioned that to anyone. Bringing it up would only sound petty, like sour grapes for being scorned.

"Look, I didn't want to say this, but..." Tawna sighed. "It's Nadia. She's being a total bitch to Darius. She's got this new boyfriend who's in the marines."

"Very interesting," Eve said, in a dry tone that suggested she thought it was anything but. "But that has nothing to do with Sophie."

"Exactly." I glared. "Nadia and I never saw eye to eye, but good for her if she's got a fit new boyfriend. Fair play."

"You don't understand," Tawna replied. "It's not about that. This guy Nadia's been seeing... he's getting his feet under the table. Summer's started calling him Daddy. He's taking them to Florida in the school holidays too, because Summer's desperate to meet Mickey Mouse."

I couldn't help but smile. Summer would love that. She watched the *Mickey Mouse Clubhouse* on a loop, knowing which Mousekatool was most useful in any given situation because she'd seen every episode twenty times before.

Tawna scowled, mistaking my fond memories for cruel amusement. "You might think it's funny, but Darius is really hurting. This guy's trying to muscle his way in and take his place as Summer's dad."

"Muscle." Eve giggled. "That's funny." When Tawna looked at her blankly she said, "Because he's a marine, get it? He must have massive muscles. I bet he's ripped."

"I'm sure he's upset," I said, ignoring Eve who was still chuckling to herself in the background, "but I don't know what he expects me to do about it."

"Summer needs her dad in her life. Her real dad, not some flavour-of-the-month replacement."

My chest spasmed at the thought of Summer and her crooked gap-toothed smile. When Darius and I had first got together she'd been a toddler, and I'd watched her grow into a chatty, confident little girl. And I'd loved her so, so much. There had been a time where I'd genuinely thought I'd be her stepmum one day.

"He needs people he can trust around him right now, people who can support him. It's not only about him, it's Summer too. Think about it, yeah?"

"I'll think about it," I found myself saying. "Although I don't see how anything I could do would make a difference."

"Soph..." Eve warned.

"You heard Tawna, it's not just about Darius," I said, as much to convince myself as her. "Summer's more important than anything that's happened in the past."

"But it's not your battle," Eve started. "Darius is big enough and ugly enough to deal with this himself."

I didn't say what I was thinking – that Nadia was such a bitch that it wouldn't surprise me if she was playing yet more games, with Summer as a helpless pawn. She was the sort of person who stored up failures and used them as ammunition in future arguments, and Darius, too afraid to rock the boat and have her cut off all access, would be bullied into going along with whatever Queen Nadia suggested.

I knew, deep down, that as soon as I'd said goodbye to the girls, I'd be on the phone to Darius finding out what I could do to help. I might have deleted his number from my phone, but that didn't make a jot of difference. How could it, when I knew that number off by heart?

I watched a tear-jerker of a romance on Netflix with a spoon and a tub of chocolate ice cream for company (not Häagen-Dazs, unfortunately – Aldi special, at a fraction of the price) as I steeled myself to make the call.

By the time I reached the bottom of the tub my stomach hurt and I feared I might be sick. The sweet creaminess coating my throat was no longer pleasant, and although I wasn't quite at the Bridget-Jones-listening-to-*All-By-Myself* level of wallowing, I wasn't far off. The film had been a bad choice. *Calm down, Sophie,* I thought, breathing in through my nose and out through my mouth. *Clear your head.* I'd learnt the technique from sexy yoga guru Leo in the YouTube video I watched when I was feeling healthy and virtuous. Sometimes, rarely, I even joined in with the exercises.

I focused on my rhythmic breathing until I felt calmer and stronger. Stretching across the settee, knocking over the empty ice cream tub so the gloop-covered spoon landed on the rug, I retrieved my mobile and dialled the eleven-digit number that was etched in my brain.

Five minutes later it was over; Darius and I had made arrangements to meet the following week. I rang Mum immediately after because although the romantic film had made me believe in happy-ever-afters I couldn't believe I'd contacted Darius. I couldn't decide if it felt like a step forward or a step back.

Mum's jubilant chatter about how she'd started knitting for the twins was a welcome distraction from my confusion. Not only that, the conversation prompted me to rifle through the craft supplies I'd stashed away in plastic storage crates on top of my wardrobe.

I needed the comfort of crafting, the security of it. Creating something new always helped me organise my mind; working methodically through a pattern to make something from nothing being a fail-safe way of sorting out the jumble of mess inside my head. If a twisted ball of wool could be transformed into something useful and practical with nothing more than a crochet hook, then surely the knots of confusion in my brain could be worked out too.

I spent a solid cathartic hour sorting through my stash after talking to Mum. There were so many materials I'd impulse-bought; skeins of scarlet thread to make Christmas decorations, balls of soft merino wool to knit winter hats, fat quarters of fabrics I'd planned to stitch together to make an heirloom patchwork quilt. There were half-completed cross-stitches and tapestries, miniature bottles of glass paints and a dented metal tin containing an assortment of pretty buttons and beads. So much potential waiting to be made into something beautiful.

I chose a thick, fluffy wool that was soft to the touch, a bright raspberry shade that left me craving sorbet and cosmopolitans, and selected the thickest needle from the wrap containing my crochet hooks. My fingers automatically formed a pretzel-shaped loop and started a chain, and before long I had the beginnings of a scarf. The repetitive motion brought calm, and working without a pattern freed my mind from thoughts of Darius. Best of all, it hadn't felt like a waste of time because the scarf was growing, absorbing my mixed emotions and turning them into something productive.

Four balls of wool and three hours later, I'd finished the scarf. Although it was a simple pattern and just one colour, I'd been pleasantly surprised by the result. Having taken a break from my hobby after furiously felting my way through the split from Darius (nothing quite like stabbing something with a pronged needle and concealing it as art rather than voodoo), I revelled in the sense of pride that took over as I held the scarf in my hands. It wouldn't have existed if it wasn't for me. It'd still just be wool, four spherical balls.

Searching through my supplies, to look for a way to embellish the scarf, I was disappointed. Although there were reels of ribbons – matt and satin, patterned and plain – I couldn't see anything suitable.

There were plenty of ends of wool though, leftover threads from previous projects – a small amount of rose-pink from when I'd made a bonnet and booties set for Marcie's little granddaughter and an off-white that I'd used to knit a matinee jacket for Noah. The texture of the wool against my skin brought back all the emotions I'd felt when knitting it – the joy for Nick and Chantel and the excitement at our family growing, tinged with a hint of sadness – envy even – that it wasn't me, as the oldest child of my generation, providing Mum and Dad with their first grandchild. Maybe I'd start making something for the new babies soon, once Chantel had her sexing scan.

Crafting is powerful. Mindful. Wonderful. To me it's a form of therapy, keeping my mind and my fingers occupied when I feel stressed.

Why had I ever let Darius dampen the joy making things brought me? I'd taken his unkind remarks to heart, let his opinions affect my own decisions. I'd compromised myself a thousand times over.

Moving the small skeins of wool to one side, I pressed the lid of the box closed and moved the crate back to its usual place. Up there it would be out of sight, but no longer out of mind. I was mentally making a list of the people I could make gifts for this Christmas, even though it was only April. There were card-making supplies in the box too, patterned squares of paper, rubber stamps and all kinds of stickers and washi tapes. The possibilities were limitless.

The realisation that I could have new things without spending money hit me. I didn't need to buy things, I could make them, or refashion what I already had. Etsy sites were full of upcycled goods people had added their own detail to to make them more desirable.

I held that thought as I looked at the scarf, draped over the back of the settee. A few crocheted flowers sewn around each end would give it a cute kitsch look.

I pulled a thinner crochet hook out of the wrap which I'd purposely not packed away and began creating, glad there was something in my life I could control. Crafting is magical. Crafting is my remedy.

MAY

I'd been floored when Darius had suggested meeting at McDonalds. Usually he'd have put forward the idea of a bistro at Sunday lunchtime, somewhere small and exclusive, an upcoming place that would be the most in-demand booking in the area the following month. But when he'd texted to confirm the meeting he'd mentioned Summer would be with him, and that she'd been pestering him for junk food all morning, so the fast food joint it was. My heart had clenched with love at the thought that I'd finally get to see Summer again.

The place was rammed – full of families giving in to their little treasures' demands for Happy Meals – and so very, very noisy. I get why it's popular. The food might not be the most nutritious, but it's warm and quick, and kids eat it without kicking up a stink.

I pinched some French fries between my fingers before popping them into my mouth. Their salty flavour started my mouth watering so I sipped my Diet Coke to quench the onset of thirst, all the while wondering where Darius was. He was late.

A man sat down next to me, smiling apologetically as his two sons bickered loudly over the plastic toys that came in their boxes of food. The older boy, a freckly red-head with a gappy grin, eventually gave in, handing his sibling the more-coveted toy, which looked to me to be identical to the other, but orange, rather than yellow.

I was shoving another handful of fries into my mouth when Darius appeared at the top of the stairwell. His eyes skimmed the crowds before falling on me and a grin broke out on his face.

With his wavy dark hair and his prominent features he looked handsome, and he was, as ever, immaculately dressed. His pristine white shirt was unbuttoned at both the top and the bottom, which would look knobbish on most men, but Darius pulled it off because he was annoyingly attractive. The same went for his shorts – knee-length and a sandy shade a designer would probably describe as camel – which should by rights be hideous. Darius managed to make them look stylish. I barely noticed the tray he was holding, I was too busy taking in the familiar contours of his face.

As they drew closer I caught my first glimpse of Summer, dressed in clothes as bright and sunny as her name would suggest. She was noticeably taller than the last time I'd seen her. Her glossy dark hair was shorter; no longer well past her shoulders, instead cut level with her jawline with a gigantic red bow clipped to the crown of her head. She looked older than seven, and I deserted my lukewarm fries and half-empty drink to run and greet her.

"Summer!" I pulled her into my chest, dumbfounded to find she was so tall that her head propped up my breasts. "I'm so glad to see you."

I didn't want to let her go, but stood back to appraise her. Everything about her was exquisite, from her dark eyes to the deep pink of her lips. She looked like the children you see in adverts for kids clothing. No grubby hands, no ketchup stains on her sunshine-yellow T-shirt. She was pure and sweet, and bright as the proverbial button, and seeing her in the flesh was acutely painful.

"I'm staying with Daddy this weekend," Summer said, matter-of-factly, her accent pure Liverpudlian. "Mummy and Daddy Rob are on holiday."

Darius interrupted before she could elaborate. "Come on then, Summer, let's dig in before our lunch goes cold."

We sat around the plastic-topped table; Darius and Summer wolfing down their burgers as though they'd not eaten in weeks, whilst I nibbled at my chips, which were far less appealing cold. Even their appearance was disappointing; soggy and saggy and limp, adjectives that are never positive no matter what they're describing.

"I thought we were going to talk." I nodded pointedly in Summer's direction, knowing we'd not be able to openly discuss Nadia if Summer was sat with us. Summer was a clever girl who picked up on everything, and from the information Darius had given me over the phone, the conversation wouldn't be suitable for little ears.

"I thought we could go somewhere afterwards. Summer can burn off some steam and we can catch up properly." The way he said it, slowly and purposefully and with his eyes lingering on me, caused my stomach to flip. I couldn't decipher if it was with lust or fear.

When we'd been dating, Darius and I would take Summer to soft play whenever she was in Newcastle. She'd loved the ball pools, and I'd find myself climbing in with her, pushing the disturbing stories of toddlers who weren't yet toilet trained having accidents amongst the rainbow-coloured balls out of my mind. At first I'd been sure people could tell I wasn't her mum, but I soon realised people don't scrutinise for a family resemblance. If they see a woman of child-bearing age with an infant they make assumptions, and although I knew it was wrong, I'd let them. I would never have introduced myself as Summer's mum – that would have been weird – but I didn't correct those who'd said "oh, isn't she a darling! You must be so proud" or, "I bet she gets away with murder with that cheeky smile, doesn't she?" I was only playing a role, but it was one I loved.

"Can we go to the trampoline park? Please, Dad. You know I love it there."

Summer pressed the palms of her hands together as though praying. Her voice carried the merest hint of whininess. She knew how to play the game. Where Darius was concerned, Summer could get away with murder.

"Whatever you want, precious girl." He grinned before taking a bite of his Big Mac. He swallowed down the burger before turning to me and saying, "And I'd like to see Sophie on a trampoline."

"What? No! I'm not dressed for bouncing." I was wearing a plain white balconette bra rather than the industrial-strength support I'd have gone for if I'd have known trampolines were on the cards. I'd only chosen it because it wouldn't show through my T-shirt.

"You'll be fine. It's only a bit of fun. It's not like you need a gym kit. They'll let you bounce in your everyday clothes."

"I wasn't about to dig out my old school leotard." My voice hissed through my teeth. "I was thinking of..." I stopped short, thinking better of mentioning my boobs around my ex, but my eyes automatically looked down at my chest, and Darius's followed.

"Oh..." He dragged the word out so it sounded like it had twenty-two letters rather than two, and raised his eyebrows suggestively before saying, "I don't really see the problem."

Of course he didn't. There was probably nothing he'd like

more than watching my unrestrained puppies jumping freely like… well, like unrestrained puppies.

"How about the soft play? Are you sure you don't want to go? You used to love it there, Summer." The desperation was obvious in my voice, and Darius smirked as I squirmed.

Summer didn't notice my discomfort, instead adding stickers to the plastic toy that had come with her meal. "I'm too old for soft play, So-So," she said, as though it was an absurd suggestion. "I'm not a baby anymore."

My heart melted as she used the nickname she'd given me the first time I'd met her. She'd been two, with a lisp, and Darius and I hadn't been dating long. Sophie had morphed into Sosie, which in turn had been shortened to So-So. There was no one else in the world who called me it. It was music to my ears.

"I know you're not, pet. I was just thinking of how much fun we used to have in the ball pools, that's all."

"And we'll have fun on the trampolines, I promise. I'm really good," she said, with a child's innocence. "I can even do somersaults. Daddy Rob taught me how."

Darius flinched, and I felt his pain.

"Okay," I found myself saying, despite my better judgement, "we'll go trampolining."

I needed to know exactly what was going on. Whatever it was sounded serious. Serious enough, even, to risk giving myself a black eye from bouncing around on a trampoline with insufficient support for my knockers.

❧

The trampoline park was exactly what I expected – loud, dark and overrun with excitable kids. My legs were like jelly after five minutes on one of the small square trampolines that lined the floor, and I resorted to tentatively bouncing with my arms tightly folded over my chest to stop my boobs jiggling.

Darius watched with amusement as he bounced up and down, barely breaking a sweat. I on the other hand, felt like I'd had a real workout.

"Relax a bit," he encouraged. "It'll be far more fun if you throw yourself into it."

Far more fun for him, he meant, copping an eyeful.

"We're not here to actually trampoline," I reminded him, bending my knees as I landed to bring myself to a standstill. "We're here to talk."

"You're right." He executed one final piked jump before coming to a faultless stop. Show-off. "Let's grab a drink."

He swept his hair out of his eyes as we moved to the café area. It was an action that used to send me weak at the knees. They weren't the most stable at that moment either, but I was putting that down to the trampolining and using muscle groups that had been in long-term hibernation.

The café was typical of the place, selling brightly coloured slush drinks and undrinkable coffees for way over the going rate. I opted for a can of Sprite. At least then I knew what I was going to get.

"This is hard to talk about," he said when we sat down. The table we'd found was covered in rings from who-knows-how-many customers' cups. "But thanks for saying you'd meet me. I thought you were still pissed off with me."

A woman bouncing a baby on her lap tutted at his choice of language, as though her child was suddenly going to start spouting obscenities.

Darius carried on regardless. "Nadia's trying to push me out. When she first got with Rob she said I'd still get to spend time with Summer the way I always have, but now she's threatening to move in with him."

"It must be hard for you, but you can't expect her to live like a nun. She's pretty." It pained me to pay the woman who was always looking down her beautiful ski-slope nose at me a compliment. "It's surprising it's taken her this long to start a relationship, when you think about it."

"That's what's making it hard. It's been so long that I kind of thought she wouldn't find anyone else."

The comment made me wonder if Darius might be jealous of the muscular man dating his ex. No one likes to feel replaceable. I knew that from experience.

"Have you met him? Is that the problem?"

Darius laughed wryly. "Oh yeah, I've met him all right. She invited him to Summer's birthday party. That wasn't awkward at all, having the woman at Build-A-Bear Workshop not knowing which of us to call Daddy."

I winced. "Ouch."

"Yeah, made me feel like I wasn't even needed at my own daughter's birthday." His lips pursed tightly together, his chin dimpling like a golf ball. "Nadia kept draping herself over him. I know what she was doing, trying to make me uncomfortable."

"And he was acting like a knob too?"

Darius shook his head. "That's the worst thing, he was as nice as pie. Can't fault the guy, and Summer loves him to bits. Of course she does, he's buying her everything she asks for. He spent a fortune at that party on accessories for the teddy she chose, told the staff to let her get whatever she wanted. Clothes, sunglasses, shoes... I mean, did you know teddy bears needed shoes? Because apparently they do nowadays."

I nodded sympathetically, but didn't understand what any of this had to do with me. I wasn't a part of their lives anymore. What was Darius expecting me to do?

"It sounds as though he just wants to treat her. She's a lovely girl. It's not surprising that he's taken a shine to her."

"But she's not his daughter, she's mine! And if Nadia moves in with him, then Summer won't need me. She'll have 'Daddy Rob'."

"You're always going to be Summer's dad. No matter what. And you'll still get to see her just as often, maybe even more. If things go well then I bet Nadia and Rob would be glad of some time alone."

Darius sneered, his nose crumpling. It was a rare moment when he looked ugly. "I don't want to think of their alone time, thank you very much."

"I was only saying…"

"Well, don't. They can swing from the chandeliers wearing gimp masks and bondage gear for all I care. What does bother me is Nadia moving Summer to the other end of the country."

That startled me. Could Nadia do that? I worked for a family law firm, but only in the office. The extent of my input was typing up notes and keeping on top of filing. My legal knowledge was hazy to say the least.

"Rob's house is in Devon. Fucking Devon! You can't get much further away from Newcastle than that. If Summer's there then I'll have no choice but to move down south. Commuting there and back every other weekend would be impossible. It's six hours' drive each way and that's on a good day. Longer still during the summer months when all the holidaymakers are there."

Darius's expression had changed, less crumpled and more crushed. I knew him well enough to tell he was defeated, and no wonder he was so upset, if what he said was true.

"That's terrible. What would you do? Would you really move down there? You'd have to get a new job, and it's an expensive part of the country to live." I sounded like a property expert when the only experience I had of the field was watching Phil and Kirstie on *Location, Location, Location*. Darius, on the other hand, knew about house prices. Johnny's company led the property development field, and Darius's role in the firm was directly related to sales.

"Exactly, and jobs aren't easy to come by. Not decent ones. That's why I needed to speak to you."

"I can't help you get a job at the other end of the country, if that's what you're hoping for."

"It wasn't. I'm happy working with Johnny."

Darius licked his lips until they were shiny and slick. It was disconcerting thinking of the places that tongue had been. The memories made me clench my thighs together.

I diverted my eyes and studied the can of Sprite, trying to ignore the sensation that the action stirred, but it was difficult. I hated myself for even thinking it, but my body's instinctive reaction had me wondering if Tawna was right after all, maybe I should give him a second chance.

But if that was the case, then why had I still been thinking about Max? He obviously wasn't interested – he'd have asked for my phone number if he was – but still, when I remembered how it felt to have my hand knotted in his at the pub, the downy hairs of his arm skimming against my skin, it eclipsed my nostalgic Darius-induced tummy-flutters tenfold.

The silence between Darius and me was uncomfortable, but drowned out by the noise of children screeching with delight as they sprung up and down.

"Nadia did give me another option. A way of ensuring her and Summer stay in Liverpool. That's what I wanted to speak to you about. I hoped you'd be able to help."

I caught his eyes once more, the same eyes I'd lost myself in so many times before. Then I looked across at Summer, bouncing on a nearby trampoline, her hair following half a beat behind her body. She might be growing up fast, but she's still so small in the scheme of things. Her life is in other people's hands.

The thought of her being taken so far away from Darius hurt my heart. He was her father, and he adored her. Newcastle to Liverpool was one thing, but Newcastle to Devon was another altogether.

"I'll do whatever I can to help stop her being taken further away from you."

His posture loosened, the tension in his body melting away. "That's what I was hoping you'd say. Thanks, Soph. Thank you." What he said next filled me with panic. "Nadia has said she'll stay in Liverpool on one condition – that I pay her mortgage on top of the money I already give her for Summer. Six months' payment upfront." My mouth was dry. I knew where this was heading. "I wondered if you'd loan me the money. I wouldn't ask, but it's not just for me, it's for Summer."

He looked at me, his puppy-dog eyes pleading, and I inwardly groaned. If there was one thing Darius had always been good at it was pushing my buttons.

CHAPTER 12

Eve tightened her hold on my arm as she let out a long, pained sigh. "My feet are killing me already. These heels aren't meant for walking."

"Car-to-bar shoes," Tawna said cheerily. "Mine are pinching too, but just think of the alcohol. Johnny's hired cocktail makers for the night. We thought we might have a cocktail hour at the wedding, so this is their trial run."

It was the night of Johnny's birthday celebration. His annual bash was a legendary affair, as much a chance to network with the North East's most powerful business people as a social event. The Indian restaurant he'd hired out had been getting rave reviews. It boasted a rooftop terrace bar with stunning views over the Tyne, and the warm, bright evening was the perfect opportunity to try it out. Johnny was footing the bill, naturally, and the champagne would be freely flowing until the last person stumbled into a taxi. It should be the perfect night with my friends. There was just one potential spanner in the works. Darius would be there, and bound to ask if I'd come to a decision about loaning him the money. He'd said Nadia had given him a deadline – seventeenth June – and I'd promised myself that rather than rush into a knee-jerk response I'd think things through. I was determined not to let my heart rule my head.

"Is it a significant birthday for Johnny this year?" Eve asked. "I know he's older than us, but he's not forty yet, is he?"

"No he's flaming not! He's thirty-four!" Tawna gasped, insulted. "As if he'd be forty. He's not got a single grey hair, and he's in amazing physical shape. You should see his stomach. Proper washboard. There's no middle-age spread with Johnny."

Of course there's not. Johnny's the golden boy. Good-looking, charismatic, hard-working and self-motivated. Funny, but not a dickhead. Financially secure. Tawna doesn't realise how lucky she is.

"Sorry," Eve said. "I was only asking."

Her grip tightened on my arm as she walked gingerly over the uneven paving and I was relieved when the restaurant came into view at the end of the road.

"And you're sure I look all right? I'm not sure about this eyeshadow," Tawna said, batting her eyelashes to show off the glittery gold eyeshadow I'd persuaded her to try. The way it swept almost up to her eyebrows might seem excessive on some people, but Tawna had such distinct features – almost modelesque – that she pulled it off. With the eyeshadow, fake lashes and shimmering contoured highlights along her cheekbones, Tawna looked as though she'd come straight from the catwalk.

"It's gorgeous," Eve replied magnanimously, "and I love that dress too."

"Isn't it beautiful?" Tawna stroked her hand against the unmistakably expensive fabric. "Johnny told me to treat myself. 'No expense spared' were his exact words, so I took it literally." She name-dropped the designer, who'd been responsible for dressing an Oscar-winning actress earlier in the year.

My outfit was another charity shop find, but it was designer, one of the limited edition runs for a high street store that caused mini riots between fashionistas and bidding wars on eBay.

"I got this from Debenhams." Eve shrugged. She was wearing a psychedelic sixties-style mini-dress that suited her gamine figure. The bright colours were set off by a chunky bronze belt, the accent colour matching the pain-inducing heels. "Summer sale," she added, unapologetically.

"It's different when you're engaged to the host," Tawna insisted. "There are standards to meet. I'm not just representing myself, I'm representing Johnny and the business, and there are some big-name players coming tonight. I can't turn up in high street fashion."

I inwardly cursed my friend for her snobbery, whereas Eve just blurted out her thoughts.

"I don't think fat-cats from South Shields are going to know Matalan from McQueen, to be honest. Last time I came to one of these events one told me I needed to put on a few pounds because I'd 'look more feminine with curves'." She shook her head. "He couldn't have cared less what I was wearing, all he was bothered about was my body fitting his idea of what a woman's should be."

"For what it's worth, I think you're bloody gorgeous."

Eve blew me a kiss of gratitude as we climbed the steps leading up to the entrance of the restaurant. Topiary pots flanked the entrance, bright white fairy lights flashing from among the green leaves. They were only thigh-high, unfortunately. Not big enough to hide behind if I needed to escape my ex.

A smartly dressed doorman welcomed us, checking our names off a guest list he guarded with his life, and a young waitress who was probably being paid a pittance to be at the beck and call of the guests offered me a glass of bubbly. I might have been thinking about the margaritas, but as I spotted Darius schmoozing with a glamorous raven-haired woman on the other side of the room, I decided it wasn't the time to be fussy. I downed the drink in one, immediately placing the empty flute back on the round silver tray. The waitress looked bemused (and mildly impressed) as I immediately picked up another. Getting drunk from the off seemed to be becoming a habit at events, if mine and Johnny's birthdays were anything to go by.

Tawna didn't notice, being too busy hobnobbing with some big shot.

"If you carry on at this rate it'll be you clinging on to me," Eve whispered, heading towards a seating plan – a board that was placed on a large wooden easel near the cocktail bar. Names written in exquisite calligraphy were pinned around the circles that represented each table. "Take it steady, yeah?"

"I've seen Darius." I cocked my head a fraction in his general direction, trying to be subtle.

Eve craned her neck.

"Don't make it obvious." I swatted her arm. "He might notice me."

Eve thought I was hiding from him because of the past, rather than the present. She didn't know about our recent contact. No one did. "It's packed in here. You'll be able to avoid him," she said confidently. "Stay with me and I'll keep watch, let you know if he comes this way."

"I can't avoid him forever though. The wedding of the year's just around the corner, and in case you'd forgotten, he's the best man."

"Well, yes. You'll have to face up to him then even if it is a tricky situation."

Tricky? More like impossible.

"Maybe it'd be a weight off your mind if you did speak to him," Eve continued, still staring in Darius's direction, although her eyes narrowed when she noticed he was talking to a female. "Get it over and done with before the wedding."

"Maybe," I replied non-committally, although inside I was thinking *no chance*. Not until I'd made a firm decision about the money, and that would take time. I was already feeling decidedly tipsy, and in no fit state to consider giving financial handouts. "I had another dream about Max last night, you know. It made me think."

Eve smiled, taking my glass from my hand and placing it on a ledge. "You really like him, don't you?"

My cheeks warmed at the thought of him. "There was something between us, I'm sure of it, but I don't want to have to go back to the charity shop to see him. If only the universe would find a way of throwing us together."

"You're an old romantic."

"Hey, less of the old." I laughed as Tawna deigned us worthy of her attention after mixing with some of the influential guests including Norma and Fred's son, Bri, who ran one of the biggest building merchants in the area. The amount of air-kissing going on was ridiculous.

"Oh, you've seen the seating arrangements," Tawna cooed. "I made sure the two of you were together, although I'm afraid I'll be with Johnny for the main meal. You've got some interesting people to chat to on your table. Stuart from Riviera Travel is one of the most eligible bachelors around," she added, looking meaningfully at Eve.

"How many times? I'm happy being single. Genuinely happy. I've got enough on my plate at the moment without worrying about anyone else," Eve huffed.

A wave of concern passed over Tawna's face. "What's on your plate? You never told me anything was the matter."

"It's nothing," Eve answered, with a hollow laugh and a wave of her hand.

I frowned. She might be trying hard to play it down but I knew my friend, and her actions left me curious and concerned. I hoped her mum hadn't gone downhill.

"It's just work stuff," Eve insisted. "And I don't want to spend tonight thinking about it."

A waiter passed by with a tray laden with cocktails. Perfect timing, because I was ready for another drink, and going by the significant look Eve shot at me, I guessed she was too. We eagerly reached for the tumblers, neither of us caring which of the colourful potions we came away with.

Eve sucked up the bright-green drink through a straw, pulling a face as the alcohol hit. When I tasted the concoction I understood why. These weren't watered down jobbies, these were the real deal.

"Make sure you talk to Stu," Tawna called over her shoulder, as she was intercepted by the Lord Mayor.

"I wish she'd take no for an answer once in a while," Eve grumbled, taking another large sip of the eye-watering mixture. "All the time she's on at me to find a man. It's as though now she's found her Mr Right we're supposed to follow her lead."

"She means well," I said, and it was as though we'd switched roles. It was normally Eve sticking up for Tawna as I berated her actions.

I shifted position as I noticed Darius making a beeline for us. I ducked down, hoping the stocky gent to my right would hide me from his eyeline, but as I moved I managed to step on the man's toe. He let out a high-pitched squeal that sounded more porcine than human, and I fawned apologetically as Eve dissolved into gin-induced giggles at my misfortune.

The incident had caused the man to spill his wine and a deep red stain seeped through his shirt (which was, typically, white). He looked like an extra in a low-budget zombie movie.

"I'm so, so sorry," I repeated, as he wrung out – yes, he was that drenched – the burgundy from his shirt. "It was an accident, and I didn't realise how close you were." I wanted the ground to swallow me whole, but no such luck. A quick escape was the best I could hope for. Why not add to the "Hide from Darius" fun by finding someone else I needed to avoid for the rest of the night?

"Worse things happen at sea," the man said. He was far more relaxed than I'd have been in his position. I'd be raging if someone had caused me to spill my drink over my outfit before we'd even sat down to eat, whereas he was positive and cheery. "Honestly, it's fine. I'll put my jacket on and no one will be any the wiser."

He reached for a dark grey woollen blazer from the back of a nearby chair and shrugged it on. "See?" he said, when he'd buttoned it up. "No one will know."

With the jacket on it was impossible to tell the shirt was soaked with wine.

"Let me get you another drink." It was the least I could do, and although he didn't seem perturbed, I felt dreadful.

"Waiter!" I attracted the attention of a man in a dickie-bow who was serving the wine the man had been drinking. I retrieved the last glass from the silver platter and handed it over.

"Stop worrying," the man said. "It's fine. And even better now I've got another drink. There wasn't much left in the other glass anyway."

"Looked like a lot from the state of your shirt." For someone so bright, Eve really did lack basic social skills at times. "You were soaked."

The man seemed to notice Eve for the first time. His neck turned as red as his hidden shirt.

"Oh. Yes. Well..." the man spluttered, which made me even keener to escape the nightmare scenario. It was plain to see he fancied Eve.

"We'll leave you in peace," I said pointedly, trying to steer Eve away. "The last thing you want is two crazy ladies cramping your style."

"Not at all. It's a pleasure to meet you both, regardless of the circumstances." His composure was fine when his attention was on me, but as soon as he looked in Eve's direction, he became a gooey mess, like a Cadbury's crème egg left out in the midday heat. "Stuart Burton," he said, extending out his free hand.

"Stuart." I fired a panicked look at Eve. "I have a feeling I've heard Tawna talk about you before. Are you in the travel business by any chance?"

"Why, yes," he said, proudly puffing out his chest. "Riviera. We won an award the same night as Johnny did, and really hit it off. Think that's how I got my invite, actually."

"Congratulations." Eve smiled, but I got the impression she didn't make the connection that this was the eligible bachelor Tawna was trying to set her up with. "Do you travel much yourself?"

And then he was off, sharing the merits of the South of France, as though we were the type of people who could afford to gallivant around on a luxury yacht for the summer. I smiled politely, throwing in a few well-timed nods for good measure, but I'd already switched off, people-watching instead.

That's when I noticed Max, looking animated as he talked to a man with his back to me. I was confused as to why he'd be at the event, because other than Johnny's nearest and dearest, Tawna had led me to believe everyone invited was involved in the housing or leisure industries.

I excused myself from Eve and Stuart's conversation and strode as confidently as I could in Max's direction, walking straight past Darius and Johnny to get to his side.

For one horrifying moment I convinced myself he'd

forgotten me altogether, but when a playful smile broke out on his face I found myself melting like Stuart had around Eve.

Thank you, Universe.

Although I was still aware of Darius's presence in the room, the serendipitous meeting with Max set me alight from the inside.

"Sophie! It's good to see you," he said, pulling me in for an embrace before kissing both my cheeks. Not the pointless air kisses that everyone else seemed so fond of, but proper lip-plants where every one of his facial hairs bristled against my skin, setting free a swarm of tummy butterflies.

He introduced me to the guy he'd been talking to, who turned out to be his brother, Chris – invited because he works in housing like Johnny, but as a builder – and although I was paying attention, sort of, my focus remained on Max. The stubble on his chin was longer than it had been the last time I'd seen him, scruffier and rugged, but it suited him, and when he rubbed his hand over it I resisted the urge to reach out and touch it too. His eyes sparked behind his glasses as he picked up my gaze and I quickly diverted my eyes.

"It's a pleasure to meet you, Sophie. Max has told us all about you," Chris revealed.

Hearing that made me stupidly happy. He'd been talking to his family about me!

"All good, I hope."

"All good," Chris confirmed, but his eyes wandered beyond me. "I'll catch up with you later, if that's all right? There's someone I really need to grab a word with over there."

"Where are you sat for dinner?" Max asked, as I watched with interest as Chris tapped Darius on the shoulder. I guessed they knew each other through work. "I've not had a chance to look at the seating plan yet."

He glanced at his watch, a steely silver band around his left wrist. The hands were showing it was eight o'clock. Tawna had mentioned food would be served at 8.15pm sharp.

"I'm next to Eve, but on a table with someone Tawna's trying to set her up with. She can't help herself when it comes to matchmaking."

He laughed. "But she's not tried to set you up?"

"I'm not on the lookout. And although the guy she's trying to set Eve up with seems nice enough, he's not my type."

"What is your type?" There was a teasing lilt to his voice that suggested he was fishing for compliments.

"I don't have one," I replied, not biting on his line. "I'm looking for someone kind and thoughtful rather than a man with a certain look. I used to think I liked beefcake gym-addicts, but I've tried it and I'm not sure it's for me."

I silently hoped Max wasn't the sort of man who lived in the scary bit of the gym with all the weight machines. He didn't strike me as the type, but I didn't know him well enough to be sure. Those biceps had to come from somewhere.

He bent down, his mouth near my ear, his breath warm on my skin as he spoke. "We should doctor the seating plan. Move it so our names are next to each other." He moved away, giving a mischievous little nod. "Are you up for it?"

"Tawna would hit the roof." I giggled. "She probably spent hours slaving over that seating plan."

His eyes glinted again, testing me. "She'll be too busy talking to all the important people to notice where we're sat."

"You're probably right."

Temptation ate me whole, the thought of sitting next to Max way more appealing than the prospect of making small talk with people who, other than Eve, I'd never see again in my life. Anyway, she was still talking to Stuart, the two of them engrossed in conversation. They were finding plenty to talk about even if there wasn't going to be any romance between them. I doubted she'd even notice if I wasn't sat next to her.

"So, what do you reckon? Should we do it?"

And before I had time to talk myself out of it, I stealthily swapped Max's name with that of someone's who I'm sure wasn't on our table the last time I looked. Darius Welch.

CHAPTER 13

The food had, as expected, been mouth-wateringly good. The starters and mains had been deliciously spicy and flavoursome, but not hot enough to burn your mouth off, and the sweet pistachio Kulfi had rounded the meal off perfectly.

Max was ideal company, and we spent the evening making up wild stories about the other guests. The man to our right with the outlandish moustache was a ringmaster who'd broken with convention and run away *from* the circus. The Mayor made money on the side by posing as a life model for amateur artists. The woman Darius had been talking to earlier married her husband purely to stay in the country. It was all nonsense, of course, but highly entertaining and just the tonic I needed to take my mind off Darius's presence.

I should have known my fun evening was too good to last. When my ex-boyfriend appeared at my side as the bowls were being cleared from the table it was impossible to get away from him. I'd been physically boxed in by serving staff.

"Nice to see you again, Sophie. You're looking gorgeous tonight." Darius smiled, but discomfort took over me. As he continued talking it became apparent why. "I was sure I was meant to be sat next to you."

He threw a glance of disapproval in Max's direction. Seeing the two of them side by side only highlighted their physical differences. Darius's dark hair was slicked back, the tooth mark tracks of his comb visible in the hardened gel, where Max's blond locks were brushed to one side but left to their own devices. Darius's suit was well cut, his shirt unbuttoned to reveal a few curly tufts of chest hair. Somewhere, in what felt like a different lifetime, I used to fall asleep nuzzling against that chest, the wiry hairs acting as my pillow. Max wore a white shirt and smart navy cords, but everything about his look was relaxed in comparison to Darius. And that was without mentioning the difference in emotions that being near them instilled in me. When I'd been alone with Max I'd been laughing, comfortable in my own skin. Darius's approach set me on edge.

"I saw. I assumed it'd been put there in error, which is why I moved it."

His jaw dropped. "Didn't you want to sit with me?"

I tried to remain patient but clear. "This is supposed to be a nice social event, and you're my ex."

At this revelation Max quietly slunk off to where his brother stood at the bar. Max said something to him and then, in unison, they looked over, both wearing stony expressions that made me feel uncomfortable.

"That's no reason for us not to get along, Soph. We got on so well at the trampoline park. Summer's been talking about how wonderful you are ever since. She's still your number one fan. Speaking of that day, have you made a decision about the loan yet? Nadia's breathing down my neck."

His flattery wasn't enough. I was annoyed that Darius coming over had pushed Max away when we'd been having such a fun night, and angry to be back on the subject of the money. It felt like days of old.

"I really don't want to do this now." The room was airless, and that combined with the mention of Summer sent my head whirring like a fairground waltzer. "I told you I'd think about it, but I need time."

"I know you'll do the right thing, Sophie. You're a good girl."

What with the patronising comment and my dizziness, I couldn't be in the same room as him a moment longer. I pushed through the crowds of people mingling near the door that led to the rooftop terrace, using my elbows to move anyone in my path to the exit out of my way, desperate for freedom.

The sky was dark as an onyx but the moon hung full and low, just beyond the glitter ball armadillo of the Sage. Normally the view of my hometown would be enough to calm me – ground me – but I couldn't relax for fear of Darius cornering me again.

I stumbled clumsily down the steps as I left the restaurant, tripping on the bottom one. I grabbed hold of the closest thing I could, one of the topiary trees lining the entrance, to stop myself crashing to the ground.

Relief coursed through me. I'd not thanked Johnny for the invite, not said any goodbyes, but none of that mattered. I could finally breathe again.

CHAPTER 14

"Did you have a good time at Johnny's party, pet?" Dad asked, eager for the gossip. With the football season over for another year he had no social life of his own so he was keen to live vicariously. "Fancy do, from what I've heard?"

"It was nice." I tried to add a cheery lilt to my voice, hoping it'd fool him. "You know what Johnny's like, he doesn't do anything by halves."

"Bri was there too, did you see him? Told me all about it when I ran into him at the newsagents. He didn't get home until four in the morning! I hope you weren't that late."

"Oh, don't worry, I was home well before that," I mumbled. Truth was, I'd been tucked up before eleven o'clock, Darius's proposition ensuring I'd fled the ball and made it back to my bed earlier than Cinder-bloody-ella.

"Are you all right?" Chantel asked through a mouthful of Mum's legendary strawberry trifle. It was as much a part of her traditional Sunday dinner as roast potatoes and Yorkshire puddings, and a particular favourite of my sister-in-law's. "You don't seem your usual self."

"Just a bit hungover and headachy," I lied. I'd had plenty to drink, but I'd not been drunk. Coming face to face with Darius had been a sobering experience. "At least that's not something you'll be needing to worry about for a while."

"Oh, it's fine to have the odd glass of wine when you're pregnant, I just don't fancy it. It was the same when I was expecting Noah. My taste buds have changed and it's just not as nice, somehow."

"I'm not drinking today either," I pointed out, digging into my second portion of trifle. I'd made sure to get plenty of custard, my favourite layer. It was Nick's favourite too, so it was always a battle between us to see who could eat their first portion the fastest and call shotgun on second helpings.

"You probably had more than your weekend quota last night," Mum chipped in, and I detected a sliver of judgement. Nick jumped unexpectedly to my defence, but Mum didn't apologise, instead pressing on by asking, "So, who was there? Anyone we'd know? Any celebrities?" as though she'd done nothing wrong.

The previous year half the Newcastle United team had turned up. Dad had been green with envy when I'd shown him the pictures I'd had taken with them.

"I wasn't really looking. I spent most of the night talking to a guy."

All eyes were on me, expectant. Even Noah, slightly less dribbly since his two front teeth had pierced their way through his bright red gums, was staring at me.

"You didn't tell me you had a new boyfriend," Mum chastised, but I knew she was excited from the way her attention was fixed on me. "So come on then, tell us all about him. Who is he, where did you meet?"

"I wouldn't call him my boyfriend, I've only met him a few times. His name's Max and he's the manager of the Hospice charity shop in town. I met him when I was shopping a couple of months ago."

"Why were you slumming it in a charity shop?" Nick asked with a laugh. "Not exactly your usual scene."

"All sorts of people use charity shops, actually," I said haughtily, remembering Max telling me about the diverse cross-section of customers that came through the shop. "I saw something in the window that caught my attention and ended up going in. Anyway, Max was serving and he invited me to his local for a drink. We didn't exchange numbers though so last night was the first time I'd seen him since then."

"This is very exciting," Mum said, her cheeks flushed. "You know we've all been worried about you since you and Darius split up."

"I'm capable of looking after myself," I said defensively, despite all evidence to the contrary.

"We know that, but it's nice to know you're opening up to new opportunities. You've had long enough to grieve that relationship, and now it's time to put all that behind you and move forward."

"I never liked Darius." Nick's comment shocked me. In all the time we were together he'd never once given the impression of disliking my ex. Nick must have read my look and known what I was thinking, because he said, "He didn't appreciate you. You're bright, you're pretty, you're funny. I know you're my sister, but you're a catch. He should have realised what he had and not taken you for granted."

It was probably the nicest thing Nick had ever said to me.

"Do you remember the way he was at our wedding?" Chantel shook her head. "He was flirting with my sister, right in front of you. I was appalled he could behave that way with you right there."

Of course I remembered it, I'd felt about two inches tall as he reeled off line after cheesy line of compliments to Chantel's younger sister, Clare. I'd laughed it off, pretending it didn't matter, but he'd hurt me.

"That was when I saw his true colours." Mum started noisily stacking the empty crockery. "I knew he was a jack the lad, but he took it too far that day."

"You never mentioned anything," I said, feeling defensive. It was as though they were belittling all me and Darius had shared.

"We tried, Soph, lots of times." Nick smiled sadly.

"Try not to rush into anything with this Max, eh?" Dad said. "Find out if he's good enough for you before you go falling head over heels."

"Yes, Dad," I replied obediently.

"Enjoy yourself, but be cautious. There's no rush." Mum smiled, her eyes resting on what was left of the trifle. "Now, who's having the last of this? There's not much left, so we may as well finish it off."

"Sophie can have it," Nick said. It was a kind gesture, especially given that mainly custard, cream and sprinkles (in other words, all the best bits) remained.

"No, honestly, I'm fit to bursting. Let Chantel have it, she's eating for three, after all."

Chantel beamed, eagerly telling me about her impending twenty-week scan appointment the following week, and Mum scooped the remains of dessert into my sister-in-law's bowl. I was excited – for her, for Nick, for all of us as she shared her joy. For once I didn't feel like the outsider. I felt part of something. Part of the family.

CHAPTER 15

Ever had a bad idea? Sitting on the floor in my bedroom, every item of clothing I owned surrounding me, I realised I'd had an exceptionally bad idea. In theory the Marie Kondo method had sounded great, and I was in the "if I have a clean house, I'll have a clean mind" mindset, but faced with the reality of the task at hand I was full of regret. I'd started the sorting process after returning home from Mum and Dad's. It had been another beautiful evening, but darkness had taken over, the sunlight replaced by the glare of the bulb in my standard lamp.

Surrounding me were ten pairs of near-identical jeans, an assortment of floral dresses and a ridiculous amount of bikinis. It was obscene. A holiday to somewhere hot where I could laze on the beach was the extent of my bikini-wearing, but from looking at my wardrobe you'd never have guessed. There were enough to keep James Bond's fancy-pieces in swimwear for the next ten films in the franchise.

Methodically, I started sorting through each of the piles. The process was satisfying, even if I did feel stupid saying "thank you" to my clothes and it took three times as long as I'd anticipated. It was pleasing to know the items making their way back into my wardrobe were the ones that made me feel like my best self. Favourite staples that have served me well.

The clothes I no longer wanted were sorted into a "sell" pile and a "charity shop" pile. Shamefully, numerous items, some of them designer, still had the tags attached. Seeing the prices printed in stark black and white on the labels made me baulk, their combined total reaching well into four figures. Although it was unlikely they'd fetch full retail price on the online auction sites, I was confident they'd attract plenty of interest. Some were from limited runs, others one-offs. I vowed to take photos and upload them to the sites, promising myself everything I made would go towards paying off my credit card.

The items in the charity pile were still in good condition but not such high quality. I crammed the clothes into a large blue Ikea bag – the floaty green dress I'd bought especially for the dirty weekend Darius and I had had in Barcelona, a pair of ill-advised white jeggings that I'd bought on a whim and worn once, a striped off-the-shoulder Bardot top I'd worn to death last summer. Leather trousers that were too tight around the thighs, and a winter coat that had plenty of wear left in it but that wasn't really "me" anymore. And jeans. So many pairs of jeans.

Cleaning out my wardrobe was a long, but pleasantly liberating, experience. It was good to regain control, to feel proactive. I didn't have a fairy godmother waving a magic wand to rid me of my debts, but I didn't need one. I'm Sophie Drew, a fully grown woman who's made her fair share of mistakes, but who's slowly but surely getting her act together.

A glance at my alarm clock showed it had taken five hours to organise my wardrobe. FIVE HOURS. No wonder I was shaking with caffeine withdrawal symptoms and craving carbs. The double helpings of trifle felt like a long time ago.

I chopped a cucumber to within an inch of its life (nothing worse than really thickly sliced cucumber – it makes me gag) and threw that and the last of the block of cheddar in my fridge between two doorstop slices of bread. Tiredness engulfed me. Family lunch followed by a session of Marie Kondo-ing had really taken it out of me. I gladly sank into my usual spot on the sofa, managing two bites of my sandwich before my head slumped back against the cushions. Patterns from the clothes in my wardrobe danced hypnotically before my eyes and I fell into a well-earned deep and restful sleep.

The sun, shining with an unapologetic ferocity, stirred me from my slumber. Confused by waking, fully clothed, on the sofa, I reached for my phone, stabbing at the screen to see the time. Shit. I'd been asleep for twelve hours straight. It was just gone nine o'clock on Monday morning, and I was late for work. Shit.

Shit, shit, shit, shit, shit.

I hurriedly changed out of my wrinkled clothes, cringing as I used half a can of body spray in lieu of having a shower, then grabbed an apple, a hair bobble and my bag before slipping my feet into a pair of shimmering gold sandals and speed-walking to the Metro stop.

When I was safely on the Metro I pulled my phone from my pocket and called the office, relieved when it was Kath who answered the phone.

"I'm going to be late."

"You're already late," she pointed out. "And Marcie's on the warpath. She's rabbiting on about a missing file. You've not picked a good day to oversleep."

"I didn't plan it, did I?" I huffed. "One minute I was eating my sandwich, the next I was dead to the world. I must have slept through my alarm."

I'd dreamt about Max again, which was another reason

waking had been a struggle. Nothing saucy, but that didn't matter. We'd been climbing Mount Everest, dressed head to toe in burnt-orange snowsuits with a couple of huskies for company. Max had still looked attractive, even buried beneath an enormous fur-trimmed hood.

"If I were you I'd stop at the supermarket and bring cakes. She's already on one. Grovelling is your best chance."

The thought of spending unnecessary money on Marcie's favourite treat – cream horns from the bakery counter – wasn't appealing. And of course, if I rolled up with something for Marcie, I'd have to buy cakes for Jane and Kath too. Marcie's wrath was even more fearsome. As my line manager she'd be within her rights to discipline me if she saw fit. My back was well and truly up against the wall.

"Thanks for the tip. If she asks where I am, tell her I'm on my way and should be in by ten." I crossed my fingers, knowing it'd be tight.

"Just get here quickly. For our sakes, as well as your own."

I exhaled as I ended the call, puffing my cheeks out like a puffer fish. Trust me to be late when Marcie was already in one of her moods. Since she'd started going through the change she was prone to mood swings. I only hoped that bribery with pastries would be enough to keep her sweet.

∮⦿

I survived the week, barely. My unplanned and unwanted Monday morning lie-in had thrown me, and I'd been playing catch-up for the rest of the week. I was convinced Marcie upped my workload to teach me a lesson. Even the cream horns hadn't placated her.

"Friday night." Jane bent down to retrieve her bag from beneath her desk. "And boy, am I ready for the weekend."

"Me too." Kath raised her arms above her head and gave a super-suggestive shimmy. "I'm out on the pull tonight. Hot, single and ready to mingle."

"Modest too." I smiled to show there was no malice in my words, whilst wishing I could have a pinch of Kath's new-found confidence. Twenty-three years she'd been married but since her divorce Kath seemed to have found a new lease of life.

"Are you out in town tonight?" Her question was directed at me. Neither Jane nor Marcie was the type to be out on the tiles to celebrate the start of the bank holiday weekend, much more likely to be settling in for the night with their significant others and a Chinese takeaway.

"I'm going to Tawna and Johnny's." I groaned, wishing I'd turned down Tawna's invite. "I'd rather have a night in, if I'm honest."

Eve couldn't make it and I wasn't in the mood for playing gooseberry. Johnny always fussed over Tawna. In one sense it was nice – showing he cared and literally couldn't keep his hands off his future wife – but it did rather drum home my singleton status. Max had been friendly at the party, but he'd still not asked for my number. Admittedly, I'd made a quick exit to avoid the awkward situation with Darius, but we'd been sat next to each other for the duration of a three-course meal. He'd had plenty of time to make a move if he'd been so inclined. I liked Max a lot, but without his number I was helpless. I wasn't brave enough to go to the shop to see him.

"Oh, I'm sure it'll be fun when you get there and the wine is flowing," Jane said. "And their house is gorgeous, isn't it? With the weather like this you might even be eating outside. What is it they call that?"

"A barbeque?" Kath suggested, a glint in her eyes.

"No! Al something or other."

"Pacino?" Kath teased, before applying a slick coat of

pearlescent baby-pink lipstick. The way it caught the light reminded me of my mum's wedding pearls. When I was small I'd loved looking at the treasures in her jewellery box, smoothing my fingers over the surface of the beads, examining the colourful stones set against backdrops of silver and gold, but the pearls had been my favourite. "Capone?"

"Al Fresco," I said, helping her out. Jane, bless her, isn't the brightest. "And I don't think it will be. They're having work done. Tawna mentioned new decking being put down ready for the lighter evenings."

"Either way, you have a good night, pet. Don't do anything I wouldn't do!" Kath quipped, which pretty much left me with my options wide open.

She breezed out of the building, waving over her shoulder as she left, and I scooped up my phone and water bottle (another money-saving effort – the amount I used to spend on takeout coffees and bottles of organic orange juice!) before following her lead and escaping the claustrophobic office.

The sounds of the city engulfed me; the aggrieved beeping of horns from irate drivers, the wailing of toddlers strapped into prams against their will, the after-work pub-goers sharing stories of their workdays as they spilt out onto the pavements.

I kept my eyes firmly on the floor as I passed the shops, not wanting anything in the windows to entice me. Three months into my new lifestyle, I was proud of myself. Twenty-nine-year-old Sophie would never have stayed within budget, but thanks to some manic online selling and savvy food shopping, the more mature me was rapidly decreasing the amount I owed.

Looking at the ground was my undoing, and the reason I found myself bumping, quite literally, into Max.

"Oh! I'm sorry!"

"Sophie." He sounded surprised. "I wasn't looking where I was going."

"It's fine, I wasn't concentrating either."

"I'm meeting some friends at the pub and I was texting to see if they were already there." He waved his handset as though to prove his point, pulling an apologetic face. "You're not hurt, are you?"

"No, no, I'm fine. I feel like a divvy, that's all. You must think I'm a total klutz."

His eyes connected with mine. His pupils looked enormous, magnified by the lenses of his glasses. "I didn't think anything of the sort."

My lips were dry, and embarrassment, like a weight pressing down on my tongue, stopped me from speaking.

"You're welcome to join us at the pub. It's nothing fancy, just a good old-fashioned boozer that serves decent real ales, and a group of us talking about music and films."

"Umm..." The weight was still there, stopping me from saying anything coherent.

"It'd be nice to spend some time with you. I was looking for you at Johnny's party, but after the meal you vanished. You're probably busy though. It's Friday night, of course you've already got plans. I just wanted to buy a drink to apologise for barging into you."

I remembered grumbling to my workmates about the prospect of spending the night playing third wheel to Johnny and Tawna and their couple friends. A night in the pub with Max and his mates was tempting.

"No, I'd like to come."

"You don't have to say that to be polite. I understand if you're meeting other people, or if you're washing your hair..."

"Max." I held up my hand to halt him. "I'd love to come for a drink with you. I'm going to Tawna and Johnny's later, but as long as I only stay at the pub for an hour or so I'll have plenty of time."

"If you're sure?"

"I'm positive."

"Great. We're meeting down here." He pointed down a side street towards a pub I'd walked past hundreds of times but never been inside, and as we walked, he told me about the people we'd be meeting up with. "There's Iain, Oz and Archie. They're the guys in the band that were playing that night at the pub? I roadie for them from time to time, and Oz's girlfriend usually comes along when she finishes work. They're a good bunch, I promise."

"I can't imagine you'd be friends with anyone unless they were dead nice. Although I've got to say, I thought the one with all the tattoos looked a bit intense."

"Archie? He's a softie. The tattoos and eyeliner make him look tough, but it's all part of a stage persona. The band's his life. He really wants to make a go of the whole music thing."

"They were good. That last song I heard before I left, the one with the long guitar solo, was great."

The haunting riff had kept catching me unawares, playing on a loop somewhere in the back of my mind.

"It's not bad, is it?" he said, shyly adding, "I helped write that one. I'm not in the band, but I hang out with them when they're writing, sometimes."

"You've got a talent."

"Thanks, but I only play guitar for fun. I'm a roadie, not a rock star. Oz on the other hand... he's one of life's hopeless dreamers."

When we reached the pub, Max held the door open to let me enter first. The inside was much smarter than the peeling whitewashed exterior suggested, with high wooden tables flanked by barstools around the edge of the room and an island bar at the centre.

The pub was quiet for a Friday, presumably due to its off-the-beaten-track location. I spotted Max's friends sat at a table near the window and a fleeting flash of anxiety that they'd hate me for imposing on their night out washed over me.

When the tall skinny man with cropped golden hair who I recognised as the lead singer in the band stood to greet me and, with a humongous smile, introduced himself as Iain, my fears slid away. Archie moved his jacket from an otherwise-empty stool and invited me to sit with them and Max asked what I wanted to drink.

They were good company, and their friendly banter suggested they'd known each other a long time. The conversation flowed as they invited my opinion on everything from storylines in the soaps to current affairs. Time ran away from me, and only when my phone vibrated in my pocket did I realise I hadn't rung Tawna and let her know my plans had changed.

Hurriedly clicking the green "accept call" button, I made my way out of the pub to a quiet small back courtyard.

"Tawna, hi."

"Where the hell are you?" she hissed. I could picture her expression. I'd seen it a million times before when things hadn't been going her way.

"I'm so sorry," I gushed. "I meant to phone to let you know I'd be a bit late, but it sort of slipped my mind."

"Are you ill?"

There was concern in her tone and for a moment I considered lying, telling her I thought a migraine was coming on, but in the end I couldn't bring myself to do it. It didn't feel right.

"I'm fine. I ran into Max in town and I've gone for a few quick drinks with him and his friends."

"Right."

An uncomfortable pause let me know she was silently

seething. I awaited the inevitable onslaught, but when it never came it was left to me to break the silence.

"I'll be on my way when I finish my drink, promise. I'll be with you in twenty minutes, half an hour tops."

"Okay," Tawna conceded with a sigh of resignation. "But hurry up. I've been cooking all afternoon and I don't want the food to spoil. Everyone's asking where you are."

"Twenty minutes," I repeated, thinking I'd far prefer to spend the night in the pub with Max and his friends than go and face Tawna's wrath. She'd always been good at keeping hold of grudges. She'd still not forgiven Leanne Dixon for breaking her Tamagotchi back in primary school, bringing it up every time we bumped into her.

"I'll see you then," she said, before brusquely hanging up.

"All right?" Max asked, as I re-entered the pub. "I got you another drink in." He slid a glass of wine across the table towards me.

"I've got to go." I gave him an apologetic look. "That was Tawna, wondering why I hadn't turned up yet. She didn't sound happy."

"I hope you put the blame on Max," Iain joked. "He's the one who led you astray."

"Guilty as charged." Max held up his hands. "Sure I can't persuade you to stay for one more?" He looked at the glass of wine. "Seeing as it's already waiting for you?"

I wanted to say yes. I really, really wanted to say yes. But the words that came out of my mouth were, "I can't. I should have been there half an hour ago."

I reluctantly gathered my belongings, slung my bag over my shoulder and draped my coat over the hook of my arm. It wasn't as though I needed to wear it; it was a mild evening, and the bus stop was close by.

"See you soon though, yeah? Give me a call or a text?" He

looked apprehensive as he took a business card out of his wallet and handed it to me. My fingers tingled at the contact, and the charge was still buzzing through me as I pushed the card into my coat pocket for safe keeping.

"I will," I said with a nod before smiling at Iain, Oz, Archie and Oz's girlfriend, Isla. "And it's been lovely to meet you all. Enjoy the rest of your night, yeah?"

There was a spring in my step as I walked out of the pub. Fingering the rectangular card in my pocket as I made my way towards Percy Street bus station, all I could think about was how soon I could text Max without coming across as desperate.

CHAPTER 16

Building up the courage to knock on Tawna's door was even tougher than it had been the day of the dress shopping fallout. I knew she'd be mad at me, and when she opened the door my suspicions were confirmed.

She looked so cheesed off. "Seriously? You ditched me for him and didn't even have the courtesy to ring? I'm hurt, Soph, really hurt."

"I thought you'd be happy I'm socialising," I replied, knowing I sounded churlish. "You're the one who said I was turning into a recluse."

"That's why we invited you in the first place, to get you out of the house, because you never seem to want to go out in town with me and Eve these days. If it hadn't been Johnny's birthday last week, I wouldn't have seen you then either."

"That's not true..."

"It seems that way to me," Tawna said haughtily. "And what am I supposed to say to Darius? He's been here for almost an hour already waiting for you to arrive."

I froze, despite the warm air of the evening.

"Darius? What's he doing here?"

Since Johnny's party I'd had tightenings in my chest when I thought of him and what he was asking of me, and not of the pleasant variety this time.

She folded her arms across her chest. "He needs to be surrounded by people he knows and trusts right now. He's vulnerable. I'm doing you both a favour here."

There wasn't an ounce of shame in her voice. What right did she think she had to try to push me and Darius back together?

After the lovely evening I'd had with Max and his friends, I was fuming at her meddling. "It's not your place to set us up. This is real life, not Blind bloody Date." I was so close to telling her about mine and Darius's recent conversations. "Why do you always think you know what's best for me? I'm a big girl, I can make my own decisions, and I don't want to see him right now."

"Please, Soph," she begged, widening her eyes until she looked like bloody Bambi. "Come in and have a drink and a chat. It's only a dinner party."

I shook my head. "You should have told me he was here."

"But then you'd never have come. When he tried to talk to you at Johnny's party you literally ran out on him."

"Exactly! That should tell you everything you need to know! I can't say it any plainer than this – I'm not coming in."

She shrugged, and I realised there was no point arguing on her doorstep. This was just the latest in a long line of things that Tawna did without fully thinking them through.

I turned to leave before I said something I might later regret, either about the money predicament or Tawna herself.

"What am I going to tell Darius?" she called after me. I was already halfway down the drive.

"Say whatever you want, I don't care." I was shouting, but it didn't really matter. No one was going to hear me from Tawna and Johnny's sprawling garden which could do a good job of masquerading as a country estate. "And for fuck's sake, stop interfering in my life!"

I upped my pace to a run, furious at Tawna's audacity. How dare she lull me to her dinner party under false pretences? How dare she?

I pulled my phone from my pocket to call the only person who'd understand how frustrating Tawna's insistence that she knew best was.

Eve answered on the second ring and only when she suggested meeting the following day because she couldn't make head nor tail of my incoherent rantings did I finally begin to calm down. Good old Eve. At least I could rely on her.

"Hiya."

Eve bundled me into a hug and I was overwhelmed by how grateful I was to have her to lean on. The combination of stress and lack of sleep had left me overwrought, and I fought back my tears by burying my head into the scratchy fabric of her jacket.

When she'd suggested meeting at the small, squat, ugly building from the 1960s that doubled as our local library I'd been less than impressed. I'd got so used to walking straight into Waterstone's and buying the books I wanted that when I thought of libraries I imagined falling-apart paperbacks smelling of stale cigarette smoke and librarians dressed in tweed.

It had been years since I borrowed anything. Could library memberships lapse? I didn't even know if the plastic card they'd given me was buried in amongst all the crap I carried around in my wallet anymore. I'd probably chucked it to make room for another coffee shop loyalty card.

"Thanks for meeting me. I really needed to talk to someone who'd understand."

"You've been there for me, and you know I'll always be here for you," she said, "and I didn't have anything planned today other than returning these."

She pointed at the stuffed tote bag slung over her shoulder. The natural cotton strap strained at the seams under the weight of the contents.

"You weren't wrong when you said you had a few books to return."

"Oh, you know how it is... you go in for one book and come out with a dozen." She smiled an embarrassed smile as we entered the foyer.

"I'm not exactly a regular here," I confessed.

Eve stared blankly, as though I was speaking a foreign language. "But you should be! Libraries have been closing all over the city – if we don't use them, we'll lose them."

"I don't read as much as you." Understatement of the century.

"Even if you only borrow one book every three weeks it shows the demand is there, plus they loan out DVDs too. And they've got computers, free for members to use."

"I don't need computers. I've got the laptop at home, and I only use that for Netflix."

She gave me a pithy look as she placed her books into the mouth-like space of the scanning machine before stacking them neatly onto a trolley ready for reshelving.

"I'm going to be a while," she said, "I've reservations to collect and there's a biochemistry book I was hoping to find too. It's supposed to be groundbreaking."

Her enthusiasm made me smile. "Don't worry, you take your time. I'll browse."

"You're sure?"

"Absolutely."

"Meet you out the front in fifteen minutes, and then we can go for coffee? Then you'll have my full attention and you can tell me all about Tawna and her meddling."

I nodded, before heading to the fiction section. Eve might be all about facts, but for me reading was about escapism. The books I'd enjoyed most were set in exotic places far away from Newcastle – I'd loved *The Beach*, and *The Island*, and *Captain Corelli's Mandolin*. A hot-pink spine grabbed my attention, the swirling script of the title written in a bold, bright yellow. It stood out from the others on the shelf and I silently applauded the cover designer's choices. The title rang a bell, and I wondered if it was the book Anna told me she'd enjoyed on the plane journey back to Austria after my birthday party.

Using my index finger, I pulled the book out from where it was wedged and turned to the back cover to read the blurb. It was about a woman who left her husband to run a vineyard in France, and just so happened to fall in love with a handsome sommelier. How convenient. The cover boasted a quote from a bestselling author which piqued my interest all the more.

I flicked to the first page and started to read. The style was light and breezy, the protagonist a sassy, strong woman ready to embrace her dreams. I gobbled up the first chapter without realising it, keen to find out more about this fictional character's journey. I was still lost within the book's pages when Eve tapped me on the shoulder, dragging me abruptly back to reality.

"Found something you like the look of?"

"It's okay." I moved to put the book back in the space on the shelf.

"Take it out, if you're enjoying it. Nothing beats a bit of escapist bedtime reading." Eve's arms were laden with books, mainly thick academic tomes. They didn't look like the type of reads to wind down with after a stressful day at work to me.

"I'm not sure I've got my library card. And even if I have, I don't know if it's still valid."

"You can borrow it on my card if not. I'm not up to my limit on loans."

I pulled the book back down from the shelf, the thought of following the character's progress giving me pleasure.

"That's great, thank you."

I tucked the book under my arm to retrieve my purse, willing my underused library card to be hidden between my debit card and my Tesco Clubcard. When I saw the distinctive black plastic peeking out I nearly whooped with delight. The book was coming home with me.

Eve and I scanned our books (her selection taking significantly longer to process than my lone loan) and made our way back through the foyer, plastered with posters for playgroups and yoga classes, local history groups and farmer's markets. A flyer near the door caught my eye.

"Look at that!" I exclaimed, my voice squeaking with excitement. "They're doing a showing of *Dirty Dancing*!"

Eve, Tawna and I must have watched that film every day the summer after we sat our GCSEs. We'd quote back the classic lines about corners and watermelons, but act smug and superior when we knew the less famous lines verbatim too. We'd all fallen head over heels in love with Patrick Swayze, and although we'd worked our way through his back catalogue none of his other roles had got us as worked up as red-hot dance instructor Johnny Castle. Patrick was the only celebrity who'd ever given my main man Milo a run for his money.

Eve moved closer to the poster to read the small print. "Film night, free to attend, bring your dancing shoes,'" she quoted.

"Sounds good. We should come."

"Really?"

"Yeah, it could be a laugh. And as it's free we can always

leave early if it's a bit crap, which it won't be, because Patrick Swayze on a big screen could never be anything less than perfection."

"You're right, we should do it as a hen do for Tawna, it's two weeks before the wedding. Let's put our names down at the desk," she said eagerly, making her way back into the library.

I didn't want Eve to know how tight things were money-wise, but the freebie factor had clinched the deal. After so long paying for everything with the credit card without a thought for the cost, staying within my means was a difficult adjustment. I needed to get the pile of Marie Kondo-ed clothes I planned to sell listed on eBay, and fast. The more I read about interest rates on credit cards, the more of an idiot I felt for becoming so reliant on it in the first place.

When Eve had registered our interest in the screening we headed out, strolling past the small run of shops – a bakery, a pharmacy, a convenience store – before stopping outside Pam's Café. It wasn't the smartest establishment, being an out-of-town greasy spoon, but it was cheap and cheery; the eponymous Pam a bubbly lady with a personality large enough to rival her expansive bosoms. Pam's was an institution in these parts, her legendary fry-ups the perfect way to tackle a hangover, and at a price that didn't break the bank. Saturday mornings were her busiest time. Peering through the window I spotted a free table in the centre of the room. Not the best seat in the house, but it'd do.

"I need to tell you exactly what Tawna's done this time. Even you won't be able to believe her gall."

"Whatever she's done it can't be as bad as when she pretended her Nana had died to get out of going on a date," Eve stated, referring to the time Tawna had had a sudden change of heart about a boy she'd been dating (and he had been a boy, because she'd been a girl. Admittedly, the case in question was fourteen years ago when we were in Year II, but it remained the unscrupulous act which cropped up in conversation every time Tawna overstepped the mark, which was fairly frequently).

"It's not far off." My shoulders tensed as I replayed the conversation, my anger reigniting. "She invited me for tea under false pretences. Made out like she wanted my company when really it was a ploy to get me and Darius to spend time together. And she had the nerve to make out I was the bad guy for turning up late!"

Eve gasped. "She's unbelievable. Why would she think it's okay to invite Darius without telling you? I know she's pulled a few stunts in her time, but this is ridiculous."

"Yep, it's a whole new level of low."

Pam waddled over, her nylon maroon dress half-hidden by a pinny way too small to protect her clothes from flour or sugar. It looked more like something kinky Kath might buy on one of her trips to Ann Summers.

We placed our orders – I justified the large bacon buttie with the logic that it'd cost as much for me to buy the ingredients and eat at home – deciding not to splash out on a coffee, instead sticking to the complimentary tap water provided. Eve ordered a supersize farmhouse breakfast alongside a large filter coffee, and then I launched right back into the conversation and there was no mincing of words.

"I've had it up to here with Tawna. I don't know what's got into her. First there was the birthday party I didn't even want, and now she's trying to fix me up with Darius when I've told her I need time to think. Sometimes I don't know why we're still friends with her."

"I'm sure she doesn't mean any harm..." Eve surprised me by standing up for our mutual friend when Darius was involved.

"It doesn't matter if she means harm or not, she shouldn't be interfering! She doesn't listen, she bulldozes in as though I'm a kid. I don't know why you're defending her."

"I'm not."

"It feels like you are." Everyone in the café turned to look at me, my volume out of control once more. Even Pam, who was probably wondering what was causing a commotion, looked. She's had all sorts kick off in her café over the years. Fist fights, slanging matches, even the Great Salt Episode of 2016 (where a scorned wife emptied every salt mill in the place over her philandering husband's head. Talk about a mess, in every sense of the word).

"Ssssh." Eve brought her index finger to her mouth, as though by treating me like a naughty school kid I'd automatically quieten down.

"Sorry, Eve, but she overstepped the mark."

A dark thought pushed its way to the front of my mind. "Did she tell you she was planning this?"

"What? No! I can't believe you'd think that!"

I didn't believe it, not really, because Eve was one hundred per cent "Team Max". Plus, with secrets not being her forte, there'd be no way she'd have been able to keep her mouth shut if she and Tawna had been in cahoots.

I let out a long sigh. "I'm sorry, I just had to be sure."

"You know my feelings about Darius. He wasn't good for you first time around, so I'm not going to be his number one fan now. If you decide to give it another go then I'll bite my tongue and let you get on with it, but for as long as you're asking for my advice it's going to be a no from me on that one."

"Simon Cowell had better watch out," I said, knowing there was no way I could tell her about Darius's request for a loan. She'd go ballistic. She already hated him. "Eve McAndrew is gunning for the role of the mean one on *The X Factor*."

She poked her tongue out in retort. "I just don't want to see you making the same mistakes again. Tawna's so immersed in her little wedding bubble that she's forgotten how heartbroken you were when you and Darius broke up. And I don't want to speak badly of her, but she's biased too. He is Johnny's best friend, after all."

"Exactly. But that doesn't mean he's right for me." The words came easily because I'd said them so many times it was like reciting lines from a script. If only I was as convinced as I sounded.

"Exactly," Eve echoed, not picking up on my concerns. Maybe I did have some acting ability after all. "And you did the right thing telling her off. Don't let her try to push you together if it's not what you want."

"Last night, when I was with Max and his friends it was so relaxed and lovely. There were no pretences and it was a laugh, you know?"

My heart picked up pace and although I was trying to play it cool I wasn't doing a very good job as Eve smiled kindly and said, "That's what you need, someone you can be yourself with. You shouldn't have to be someone you're not, because you're already amazing just as you are."

"Now you're the one being biased." Her words reminded me of Nick's comments about how I deserved better than Darius.

"I'm being honest," she corrected. "The way Darius tried to change you always made me cross, not to mention that he had no respect for you. You didn't need the fake tans and the nail extensions and the overpriced dresses. You're beautiful."

That made me laugh out loud, because I didn't feel it. My hair desperately needed a wash and lack of sleep had left my skin a dull, washed-out grey. Make-up could probably have fixed it, but I hadn't had the inclination knowing we were only staying local. The old Sophie, the one Darius had shaped and moulded, would never have left the house without her war paint.

"That proves you're either blind or lying, but thank you anyway. You're a good friend. Unlike others who shall remain nameless."

"Don't be too hard on her, Sophie. What she did was wrong, going behind your back like that, but it's done with love. Talk to her. Let her know how you feel and she'll soon realise how out of order it was."

"I don't think I'm ready to speak to her yet."

"Well, you'd better get ready, because we're meeting her in..." Eve looked at her watch, "...ooh, three hours' time."

I rested my elbows on the table, allowing my face to fall into my hands.

"I'd forgotten about the dress fitting," I moaned.

"Call her," Eve instructed, as Pam unceremoniously placed our brunches in front of us. "Eat up, and then do it. Clear the air. You'll feel better once you've talked it through."

"Maybe. But unless she apologises there's no way I'm going."

I flicked back the lid on the brown sauce, flipped open the stottie and smothered the bacon in the tangy sauce. The smell made my mouth water.

"She'll apologise, I'm sure of it. And we can tell her about her hen night with Patrick Swayze."

"If it was him she was trying to set me up with it wouldn't be a problem." I laughed, pressing the lid of the stottie back on top of the base. Sauce oozed temptingly out of the sides.

"If it was him she was trying to set you up with then neither Max nor Darius would get a look in."

CHAPTER 17

My eyes sprung open, despite my eyelids apparently being made of lead. I wasn't used to sharing the duvet. There hadn't been anyone since Darius, so being kicked in the shin as my bed-partner writhed through a bad dream was a pretty rude awakening.

"Eve," I moaned sleepily, prodding her in the ribs. "Stop it."

My friend jolted at the contact, all four of her limbs extending. I was not only kicked, but whacked around the face as well. Great. Some thank you for letting her stop over after getting totally sloshed.

After the dress fitting (which hadn't been as awkward as I'd thought it might have been, because Tawna's flattery about how much the dress suited me weakened my hard-nosed exterior) the three of us had come back to my house, watched a film and drunk into the early hours.

Three home-measure gin and tonics later I'd brought Darius into the conversation. I felt bad bringing up something that had the potential to ruin such a lovely night, but I couldn't not.

"You understand though, don't you, how inviting both of us

to your place might make him think I want to get back with him?" I'd said.

Tawna had looked puzzled. "Why would he think that? It was me doing the inviting. It was nothing to do with you."

"He doesn't know that though, he probably thinks I put you up to it. You know how full of himself he is. He finds it difficult to believe anyone can resist him."

"You used to be so happy together, Soph. I just want you to have that smile on your face again."

"Stop trying to force my hand! If I do decide to get back with him it'll not be down to you sticking your oar in."

Tawna's face puckered which in turn made me feel guilty. When Eve said she'd never deliberately want to hurt me she was right. We'd been friends since we were five and she'd scooped me up when I'd fallen over in the gravelly infant school playground, taking me to a dinner lady in a checked green pinafore who'd doused my knee in Dettol (which had hurt like nothing else). She'd been looking out for me in her own inimitable way ever since.

"I don't need Darius to make me smile." I took a swig of my G&T, swirling the clear liquid around in the glass so the ice cubes jangled against the sides. "I'm capable of finding my own happiness." The words were nothing more than bravado really, but perhaps if I said them enough I'd start to believe them?

"You are," Eve agreed, "which is why I want to hear more about Max. Are you going to call him? And when do we get to meet him properly and see if he's worthy of our Sophie?"

"We kind of left it up in the air," I admitted. "You can meet him at some point, but not yet, it'll only scare him off."

"You met his friends," Eve stated, "and what are you trying to say? That we're scary?"

"Not scary, but when it comes to my boyfriends the pair of you act like my gatekeepers. Just this once I want to do things my own way and at my own pace rather than be swayed by your opinions, good or bad." I knew my friends were still in opposite corners of the boxing ring, with my heart in the middle. If it was going to get pummelled, I needed it to be on my own terms. "Can you both promise that from now on you'll let me get on with it? I might make the wrong choices, I might make my own mistakes, but that's what they need to be – mine. What I need from you two, more than anything else, is support. Unconditionally. Can I rely on you for that?"

Tawna and Eve smiled and nodded, and my heart burst with love for these women, the friends I'd walked through life alongside for the past quarter of a century.

"You can rely on us." Eve raised her glass in a toast.

"Unconditionally," Tawna added, touching her glass to Eve's.

A tinkling sound rang out as my own glass chinked against theirs, a sense of contentment filling me as I knocked back the last of my drink.

The morning after, in the cold light of day, I wished I'd gone easier on the booze. It had been nearly two in the morning when Tawna had finally phoned Johnny to come and collect her. It had been easier for Eve to stay the night than go back to the bedroom of the terraced house she'd grown up in and never left. She'd climbed into my king-sized bed with me and we'd talked sleepy drunken nonsense until we couldn't keep our eyes open a moment longer.

Eve claimed the candyfloss pink cover as her own as she spun around, pulling the duvet over her head until she resembled an enormous marshmallow. I gave up trying to sleep.

My brain jiggled within my skull, like a bolt had come loose somewhere, as I climbed out of bed. I wondered if I may actually be falling apart. The order of the day was a couple of paracetamol and a vat full of coffee.

Two large mugs of coffee and two painkillers later, I felt

marginally more human. Being the kind and generous soul I am I poured another coffee to take to Eve, and popped two slices of bread in the toaster. After a slow start I was just about up to stomaching solids. Whether Eve would be remained to be seen.

When the toast sprang up I added a thick, gloopy layer of Nutella. The joy I'd had at finding a reduced jar of the real stuff rather than settling for a supermarket-own brand had been ridiculous. It came to something when other people were celebrating babies, weddings and promotions and my excitement came via a discounted jar of chocolate hazelnut spread.

"Wakey wakey, sleepyhead!" I chirruped, placing the spotty Emma Bridgewater tray on the bedside table before drawing back the curtains. The daylight rushed in with such intensity that I squinted at the glare. Unsurprising the blazing sun didn't go down well with Eve.

"Let me sleep," she growled, face-planting herself into a pillow. "Any real friend would."

"Real friends bring breakfast in bed," I corrected. "Wake up and smell the coffee."

At the mention of coffee, my friend stirred. Her bedhead made me smile, and although she grumbled as she pulled herself into an upright position, the soft moan she emitted after the first sip told me she was grateful for the caffeine kick.

"Thank you," she said, spotting the toast. "This is exactly what the doctor ordered."

"Don't say I never do anything for you. And of course you're welcome to have a shower here when you're ready. There are clean towels in the bathroom cupboard."

"I'll take you up on that, even though I don't have anything to change into," she said, pulling a face. "I'm convinced I can smell myself." She tentatively lifted an armpit, tilted her head and sniffed, before recoiling. "Urgh. Either way, I need that shower."

"You can borrow something to wear. Take a look through that pile and see if there's anything you can refashion." At least my procrastination over the charity shop pile benefitted someone.

Eve wasn't as curvy as me but she was a similar height. Borrowing my fitted clothes would be out of the question – they'd hang, baggy and shapeless, around her chest due to her lack of boobage – but boho dresses might be passable with an accessory belt casually slung around the waist and would be on trend with festival season coming up.

"I will, thanks."

We sat in amiable silence as Eve allowed the coffee to work its magic, and I tried not to get uptight about the toast crumbs falling on my bedclothes. I'm like the girl in the fairy tale *The Princess and the Pea* when it comes to sleep. Darius had peeled off a plaster in bed once and not thought it necessary to take it to the bin in the en suite. I'd freaked out big time when my foot had skimmed against the soiled plaster, convinced it was a rodent. He'd thought it hilarious; I'd thought it disgusting and unhygienic.

By the time Eve was fed, showered and dressed in a floaty knee-length dress (that, although loose, looked okay with a belt), I was ready for fresh air to bring me fully back round. I suggested we walk around the block to get a lungful of the good stuff. Although Eve looked fresher than before, she seemed quite content curled up in the corner of the settee watching repeats of the third season of *Gilmore Girls*, so I was surprised when she agreed.

The air was infused with a summer aroma that almost knocked us out, the sizzling sun penetrating right through the bare skin of our arms until our bones radiated the heat.

The area was quiet on a Sunday, but an unnatural-for-a-weekend buzz of life hummed from the playground of the nearby primary school. As we got closer I noticed the rows of cars lining the back wall of the school, wallpapering tables in front of them piled high with everything from toys to books to clothes. It was like Max's charity shop, but thirty-fold.

"Oh, look. A car boot sale. It's years since I've been to one of these." Eve sounded reflective.

I almost told her there was a good reason why she'd not been to one recently, because they're full of tat other people are trying to get rid of, but then she added, "My mum used to love a car boot sale, remember?"

The thought of Lucille McAndrew brought a smile to my face. She was one of the quirky mums; usually found wearing clothes that mismatched but that looked funky in a retro, hippy way; her tangled hennaed hair tumbling down past her shoulders. Mrs McAndrew had always had an open house, the back door leading into the family's small, disorganised off-shot kitchen as well-used as a swanky hotel's revolving door. Tawna and I had all but lived there as teens, because Eve's mum had been far more relaxed than our parents. Her opinion had always been "if it's a choice between you doing these things in the park or doing them under my roof, I'd rather it be here where I can keep an eye on you". That had led to nights drinking bottles of Apple VK as though it was going out of fashion (which to be honest, it had been) in Eve's bedroom, and Tawna even brought her first boyfriend, a spotty boy called Richard who had a habit of saying "cool" far too regularly, into Eve's bedroom when Eve was on a school trip to the WWII battlefields. Eve had been disgusted on her return, insisting her mum put her sheets through two 90 degree Celsius cycle washes in case any bodily fluids remained on her bedding.

"Are we going to have a look around?"

The cardboard sign tied to the wrought-iron gates stated, in large red capitals, FREE ENTRY. It seemed unlikely anything being sold would encourage me to deviate from my enforced non-spending ban, so the car boot sale seemed like the perfect mindless activity to bat away the hangover blues.

"We could," Eve replied, but the way she pulled her mouth awkwardly to one side suggested she was unsure.

"We don't have to..." I began, at the same time as she revealed, "I'm trying to save money."

I found it hard to hide my surprise. Eve always made out she was doing fine financially, thank you very much, and although I didn't know exactly how much she earned, she had a graduate job. I assumed she'd not have worries when it came to money, but maybe this was what had been bothering her at Tawna's party, when she'd tried to convince us that her only troubles were work-related.

"For anything in particular?"

She looked at the ground, shifting her feet in a nervous jig. "Well, I'm wanting to get my own place. I can't stay in the house forever anyway – it's going to have to be sold sooner or later. Sooner, actually. Mum's care is costing more than I'd estimated but she's adamant I stay in the house and won't even consider selling while I'm living there. That's why I'm trying to get enough to put down a deposit on a flat. If I move out she'll see I'm able to stand on my own two feet and then the money from the house sale can go on her care."

She flicked a flyaway strand of hair out of her face and planted a fake smile.

A bitter taste filled my mouth. "It makes me sick how people who've worked hard all their lives are expected to sell their homes when they need care."

"It gets to me too, but there's no other option. I was angry at first, but I've accepted it now. I'm fortunate, I earn a decent wage and my outgoings aren't that bad, it's just I've got used to having a disposable income. The past few months I've been putting aside as much as I can afford, and along with my savings I'm already halfway to a deposit."

I put my arm around my friend's shoulder, pulling her in close in a sideways hug.

"Why didn't you tell me sooner?" What amazed me most was how she'd managed to keep it to herself when anyone else's secrets are spilled within seconds.

"I only made the decision just before your birthday, and I wanted to tell you, but I had this sense that you were distracted. I didn't know if it was down to the milestone birthday or something else, but you weren't your usual self. Then you went off the radar..."

"I'm sorry. I should've been there for you when you needed me most." If I'd known I would have been banging her door down with a bag of her favourite sugar-coated jam doughnuts in one hand and a bottle of something strong in the other. "I had my head up my bum. New Year and my birthday made me reassess everything and when I realised how much I was spending it was a wake-up call. I've been trying to make cutbacks too."

"You taking a step back from the social scene did me the world of good too, to be honest. I stopped spending as much on nights out and made more time to see Mum. If you saw her now, Sophie, well, you wouldn't recognise her. Sometimes, rarely, she's the same as before, but there's an emptiness in her eyes as though she's looking but not seeing. She knows who I am, mostly, but she talks about the past as though it's the present. She was even talking fondly about my dad the other day."

"No way. I don't think I've ever heard her mention him without an expletive attached to it somewhere."

Eve smiled. "I know. It's bizarre. Although I have to admit it's been nice in a way. I knew they must have loved each other once, but after all those years of her cursing him, it's been good to hear her reminisce about the happy times."

"I always imagined the two of them as being totally in love with each other, lacing daisies into each other's hair," I said with a fond smile. "I bet the love they had was all-consuming. A lifetime of love in one summer."

Eve's dad had moved to London when she was a baby, which was probably why Lucille – even with all her hippy-dippy talk about free-love – found it hard to be positive about him. It couldn't have been easy being a young single parent.

I'd met Eve's dad a few times over the years. We'd spent a week with him once, staying in the flat he lived in above the tattoo parlour he ran (nothing like the sterile places you see on every corner these days. This was a grim, dark shop that smelled of mould and weed, around the corner from Chalk Farm tube). He'd been friendly and laid back, with the same wide easy smile as Eve, but dressed like he ought to be at Woodstock, with a loose cheesecloth shirt, flared blue jeans and a heavy statement pendant swinging around his neck.

"They were young. Eighteen, the pair of them."

"So young."

"And I don't blame Dad for leaving. Even now he's like a kid, so imagine what he must have been like then. The way Mum's been talking about him, I can tell she was love-struck. 'Greg with the dimple' she keeps calling him. I never even knew he had a dimple. He's had that bushy beard for as long as I can remember, well before the hipsters brought them back into fashion."

"Any fashion comes back round if you wait long enough."

"Very true."

We drifted into the car boot sale as we talked. The amount of unwanted stuff was insane, especially kids' toys. Every car seemed to be selling a plastic dolls house or two-storey garage and the tables were piled high with jigsaws (probably with half the pieces missing) and assorted board games. There were also indiscriminate items, like a glitter lava lamp, a mug tree, a set of oversized cushions... anything people had bought and then regretted, or more likely been given for Christmas by someone who didn't know them especially well.

Nothing grabbed my attention, but Eve made a beeline for the back of a black 4x4, eagerly grabbing my arm to pull me towards whatever it was she'd spotted.

When we reached the trestle table, I knew immediately why she'd dragged me to this car. There, slap-bang in the centre of the other life detritus, was a serving bowl I'd seen many times before. Not the exact one – that would've been impossible, because the version I knew had been accidentally broken fifteen years earlier – but still, the similarity was striking.

"Sophie." Eve's grip tightened on my arm until I could feel each of her fingers digging into my flesh. I imagined the small round bruises the size of five-pence-pieces that the pressure would leave on my skin. "It's Mum's bowl."

I didn't correct her. We both knew it wasn't the actual bowl.

"I've got to have it," she said, letting go of my arm to touch the bowl. "It's ugly, but..." She ran her fingers along the rusty orange, olive green and tan pattern that followed the ripples of the fluted edge of the bowl.

"I know."

The bowl was so retro it was untrue, but even looking at it I could taste Lucille McAndrew's lunch offerings. Tossed salads dripping in balsamic vinegar, spiced lentil dahl, enough pasta to feed the whole street... for a moment I was a teen again, sat around the drop-leaf table in Eve's dining room, being exposed to vegetarian foods my own parents would never have dreamt of serving without a side order of chicken or steak. It shocked me how an inanimate object could bring back such evocative memories.

"Let me buy it for you." I reached into my bag to pull out my purse, before asking the woman how much she wanted for the bowl.

She asked for a nominal sum before telling us the bowl had been a wedding present.

"My mother-in-law gave it to us," she confided, quietly. "It's not to my taste but she told me it was a family heirloom. I've only kept it for the past forty years to be polite."

"Won't you get into trouble for parting with it now?" Eve asked.

"She died in March. It was a relief, in some ways. She never thought I was good enough for her son even though I've been working full time, raising four boys, running a home... She criticised me once for buying a birthday cake for my youngest's tenth birthday – it was one of those caterpillar ones they sell at Marks, you know? He'd been dropping hints about that cake for months, so of course, I bought him one. 'Shop-bought, Andrea?' she'd tutted. 'I always made cakes for my children. I always think you can *taste the love* in a home-made cake.' Dale's twenty-two now and he asks for that same cake every year. But with each birthday I remember how much that comment hurt."

"We had a bowl just like this when I was growing up so it has nothing but good memories for me," Eve said, hugging the bowl to her chest. "My mum would fill it to bursting and then anyone who was at our house at mealtime was welcome to dig in. She was the best cook."

"She really was," I agreed, my eyes misting over.

I offered the lady a note, but she didn't take it, instead shook her head slowly. "You girls have the bowl, it obviously has a sentimental value. It wouldn't feel right to take your money. Enjoy it, and make sure it gets used. It's been at the back of our kitchen cupboard for goodness knows how long. Fill it up with some of your mum's recipes."

A lump rose in my throat at the kindness of the gesture.

Eve clutched the bowl like it was her firstborn child as she gushed her thanks, her delight in the object filling me with pleasure. It was worth the stinking hangovers that forced us out of the house and into the world to see her happy.

"Thank you so much," I said. "You've no idea how much this means to us."

"Oh, I think I do," she said gently. "I could tell from the way you were pulled to it. You're meant to have it."

We said our goodbyes and shuffled along to the next table, chock-a-block with CDs of nineties artists I'd long forgotten and DVDs of popular comedy series. We passed a table covered with a jumble of children's clothes that looked as though they'd seen better days, then came to another which displayed, amongst other things, a manky looking foot spa, a pineapple shaped ice holder and the world's ugliest Toby jug.

As I reached for a simple glass vase to examine its condition, my hand skimmed that of a man. When I looked up I found myself once again face to face with Max.

I quickly drew my hand back towards my body, but the heat of my cheeks told me I was blushing.

"Sophie!" He sounded surprised, but he couldn't have been any more surprised than I was.

"Max," I managed, but although his name was about as short

as they come I still fumbled over it. What was it about him that got me all flustered? "This is my friend, Eve," I said finally. "I don't know if you remember her from Johnny's party?"

"By sight," he said, with a radiant smile. "Lovely to meet you properly, Eve."

I noticed him taking in the bowl as he offered his hand, probably wondering what possessed her to buy such an ugly, dated piece of tableware.

"You too." Eve carefully juggled the bowl in the crook of her arm to accept his handshake. "It's about time, Sophie's always talking about you."

I shot Eve a glare.

"Really?" His eyebrows rose above the upper rim of his glasses.

"Maybe not always," Eve hurriedly corrected, the corners of her mouth twitching the way they always did when she got nervous. I continued to stare, prompting her to dig herself out of this hole. "Just a few times. Probably only once or twice, actually."

"I thought you might have phoned," he said, and the way he looked at me was so intense that it was as though he was looking right inside me, as though he could see my soul laid bare.

I liked him. A lot. If it hadn't been for Darius taking up so much brain space I would have phoned him, for sure. But something in the back of my mind was sowing seeds of doubt. Was I really ready to jump headlong into a new relationship?

JUNE

CHAPTER 18

Going back to work after a bank holiday weekend was never anything other than bog-awful, but having Kath, Jane and Marcie's full attention made it marginally more bearable. They'd spent all morning grilling me for information about my weekend, and as I gave them the full story, from how Tawna's Friday night matchmaking attempts had backfired right through to the meeting with Max at the car boot sale, they oohed and aahed in all the right places. By the time I'd told them everything, they were armed with questions which they fired at me at pace.

"Are you going to see Max again?" (Jane)

"Did you invite him back to your place?" (Kath)

"What happened to the vase? Did you buy it?" (Marcie)

"What did Eve think of Max?" (Jane)

I answered as honestly as I could. "I promised to drop some unwanted clothes into the charity shop soon so I'll see him then. Of course I didn't invite him back to my place. Neither of us bought the vase; it had a hairline crack along the bottom and we thought it would leak. Eve thought Max was lovely, but I think she'd say that about anyone who wasn't Darius. Any more questions?" I'd laughed, while secretly enjoying my moment in the spotlight. The weekend debriefs usually centred on Kath's latest conquests rather than my messed-up attempt at adulthood.

"So is Darius finally out of the picture for good?" Marcie asked, to looks of disbelief from our colleagues.

I avoided making eye contact, not wanting to think about the money he'd asked me to loan him. We were already in June, I had little more than a fortnight left to make a decision about whether or not to give him the cash. And as lovely as Max seemed, the same thought played on repeat in my mind – could someone I'd known a matter of months compare with the person I'd thought was my forever?

"Obviously. Duh." Kath's look was scathing.

"She loved Darius for years," Marcie snapped back. "You can't rub those feelings away. Our hearts aren't whiteboards that can be wiped clean."

Trust Marcie to go for an office-based analogy, I'd thought, wondering why people were again doing that irritating thing where they talked about me as though I couldn't hear them.

"He doesn't deserve our Sophie," Jane said and, like a mother hen, passed me the tub of luxury rocky road chunks, as though they were the answer to all my problems. The decadent dark chocolate melted unveiling the springy texture of the marshmallows and a raisin burst, its tangy juices mingling with the chocolate. It was orgasmic, briefly taking my mind away from the battles of my heart and head. My junk food intake was mainly limited to whatever was going begging at work and so the good stuff tasted particularly divine.

"You don't need to worry about me," I said, through a mouthful of chocolate. "I know what I'm doing."

I tightly crossed the fingers on both of my hands. Know what I'm doing? Yeah, right.

I still hadn't made my mind up about giving Darius the money. Trying to rid my mind of Summer's innocent face had been all but impossible. In a particularly hormonal moment, I'd considered calling the credit card company to see if they'd issue me with another card on my account seeing as I'd paid well over my minimum repayments, but every time I'd started dialling the number I'd quickly pressed the "end call" button, knowing they'd laugh me out of town. It would only ever have been a query, not an action, but like Marcie and Tawna have pointed out, Darius and I have a history. There's a sense of loyalty and although I hated to admit it, even to myself, there had been moments recently when being near him had made my stomach clench in a not-entirely-unpleasant way.

But then there was Max, who seemed to be a decent, kind man, driving me to distraction. I didn't know him well enough to judge his character – he could be into bondage or hurting kittens or something really perverse like eating baked beans cold from the tin – but there was a definite attraction. Would it be worth risking everything on the unknown? Everyone has flaws, but at least Darius's were familiar. Nothing he could do would surprise me, and maybe it really was better the devil you know: since starting my challenge I'd become so used to the "make do and mend" mentality that the thought of a new anything, even a new man, seemed unnecessary and frivolous.

But Max makes you happy, said a little voice in my ear. *Think of how free you feel when you're with him.*

But Summer, whispered a voice in my other ear, *but Summer. But Summer. But Summer.*

By the time Saturday rolled back around, I'd done enough overthinking to last me a lifetime. Tawna called with the sole purpose of letting me know Darius had been asking Johnny after me on a lads' night out (reminding me the deadline for the loan was just over a week away, as if I could have forgotten), and Eve had been gushing about Max's positive attributes with such gusto that it wouldn't have surprised me if she'd announced she was going to make a play for him herself. Well, not quite, because Eve wasn't like that, but she'd delighted in reminding me how he'd been interested in me and my well-being. "Not like Darius," Eve had said snarkily, "where everything was always about him." That was when I made the decision to be proactive and ask Max on a date. A real, honest-to-goodness date.

When I reached Max's charity shop (because that's what it'd be known as forevermore in my mind) it was much warmer, and the heat, combined with lugging the bags full of Marie Kondo-ed clothes (which seemed far heavier after carrying them for a while with the handles cutting into my palms) meant I was a sticky mess. It was almost enough to make me wish I'd picked up the phone and rung Max rather than being hell-bent on doing this in person.

The door was closed, unlike the last time I'd been there, and I debated whether or not I could open it by pushing the handle down with my bum so I didn't have to put the bags down. I was preparing to carry out the manoeuvre when the door swung open.

"Come in, come in," sang a rainbow-haired teenager wearing a pair of denim dungarees. She was young enough for them to look like a fashion statement rather than as though she'd been painting and decorating as a sideline. "I saw you through the window and wondered if you were dropping off donations."

I lifted up the bags and grinned. "Yep. My wardrobe was in dire need of a sort out."

"We're always glad of good quality women's clothes," the girl said, relieving me of the bags. They must have been even heavier than I'd thought as she hunched double, the bags plummeting to the floor as she said incredulously, "What have you got in here? Lead weights?"

"There are a few pairs of jeans," I admitted, thinking of the high street denim I'd almost put on eBay, before realising they'd cost a fortune to post. "Oh, and a fur coat. Fake, not real, obviously." The black fur peeped out from one of the bags, as though a panther was trapped inside waiting to pounce.

"Thank you," she said, shaking the sting from her hands.

I clenched my hands into fists before flicking out my fingers to stop rigor mortis setting in. The deep red mark that followed the curve of my lifeline where the handles had left their imprint was bad enough.

"I'll take them out the back to the stockroom when it quietens down in here," she said.

Her comment made me realise the shop was busy – not quite the Metro Centre on Boxing Day, but there were a few people browsing. A woman pushing dresses along a rail, the hangers scraping like nails down a chalkboard. A mum and a young girl rifling through the dog-eared basket of children's books. A man in a turquoise polo shirt flicking through the vinyl. Max was behind the counter, serving a pocket-sized grey-haired lady with one of those annoying wheelie trollies that women of a certain age drag behind them, clipping at the heels of anyone who dares to obstruct their path.

My heart beat faster at the sight of him, and I had to internally tell myself to calm down. There was no rational reason to be nervous, especially as last time I was in this shop I all but thrust my 38DDs in his face.

I turned my attention back to the young girl. "You're welcome. Better someone can make good use of them."

"Oh, I'm sure they will." The girl grinned, flashing two rows of gunmetal grey braces. "You'd be surprised at how many people come in here hoping to find a bargain. Although," she leaned in closer, as though about to share a secret, "I think half the women who come here only want to talk to Max." She flicked her head in the direction of the counter and I couldn't stop my eyes following hers. He was leaning forward as he handed the customer her change, a wide and friendly grin on his face. "Everyone likes talking to him. He makes people feel..." the girl searched for the right words – I recognised the reaction – "he makes people feel special."

The girl looked at the floor, swaying from side to side so her rainbow hair swished behind her like a multicoloured waterfall, soft waves of pinks and greens and blues tumbling forward over her shoulders. She was like a unicorn in plain sight.

"I know Max, and you're right. He does make people feel special."

The girl's head pinged up, her eyes wide and startled. "Are you his girlfriend?" she asked in a tentative whisper.

I shook my head. "No, just a friend."

She visibly relaxed at my reply, even though she must have known her chances with him were close to zero, however much she fantasised about him; she can't have been more than seventeen.

"He's nice, isn't he?" she said, gazing dreamily in Max's direction.

Max looked over, as though he could sense our gaze, raising his eyebrows so they bobbed quizzically over the upper rim of his glasses. The girl quickly turned away.

"He is."

"I'll leave you to look around," she said, embarrassed,

wincing as she picked up the bags again and made her way towards a doorway at the back of the shop. I had the distinct impression she was looking for an excuse to hide and the storeroom was the best option. "Thanks again for the clothes."

With the girl out of view and my heart thumping against my chest I moved towards Max and the counter. Even with my nerves churning I recognised the sensation of a playful smirk creeping onto my face as I replayed the conversation I'd rehearsed on the train one last time before I said the words aloud.

"Hello, you." He pressed his elbows against the counter, placing his head into the cup made by his hands. "What brings a nice girl like you to a place like this on a Saturday lunchtime?"

"You know... just donating some things I no longer need."

"And here I was thinking you'd come to see me." A cheeky twinkle sparkled in his eyes.

His comment buoyed me with bravery. "That might have played a part in it too."

"Really? Because you never phoned..." His voice was light, but I sensed there was something serious buried beneath the words.

"Actually, there was something I wanted to ask you, and I thought it'd be better face to face."

"Fire away."

My palms were sweating but I resisted the urge to rub them against my beige linen trousers. Damp patches would be all too obvious.

"I wondered if you'd like to get together some time. That night at the pub with your mates was fun, but I thought we could go somewhere, just the two of us?"

"Are you asking me on a date, Sophie Drew?" The way he stared at me, teasing and testing, filled my stomach with a mass of fluttering butterflies.

"Yes, I suppose I am."

"And where were you thinking of taking me on this date? After all, I already took you to the best drinking hole in the city," he joked.

"You plied me with alcohol in a backstreet boozer," I replied, giving as good as I got. "Maybe a picnic, or a trip to the coast? We could eat ice creams with all the toppings until we feel sick."

"Ice cream sounds great. When are you free?" That was when I knew he wasn't going to turn me down.

"The forecast said tomorrow was going to be nice..." I twiddled my hair around my fingers.

"I'm busy until two, but we could go after that?"

"Perfect." It meant I could have a lie-in and still have time to wash and dry my hair and apply enough make-up to make it look like I wasn't wearing any.

"Perfect." He beamed and we made arrangements.

I was already mentally running through my outfit options and whether the polish on my toenails needed touching up. Doing my own pedis saved money, but my efforts didn't last as long as the salon standard ones.

Five minutes later I floated out of the shop as though I was riding on a bubble, like an extra in a Katy Perry video. As I closed the shop door behind me a unicorn glared back at me, its colourful mane in juxtaposition to the dark expression on its face. Except it wasn't a unicorn at all. The girl with the rainbow hair must have overheard our conversation. She looked completely devastated.

CHAPTER 19

The following afternoon my stomach was flipping somersaults. It was all I could do to stop myself peering out of the window to look for Max's car. He'd told me to keep an eye out for a silver Mini just after 2pm, but I'd overestimated how long it would take me to get ready. By 1.42pm I was already drumming my fingers against the white gloss-painted windowsill, my chest fizzing with a combination of hope and first-official-date nerves.

I rifled through my bag for my phone, and for no particular reason found myself thinking the worst – that he'd send a last-minute message saying he'd changed his mind, or had a better offer from a member of his charity shop fan club.

I'd been about to put the handset back into my bag when my phone vibrated, the familiar ringtone making me jump. As if my heart hadn't already been racing. When I saw it was Max trying to contact me, I inelegantly swiped at the screen to answer the call.

"Hi, Max." I deliberately kept my tone light by raising my pitch. I sounded like an airhead. "Is everything okay?"

"Fine, fine," he said casually. The general hubbub of people laughing and chattering around him blended with his words. "I'm on my way now so I'll be with you in ten minutes."

The noise in the background turned up a notch, and I thought I heard a wolf whistle.

"I'll be ready and waiting. I've got a cool bag with picnic food, and some posh fruit juices."

I looked at the ice-blue bag, crammed full of cheeses, meats and savoury snacks. Although I'd promised myself I wouldn't go wild in the supermarket, I'd bought more than I'd set out to. The items in the yellow-sticker reduced section had been perfect picnic fodder.

"We'll have to leave room for ice cream though," he said, "and candyfloss. No trip to the seaside is complete without candyfloss."

The voices in the background got louder again and I heard, clearly, a child call out, "Uncle Max is taking his girlfriend to the seaside!"

Being referred to as Max's girlfriend pleased me, a smile pulling at the corners of my mouth.

"Who's that?"

"Oh, that's my nephew, Dylan. Chris, the brother you met at Johnny's party's son. He's six, and thinks girls are disgusting. I've told him he may well change his mind about that by the time he gets older."

Dylan responded in the background, "No way, girls smell," and I giggled.

"Sounds like you've got a lot of people around you."

"It's always like this on a Sunday, everyone comes round to Mum and Dad's for lunch. It's too hot for a roast today though so the barbecue's fired up instead and my nephews are splashing in the paddling pool."

"That sounds nice." A twinge of envy shot through my chest; they sounded like a really close family. Even though I got on with them, and Nick had made an effort recently so I saw more of him and Chantel, there were still times I felt like the odd one out of my siblings. In a particularly brave moment I'd mentioned my insecurities to Mum, but she'd told me I was being silly. Although her words were kind, I hadn't believed them. All the comments she'd made over the years about how proud she was of Anna and Nick's achievements had stuck with me, along with the little digs about my own choices. "It must be lovely."

"They're not a bad bunch. Except Dale. He's an idiot," Max said, a jokey lilt in his voice, presumably to annoy Dale. "Thankfully, I won't have to see him until next week now."

"One of your other brothers?" Having first-hand knowledge of how annoying brothers can be, it seemed likely. When we were growing up, nothing would give Nick more pleasure than getting a rise out of me.

"Yep. Anyway, I'm on my way out of the gate now. I'll be with you soon."

After he'd hung up I slid on my sandals, picked up my handbag and the cool bag and made my way down to the car park to wait for Max.

A silver Mini appeared around the corner shortly after and I didn't even try to hide my excitement as he clambered out of the car and greeted me with a grin. His fingers brushed mine as he relieved me of the cool bag. I had a feeling it was going to be a special afternoon.

"You're kidding me."

I shook my head emphatically. My hair couldn't look any worse for the action because the sea air was blowing through it with full force. "I promise you, I'm telling the truth."

"Never?"

"Not once."

"Then that's something we'll have to rectify. A life without crazy golf is a life half-lived."

I laughed at his horror as we sauntered along the water's edge, our feet tracing the tide marks where the dry sand met the wet.

"I don't know how I've managed to reach my thirties without playing a round," I said with a sombre nod. "My childhood was one of severe deprivation, obviously."

"It's a good job you've found me. I'm going to make it my mission that we have a game before the day is out."

"Food first though."

"Food first," he agreed, proudly displaying the cool bag. "I had one of Dad's burgers at lunch, but if you've not had anything to eat you must be starving."

"I'm pretty hungry," I admitted, hoping my gut wouldn't vocalise the rumble that was bouncing around it.

"This looks like a good spot for a picnic. What do you reckon?"

I wasn't going to argue, so Max unfurled the tartan picnic blanket and started arranging the food on the disposable plates. I was glad I'd taken the time to remove all the yellow labels showing the bargain-bucket prices, and hoped Max wouldn't notice the dates on all the packages were the same day – today.

The sky was bright, the air warm, despite the sun hiding behind clouds that were clumped together like melted marshmallows; and as we tucked into the snacks, watching the frothy spume spilling onto the sand, I was glad I'd trusted my instincts and made the decision to ask Max out, because the afternoon had been lovely, the laughter regularly punctuating our conversation an indication of our mutually dry sense of humour.

"Tell me about your family." I licked the butter off the top of a cream cracker, aware it was a disgusting habit but not really caring. I'd had enough of acting, of being someone else to try to attract love. No more pretending, no more being someone I wasn't. From this point forward I was going to be me, warts and all Sophie Drew. "Sounded like it was quite the party."

Max snorted, his nose crumpling so his glasses shifted on the bridge of his nose. "It's always like that. Any gathering descends into total chaos before long."

"Raucous family?" I asked, curious.

"Big family," he corrected. "I'm one of four brothers. Second oldest. Chris and Grant, who you've met, are married, both with kids, so any family occasion is busy and loud, even if it's just getting together for a meal."

"I didn't realise there were four of you. I'm one of three and it's bad enough."

"I'm lucky, we all get on, mostly. Sure, there were times growing up where Chris and I came to blows, but that's probably because we're so close in age. There's only a year between us. Well, a year and two days if you're being really specific."

"I think that's why I've found it hard with my siblings. They're really close to each other, and not just in age." I scrunched the fabric of the blanket between my hands. "I'm four years older than Anna, five and a half older than Nick. It shouldn't make a difference, but it does. I'm probably jealous of how close they are, and how they seem to have life sussed out as I blunder along from one disaster to another."

Tension froze in my body, my back as straight as one of the

lolly sticks that ran through the centre of the icy treats being sold from the kiosk on the promenade.

Max shuffled closer. His hand, large and warm, rubbed the exposed skin either side of my dress strap. "Today isn't a disaster though, is it? From where I'm sat it's pretty damn great."

His words gave me happy chills. He moved in closer still, sliding his hand over my shoulder blades until his arm was draped around my shoulder.

"No," I whispered, my eyes still fixed on his. "Today isn't a disaster."

And then Max's face edged closer to my own, our intentions so obvious and so visceral, and as his lips met mine and I fell into his kiss the thrill excited me as much as my very first kiss. But kissing Max was way better than kissing Colin Hammond at the Year 7 school disco. Kissing Max wasn't awkward or clumsy or to impress my friends. It felt right. Boy, did it feel right. His kiss was full of purpose without being too much. It lasted both a second and forever all at once, and when we parted I was left bewildered, like Alice spiralling down the rabbit hole with no clue what she'd be faced with when she landed.

"Wow," he said. "That was even better than I thought it'd be."

"You'd been thinking about kissing me?"

He smiled. "For weeks."

"I've been thinking about you too. Ever since that first day when I came into the shop. I couldn't explain it, but there was something pulling me to you. I wanted to spend time with you, get to know you better."

"And now you can."

When he put his arm around me, I allowed myself to slide my arm around his waist too. Even through his T-shirt the contours of his back felt so solid, so very *there*.

We sat in quiet solitude for a time. The world carried on around us – children chasing kites that soared on the coastal breeze, waves lapping at the shore like caresses, the seagulls darting and swooping in formations across the pastel sky.

Then Max affectionately patted my back, bringing me to the present, and said, "Are we having that round of crazy golf then?"

And I nodded yes, because I didn't want my life to be half-lived any longer.

CHAPTER 20

Eve and I were enjoying a stroll around the lake, having borrowed her neighbour's dog. A grumpy Dalmatian with the distinctly unoriginal nickname Spot; he wasn't enjoying the great outdoors as much as we were. In fact, he'd flat-out stopped twice, which we'd taken as a sign that it was time to wander back towards the car park.

We'd talked as we walked, Eve itching for information about the previous weekend's date with Max.

"It all sounds very romantic." Eve had a faraway expression on her face as I replayed the minutiae of the date, especially when I told her how Max had shown me how to master my crazy-golf swing. It sounded cheesy even to me, how his body had pressed against mine as he stood behind me, the sparks flying as he'd repositioned my hands on the well-used club, but Eve was right. It had been romantic. More than that it had been real and true. "I'm so happy for you, Sophie. It's been a long time since you've had a nice guy in your life."

The pointed jibe at Darius didn't pass me by, but I ignored it, not wanting thoughts of him to complicate my beautiful memories. I'd not thought of him when I'd been at the beach either, I'd been too busy being present and enjoying Max's company.

"Max is so sweet, Eve. He really listened to me when I spoke to him, and I felt like I could have told him anything in the world and he wouldn't have judged me. And you should have heard him talking about his family, it sounds like they're so tight-knit."

"Nothing more attractive than a family man," Eve agreed, her eyes lighting up. "A man who appreciates his own parents is perfect Daddy material. It's scientifically proven."

I didn't dispute the accuracy of that fact, instead imagining Max cradling a newborn baby in his surprisingly toned arms, gazing adoringly into its eyes with all the love of a doting parent. It was like one of those black and white art shots, although Max wasn't topless in my mind. (Although I'm sure if I knew what to expect he'd be half-naked in my head, we'd just not reached the topless stage yet. That said we'd not reached the baby stage either, but I had no trouble conjuring up an image of him with a child.)

"Sophie?" I realised I'd been lost in my daydream and blanking my friend.

"Sorry, I was thinking of something else." The man I'd been on one proper date with holding our baby. What was I becoming?

"I could tell. You had this dopey look on your face."

"Dopey?" I laughed. "Thanks a bunch."

"You know what I mean. Looked like you were miles away."

"Thinking about Max, that's all," I replied, with a grin that probably confirmed the dopey comment a million times over.

Eve rolled her eyes, but with a smile that showed she wasn't really judging me. "You are such a smitten kitten, Sophie Drew."

"I'm trying to play it cool, so I've been careful not to bombard him with messages. I don't want to come across as desperate. He sent me a message earlier and I'm challenging myself not to reply until I get home tonight."

Eve looked unsure. "Playing games isn't a good way to start to a relationship."

"Men don't like needy women, Eve." Or so all the internet articles I'd been reading had said.

"But no one likes being ignored," she replied.

The gloomy raincloud that had hovered in the distance edged closer, the first spots of rain falling as we reached Eve's car, relieved we'd made it before the heavens opened. Trust there to be a downpour when we had plans to go to a music festival that evening with Tawna and Johnny. The park would be a quagmire.

As Eve put her key into the ignition, our mobiles beeped in unison. Different notification tones, but there was only one person it could be – Tawna.

Both of us looked wordlessly at our incoming messages, digesting the information before us.

"I can't believe she'd do this. Even for Tawna it's unbelievable."

Eve's skin turned a funny shade of green, like mushy peas. "What the hell is she playing at?"

I looked back at the screen, rereading the message in case I'd misunderstood, but no.

Booked the hen do! We're heading to NYC June 17th - 20th!
I'll let you know how much you owe me later. #GirlsOnTour

The thought of how much four nights in New York would set me back made me feel sick, and there'd bound to be additional expenses too, because who goes to America to sit in a hotel room? Not Tawna Maguire, especially not on her hen do. Meals out and Broadway shows would fill our days, along with shopping sprees on Fifth Avenue and cocktails in exclusive bars. It made me nervous. Not to mention that my annual leave was rapidly running out, and June 17th was less than a week away…

"We could ask her to scale it back?" Eve said, but her words were devoid of optimism. No way would Tawna change her plans. Once she set her heart on something, she got it and damn the consequences.

"Not a chance."

Eve sighed. "I'll be dipping into my deposit savings then. I'd hoped I'd be applying for a mortgage before the wedding, but looks like that idea's out of the window."

I didn't let on that I'd be struggling to find the money at all. My wages were due in my current account on Tuesday but they were hardly generous to start with. I'd have to do another sweep of my wardrobe to see if there was anything else worth selling. I didn't have vast amounts of money floating around, but then who did? Not me and not Eve, that's for sure.

"I might tell her to invite someone else in my place." I was furious that she'd put us in this predicament. "I do love her, but she's so detached from what life is like for us mere mortals. I bet she paid for it from Johnny's account. He probably won't even notice the money's gone."

"You can't get her to invite someone else. We're her bridesmaids. We've not got a choice, we've got to go."

Eve reversed out of the parking space, her lips clamped together as she checked her mirror. She looked like the emoji with the straight line for a mouth, as though she was deeply unhappy but resolutely battling on to stay calm. It didn't fool me though. I could hear her teeth grinding behind the curtain of her lips.

"I'll ring her then. Have it out."

And before I had chance to think it through, before I could plan a conversation or convince myself it was a bad idea, I'd angrily jabbed at Tawna's entry in my phone book and held the phone to my ear. It only rang twice.

"Soph!" Tawna exclaimed, her voice dripping with excitement. "Did you get my message? We're heading to Manhattan! Me, you and Eve taking on The Big Apple!"

She spoke so fast that I couldn't get a word in, chattering about what an amazing time we'd have and how the trip would be her last hoorah as a single woman.

Eve studied me as she waited at a T-junction. She raised her shoulders and mouthed, "What's she saying?"

I pulled a face that didn't answer the question, it was nothing more than a pleading look from a hopeless case.

When Tawna eventually shut up I stayed quiet. I'd not said a word since the call was connected.

"You're not mad at me, are you, Soph?" she begged. "I know it's unexpected, but it was meant to make you both happy. Please don't be mad at me. I couldn't bear it."

"I wish you'd asked before you booked it, that's all," I said, trying to be diplomatic. I was fuming, but I didn't want a fight. "It isn't easy getting time off work at such short notice. Some people at the law firm book their holidays a year in advance."

"Oh, I'm sure you'll find a way to swing it," Tawna replied with so much nonchalance that it came across as dismissive. "Even slave-driver Marcie wouldn't deny you of a trip like this. I'm sure she'll be able to get some agency girl to cover you."

She didn't mean to be mean, but I bristled at the throwaway remark. It made me out to be replaceable, and although my job didn't require much in the way of qualifications, it was still skilled work.

"It's short notice for Eve too," I added. "And her team's tiny. They can't just drag any old Tom, Dick or Harry off the street to cover her. She's got a PhD!"

"It's a once-in-a-lifetime trip," Tawna argued, "my one and only proper hen. I don't think it's too much to expect my two oldest friends, my bridesmaids, to be there with me."

I envisaged her sat with her nose in the air like a Disney baddie.

"Well, I don't think it's too much to expect to be *asked* if I want to fly halfway around the world next week," I huffed, no longer trying to hide my annoyance. Her comment about the agency girl was still jangling on my last nerve. "Even if I do manage to get the time off work it's going to be expensive."

"But so worth it," Tawna replied.

"It's all right for you. You're not working nine to five every day, with clients relying on you. You don't have bills to pay single-handedly either."

"But you'll be there, won't you?" Her voice trembled, and again I was racked with guilt. "If money's a problem, I'm sure Johnny would pay for you."

There was no way I was going to accept their charity.

"Don't worry," I said, all the while worrying, "I'll find the money. I'll be there."

"Me too," Eve called out, although her lips barely moved and her teeth remained gritted.

"You're the best friends a girl could ask for," Tawna exclaimed. "I knew you'd come around. We're going to have so much fun!"

But as she enthused about a restaurant we simply had to go to down in Greenwich Village, I switched off from her babble, staring vacantly out of the window as the fields passed by in a blur of bottle-green.

"Don't forget it's the festival tonight," Tawna chirruped. "You are still planning on coming, aren't you?"

"Yep," I managed, thinking at least the music event we'd planned to go to was free. Maybe I could smuggle some booze in in a flask, pretending it's tea. "Eve's still up for it too, but she might be late." She'd planned to visit her mum at the care home once she'd dropped me at my parents' house and returned the dog to her neighbours.

"You girls are the best," Tawna squealed. "The absolute best. I can't wait to see you later!"

I was about to put the handset back into my bag when it beeped and, assuming it was Tawna, I unthinkingly opened the text.

Hi beautiful. Made any decisions about the money yet?
I could do with knowing one way or another ASAP. D xxx

CHAPTER 21

"Mum? Dad?"

The house was still and the radio quiet, an indicator that no one was home even though I'd told Mum and Dad I'd be dropping by. When I poked my head around the door to the living room the local paper was resting on the arm of Dad's chair and two mugs of tea were left, unfinished, on the coffee table. They weren't placed on coasters, and that was when I knew in my gut that something was wrong.

I walked into the kitchen, hoping to find a clue, and there it was, written on the whiteboard Mum uses for her shopping lists –

SOPHIE,
GONE TO NORMA'S. FRED'S HAD A FALL.
COME OVER IF YOU LIKE.
LOVE U, MUM XXX

Suddenly the worries I'd built up to be so major – Darius, money, the hen do – seemed trivial. What if Fred was seriously injured?

I didn't hang about. Closing the front door behind me, I turned left and jogged the ten minutes it took to get to Fred and Norma's house.

An ambulance was parked on the driveway but there were no sirens or blue flashing lights.

I noticed the net curtains twitching in the house across the street.

Norma opened the door before I reached it, and from the way her cheeks sagged and the vacant look in her eyes I knew what she was going to say. The tears started to fall before she even said the words.

"He's gone, pet. He's gone."

The park was already rammed with people when I arrived. Couples sat on checked picnic blankets with food and drink brought from home, others standing in groups with drinks in their hands, more still browsing the food stalls. I'd not had anything other than the slice of Victoria sponge Norma had given me, which I'd nibbled at to be polite, but I didn't have an appetite.

The last thing I'd felt like doing was going to the festival, but she'd insisted.

"Fred would hate for you to change your plans because of him. Please go, Sophie. There's nothing you can do here."

And I'd replied numbly that I would.

The evening was humid, almost muggy, and the post-storm evening sun was bright enough to warrant sunglasses, although mine were at home. Raising my hand to my forehead to shield my eyes from the glare, I scanned the crowd for Eve. She'd been well up for the festival, extending the weekend for as long as possible.

Just as I was contemplating leaving, thinking I'd never be able to find a familiar face in the crowd, there was a hand on my shoulder.

"Hi there."

I didn't need to look into those deep dark eyes, or to take in the charming smile. I'd have known that Scouse accent anywhere. Darius Welch.

"Sophie! We found you!" Tawna swept me into a hug. With her cloud-like hair and the hit of her fragrance she all but knocked me off my feet, as if the events of the day weren't already enough to leave me reeling. I'd texted her and Eve to let them know about Fred, telling them I didn't want to talk about it yet in case I got emotional. Grief is a weird beast. One minute you're numb, the next you're raw with it. "It's so busy! We were just saying it was going to be impossible to get to wherever you and Eve were."

"I'm right here."

"It's good to see you, Soph," Darius said, taking a step closer. He bent down to hug me too, it was bewildering to experience his arms around me for the first time in so long, to breathe in the scent of his neck. "You're looking good."

I'd worn the jumpsuit from Max's shop, hoping that by wearing something nice I could trick myself into feeling better.

"Thanks."

I struck up a conversation with Johnny, but was aware of the weight of Darius's gaze on me.

A band took to the stage, a grungy-looking outfit with ripped black jeans and misshapen T-shirts that had faded to grey. The drummer nodded his appreciation for the faint ripple of applause, raising his drumsticks in a salute. They opened with a cover, and a slightly ropey one at that, but the crowd, there for the atmosphere, not the music, weren't bothered.

When Tawna declared she was dying of thirst, dragging

Johnny to a nearby stall for liquid refreshment, Darius and I were left alone.

"Why did you come? Tawna must have told you I'd be here. Did you just want to put pressure on me to make a decision about the money?"

His eyes caught with mine and despite my inner fury, my tummy flip-flopped. Our relationship was always about the extremes – sizzling hot or frozen out. Lukewarm was never an option.

"This isn't about Nadia, and it isn't about the money either. I wanted to see you, Soph. The truth is, I can't stop thinking about you."

"You didn't have to gatecrash a night out with my friends."

"I tried to talk to you at the party, I've asked Tawna to give you messages." He paused, looking at me with large doleful eyes. "I've loved you so much for so long. I'd give anything to go back in time and take back the awful things I said."

"You told me I was vain."

"I had no right to do that. I know that now."

"I did it because I wanted your approval." Saying that aloud made my heart hurt. "I didn't believe I was good enough for you."

"If anything you were too good for me. I know Eve hates me and says I don't deserve you. She's right, I don't. But that doesn't stop me loving you. Nothing will."

"Then why did you flirt with other women right under my nose? I wanted to feel loved, Darius. All I ever wanted was for you to love me and be there for me."

"I know." His shoulders sagged in a way that made me believe his remorse. "I'm sorry."

His apology was a surprise. Darius Welch wasn't the kind of man to admit to his mistakes.

"It was never to do with you," he said, running a hand

through his hair. A strand flopped in front of his face and he cocked his head to keep it out of his eyes. I was overcome by a sense of déjà vu which almost knocked me sideways, a distant memory of when our relationship was new. "I was weak, and I loved the attention. It was selfish of me, but at the time I didn't think of how it made you feel. I loved you so damn much. So damn much."

The music from grungy band came to a halt and I clapped as they said their thank yous, mainly because I didn't know how to respond to what Darius had said.

I'd loved him too, that head over heels love that is ten-a-penny in youth but doesn't often come around once you hit adulthood. I'd had the daydreams about our wedding day, spent hours practicing my signature as "Sophie Welch". Looking back it sounded childish, whereas at the time it had been exhilarating.

"Tawna told me about Fred. I'm sorry. I know how much he meant to you. I've let you down so many times, but I'm here for you now. Let me help you however I can."

When his hand slid around my waist it took me by surprise but a gush of nostalgia, along with the echoes of his words, stopped me from pushing him away. The spicy scent of his aftershave gave me a head rush, and the chatter of the surrounding crowds fuzzed in my ears.

"I still think of you all the time," he said, whispering in my ear. His lip caught my earlobe as he added, "What we had was special, wasn't it?"

He drew me closer, and I turned to find myself facing him. Every detail was so familiar it was as though he was in high definition. When he leant in to kiss me I unwittingly responded, the soft cushion of his lips against mine as bliss-filled as the mellow music coming from the stage. I allowed myself to float away from the harsh realities of life, unthinking and carefree, and only when Eve appeared and screamed, "I can't believe it!" did I pull away, full of confusion.

To avoid her barrage of questions I extricated myself from Darius's hold and focused my attention firmly on the stage. The beautiful melancholy tune was coming from a sole man sound-checking guitars for the next band. My heart sank as he looked straight at me, a pained expression on his face, as his fingers picked out a gentle melodic riff.

Max.

CHAPTER 22

" Aaah!"

Freshly boiled water splashed onto the back of my hand, the burning sensation stinging so much that it brought tears to my eyes. It was my own fault for not concentrating when doing the tea run. My brain repeatedly replaying the scenario all morning.

The attraction that had always been present between Darius and I was undeniable. My knees had buckled beneath me as soon as his lips had connected with mine and if it hadn't been for his arm around my waist, the large palm of his hand firmly clutching my hip, I may well have melted on the spot.

But then there had been Max, who must have seen the kiss from his prime vantage point at the centre of the stage where he was setting up for the band. The crushed expression he'd been wearing said it all – any doubts I'd had about his feelings for me were quashed. No one would look as hurt as that if they didn't care.

Darius had been sending me texts full of kind words and condolences ever since the festival, but I'd not replied. Not only was I confused, I was purposely faltering because time was ticking on and I still hadn't given him an answer about the loan. I so desperately wanted to do what was right for Summer, although I was in no fit state to make big decisions. Anyway, where I'd find the money if I did decide to give it to him goodness only knew.

"Are you all right?" Jane asked, as I placed the kettle back on its stand and ran water from the cold tap over my hand. "We heard you cry out."

"I scalded myself." I held out my hand, showing her the blotchy marks where the water had hit. "It feels like nothing's going right at the moment."

"Now now, don't be so hard on yourself. Accidents happen to the best of us, and we didn't expect you to be here at all when we heard about poor old Fred. You shouldn't be here if you're not up to it, love. You've been in your own little world all day."

So she'd noticed, and if Jane had, Kath and Marcie would have too.

"I've got a lot on my mind," I admitted, through clenched teeth because the temperature of the water against my sensitive skin stung like hell.

"Fred was like family to you. It's understandable that you're going to find it hard."

"It's not just Fred," I confessed, feeling terrible that I could even be thinking of anything else after such an awful event.

"Matters of the heart?" she enquired. "We did wonder why we didn't get an update after the weekend, but didn't like to push you for details."

"That's part of it," I said, downplaying the effect the whole Darius situation had had on my productivity, "but I need to speak to Marcie about taking some time off at short notice."

"The funeral?"

I shook my head. "I'll need time for that but there's something else too."

"Ooh." Jane grabbed a cloth from the edge of the sink and wiped the spillage from the kitchen work surface. "Planning a holiday? Getting away might be just what you need."

"Tawna's planned a holiday," I corrected. "She booked herself a hen do. The trouble is we're due to fly on Thursday, and you know how strict Marcie is about giving the full two weeks' notice for any leave."

"How exciting. Where are you off too, somewhere nice I hope?"

"New York." I found myself smiling. Getting away did sound very appealing, and I'd spent half the night uploading clothes to the online sales sites to raise funds to pay Tawna back. Since there'd been no chance of me sleeping, it had seemed as good a time as any to set to work.

"How fancy! You youngsters go all out on these hen and stag dos these days. Mine was a night down the local with the girls and we thought we were posh because we had a meal as well as drinks. We're talking thirty years ago now. It was a different time."

"I'd have been more than happy with a night at the pub. Marcie's going to hit the roof. She probably won't even say yes."

"She'll understand. It's not every day one of your best friends gets married. And don't tell her I told you this, but she's been worried about you, even before this weekend. She'll be glad of you taking some time away from the office."

"Worried? Why?"

"We've all noticed how distracted you've been lately. You know, you can always talk to us about anything that's bothering you. You probably think we're dinosaurs who can't understand, but we'll do our best and even if we can't give you any advice we can listen."

"Thanks, Jane," I said, as she threw the soggy dishcloth into the sink, "but I wouldn't know where to start. Everything's got on top of me lately."

"Let's take these teas through, grab those choccie biccies, and you can get it all off your chest," she said kindly. "Come on, now. You'll feel better for offloading."

Jane carried the tray through to our shared office, and called Kath and Marcie. "Ladies, it's time for a tea break. And be quick about it, Sophie needs us."

Before long we were sat in a circle, hands tightly wrapped around our mugs. I was dying for a biscuit too, my appetite having returned with a vengeance, but didn't want to be the person to open the packet.

"So what's troubling you?" Kath asked, her face furrowed in concern. "Besides Fred, of course. It's not Max, is it? Because if he's messed you around I'll search the streets of Newcastle until I find him, and when I do I'll string him up by his you-know-whats. No one takes advantage of our Sophie."

I rapidly shook my head. "It's not Max. It's everything. I feel so out of my depth that I don't know where to begin."

"Take a deep breath," Marcie instructed, demonstrating by inhaling in an over-exaggerated fashion. She looked like Yoga Leo. "And then when you've calmed down you can talk. Work can wait, you're more important. We're a family here, we all need to look after each other."

Hearing my line manager speak so gently, so kindly, made me want to cry. It wasn't like Marcie was a bad boss, but I'd never have had empathy down as her strong point. She was usually blunt, which probably explained why she was chosen for a role that requires ensuring we all toe the line in the first place.

"Well," I began, taking another sip of my tea to brace myself, "Tawna's booked a last minute hen do…"

"To New York!" Jane chimed in.

"…to New York," I continued. "She didn't tell us before she

booked the flights and we're due to leave on Thursday. I know it's incredibly short notice, but I'm the chief bridesmaid and I feel I should be there."

"Of course you should be there," Marcie agreed. "Fill in the annual leave form and put it on my desk by the end of the day and I'll get it signed off for you."

I was amazed. That was one of the things I'd been getting myself worked up over ever since reading the message from Tawna saying she'd booked the flights. Could it really be as simple as filling in the form and Marcie would sign it off without a fuss?

"Are you sure? It'll leave you short-staffed, and we're so busy at the moment, and I'm going to need a day off for the funeral. I don't want to let you lot down."

"You're not letting anyone down," Kath said firmly. "I can take on some of your workload, if you like. So you're not snowed under when you get back."

"You don't mind? Haven't you got enough on with your own work?"

Kath flicked her hand nonchalantly. "It's no problem, and better than getting a temp in. So that's that sorted already."

"See?" Jane said. "I told you we'd do whatever we could."

"Thank you. Thanks all of you, but that's just the tip of the iceberg," I admitted, reaching over for the biscuits. I could only resist a good thing for so long before caving.

"Like I said, we look out for each other here. So, what else is bothering you? And don't say nothing, I can tell from your body language that something's up."

"I kissed Darius."

My workmates' eyes were on stalks at that nugget of information.

"What about Max?" Jane said. "That date he took you on to the coast, it was like something out of a Mills and Boon."

"I know, I know," I moaned. "I've probably made a dreadful mistake."

"I'd say definitely," Kath muttered, barely loudly enough for me to hear. "Max sounded great."

"Ssh." Jane gave Kath a dirty look. "You're not helping."

"I've seen Darius a few times lately, and it's thrown me. One minute we were talking, the next…"

"The next you had your tongue shoved down his throat?" Kath offered.

"Pretty much," I said with a grimace. "It wasn't planned. It just felt like the right thing to do at the time."

"If it felt right, then maybe it was right," Jane added, but she didn't sound too sure. "Sometimes these things happen for good reason."

"It was the grief, I wasn't thinking straight. Besides, I feel bad for Max."

"It's not like you're married to him." Kath scoffed. "Not that that necessarily makes a difference. But you know what I mean. One kiss with your ex doesn't constitute cheating, not when you've not made a commitment to each other."

"You don't even need to tell Max," Jane said. "I wouldn't, if I were you, not at this early stage. Keep your options open."

"I disagree," Marcie interjected disapprovingly. "It's always better to be honest."

"I don't have the option of keeping it a secret even if I wanted to." I hid my head in my hands. "Max was there," I mumbled. "He saw us."

Marcie frowned. "Pardon?"

"Awkward," Jane said, a look of pity crossing her face.

"Fucking hell," Kath exclaimed. "What did he say?"

"He didn't have the chance to say anything. He was up on the stage setting up for the band and we were in the middle of a crowd."

"Maybe he didn't see you then," Jane suggested. "If he was busy."

"Oh, he saw us all right. He was looking directly at me. That's why I feel so awful. He treated me so well when we went to Whitley Bay, he deserves someone better than me. Someone who doesn't snog their ex-boyfriend."

"Give him a call. Explain." Jane made it sound so easy, not like the most awkward conversation in the history of the world. "That's if it's him you want, of course."

"I don't know what I want." I sighed, reaching for a second biscuit. "One moment I think I've got it sussed and want to give things with Max a proper shot, and the next... well. The next I'm royally cocking it up. I've probably ruined every chance I had with Max anyway now."

I couldn't bring myself to tell them about the rest of it – mentioning my debts was out of the question, as was telling them about Darius's loan request – I didn't want them to judge me, and I certainly didn't want them feeling sorry for me. I'd heard them make jokes about millennials before – about how reliant we are on our phones and how much money we spend on posh coffees and spaghetti squash. Telling them I'd lived beyond my means for so long would only fuel their hypotheses.

"For what it's worth, I think you should phone Max if you like him. Talk to him. Explain. What's the worst that could happen?" Jane said before biting into a biscuit. Crumbs landed on her blouse but she was too busy enjoying her treat to be bothered about brushing them off.

"He might not pick up, or worse still, he could answer, hurl abuse at me and then hang up," I offered, catastrophising events being something of a strength of mine. "I don't think I can do it."

"If he's as nice as you say, I bet he'd understand, but it's your call," Kath said. "Sometimes you've got to bite the bullet and have the difficult conversation. Maybe he'll be angry, maybe he'll be upset. We don't know. But talking to him is the only way you're going to get any answers."

Although I knew she was right, I was scared. That's why I finished the dregs of tea from my mug, baulking at the soggy biscuit crumbs lingering in the liquid as a result of my biscuit-dunking habit, and rapidly changed the subject back to New York.

"I'll fill in the holiday form for you now, Marcie. Thanks so much for being so understanding about it."

"No problem. It sounds like some time away could do you the world of good, and you never take time off. I can't remember the last time you had a sick day."

"I'll work extra fast this week to make up for it, I promise. Starting now." I pushed back my chair and headed towards my desk.

But despite my promises, I spent the afternoon pretending to be productive, while all the time my heart raced, my stomach churned and my brain came close to exploding. My workmates might be on my side, but I still had some important decisions to make.

CHAPTER 23

It was an early start. Closer to the middle of the night than to the dawn, so maybe it wasn't early at all, just really, really late. Early, late, whatever – the only thing keeping my weary eyes open was the double shot of espresso in my takeout Starbucks.

"I'm so excited," Tawna buzzed, not looking anywhere near as tired as I felt. Her make-up had been freshly applied for the flight, whereas if the previous day's mascara had managed to cling on to my eyelashes it'd be a miracle. "One final fling before the big day," she added, in a slightly wistful tone.

Eve smiled. "We're going to have a great time. I can't wait to touch down now."

We hadn't even boarded.

"We've got hours trapped on a plane before we get to New York," I complained. "Popping ears and crap films on the inflight entertainment system. And I'd put money on me sitting next to someone who either man-spreads or hasn't used deodorant since the turn of the millennium."

"Don't be grumpy, Soph," Tawna pleaded. "This is supposed

to be fun. All I want is to let my hair down and relax with my girls."

"In New York." My voice dripped with sarcasm, all the things I'd hurriedly sold to pay for this jaunt looming in the forefront of my mind.

"For crying out loud, just eat something already." Eve shoved a cereal bar at me, which I initially turned my nose up at before realising it had chocolate chips in it. After that I tore the wrapper off like a woman possessed. "You're always like this when you're tired and hungry."

Eve knows me well. I'm like a baby – without enough food or sleep I'm a nightmare to be around, which means middle-of-the-night departures are never going to be a laugh a minute for my travelling companions.

Adding to my grumpiness was the fact I'd still not made a decision about whether or not to give Darius the money, plus I'd wimped out of calling Max. I wanted to so badly, but I was petrified he'd slam the phone down on me. Instead I ended up continually checking my phone to see if he'd rung. But there was nothing. Nada. Zip.

That's why I, along with a group of other haggard-looking travellers who were surely also wondering why they'd put themselves through the torture of a flight at an inhuman hour, wasn't the cheeriest person on the planet as we sat in the departure lounge.

"Sorry." One bite of the cereal bar had given me enough of a jolt to remind me of my basic manners. "I'll sleep on the plane. I won't be this miserable in America, I promise."

"You'd better not be," Eve retorted, throwing me a warning look. "Just forget about your love life for a few days."

"What have I missed?" Tawna unscrewed the cap from her bottle of water and took a sip. "I feel so out of the loop. I know you and Darius were getting it on last weekend."

"Max saw Sophie kissing Darius at the festival," Eve explained.

"No! What did he say?"

"That's just it, he hasn't said anything. Sophie's too nervous of how he'll react to try to contact him and he's not phoned her either."

"Maybe that proves he's not that interested." Tawna's shrug of indifference annoyed me, but her words hurt me most. Max gets plenty of offers, if what the girl in the charity shop said was right, so why would he want to get involved with someone who kisses their ex right under his nose? I checked my phone again. Zilch.

I took another bite of the cereal bar.

"I know I wasn't the most encouraging person when you first told me about Max," Tawna draped an arm around my shoulder, "but I want you to be happy, Soph. I saw your face just now. You miss him, I can tell."

"Yeah," I replied sadly, through a mouthful of cereal bar. "He listened to me. I really thought we might have had something meaningful, but then I went and threw it all away. If only I could be more like Kath. She doesn't get attached too quickly."

I swiftly segued into telling them about her latest conquest, someone she'd met on a dating app who she'd therefore assumed to be footloose and fancy free. When they'd met in person it had transpired that he was married and looking for someone who'd be willing to join him and his wife in the bedroom.

"Surely she didn't go through with it." Eve's face was a picture – a pale ashen picture. "I'd run a mile if someone said that to me the first time I met them."

"She did. She's seeing them again too."

"Marriage should be sacred." Tawna tutted disapprovingly. "If Johnny suggested a threesome I'd tell him where to shove it."

"If he was after a threesome, he might enjoy that."

We almost missed the announcement booming out of the tannoy informing us our departure gate had opened and our flight was ready to begin boarding because we were giggling so much.

Like fools we hurried to the gate, unable to stop our faces from breaking into stupid grins as the flight attendant checked our boarding passes and passports and allowed us to board the 787 Dreamliner. I switched my phone to flight mode, which was one way of stopping me checking it. After selling so many of my favourite outfits to pay for the trip (my poor wardrobe looking exceptionally sparse as a result), I couldn't waste it dwelling on Darius or being miserable over Max.

"We're officially on our way now," Eve announced as she stuffed her rucksack into the overhead locker. "Everyone knows that the moment you get on the plane is when the holiday properly starts."

I settled into my seat. The heavy metal ends of the seat belt fastened together with a satisfying clunk and I let out a sigh of relief at the lack of man-spreading stinkers and allowed myself to rest my eyes.

When I reopened them we were on the approach to JFK. I'd managed to sleep for the whole flight.

The hotel was right in the heart of Times Square. Neon lights flashed through the window of our room and every time the scene on the giant billboards changed so did the colour of the room. It was like being inside a disco ball and that, combined with my mammoth sleep, left me raring to get out there amongst the people, the noise, the life.

The circus-like atmosphere wrapped around us as we

stepped onto the street; people staring, awestruck, at the lights flashing overhead.

Nothing could have prepared us for being here, despite its familiarity from being in so many films. The reality was different. Times Square equated to sensory overload. The deafening honk of car horns, the waft of hot dogs tiptoeing on the heavy, humid air, the shoulder-barges of tourists with a hideous lack of manners and no concept of personal space... It was amazing. There really was no place else like it on earth.

"Let's get a selfie," Tawna suggested, holding her phone out at arm's length in preparation. Eve and I obediently squashed our smiling faces against hers as she pressed the small round button to capture the moment. The picture looking back at us showed three tired but happy friends. "Thanks for coming, ladies. This is going to be the best hen do ever!"

Tawna wrapped an arm around Eve and me, and as we walked downtown towards the majestic Empire State building, it truly felt like the three of us were taking on the world, and our togetherness was so present – so vital – that I'd back us in that dual.

We were surprised to find a non-existent queue when we arrived at the landmark.

Eve frowned. "Is it closed?"

"The guidebook says it's open every day." Tawna shrugged, eyeing a suited man carrying a briefcase striding out of the doors. Seeing him reminded me that the building was more than a world-famous tourist attraction, it was also a working office block.

Tawna hurried over to the man, and from the way he looked at her, taking in the freckles on her shoulders where her strappy sundress didn't cover her skin, I knew he thought she was flirting. He salivated as she flicked her hair over her shoulder as she spoke, Tawna unaware of the spell she was casting over him.

When she skipped back, telling us to go inside and to expect a queue upstairs for the lifts to take us to the 86th or 102nd floor viewing areas, I mentioned how he'd looked like he wanted to ravish her.

"Don't be daft! I was only asking him about the opening hours. Anyway," she added, proudly waving the rock on the third finger of her left hand at me, "he must have seen that I'm engaged."

"That diamond is pretty hard to miss," Eve deadpanned. I smothered a laugh because she was right, the stone was especially dazzling in the city sunlight.

"You don't really think he thought I was coming on to him, do you?" Tawna asked, a worried expression on her face. "I know I said 'what goes on tour stays on tour' but I was only joking."

"We know," I assured her. "You're so in love with Johnny you don't even look at anyone else."

That's the difference. If I cared for Max as much as I professed to, surely I wouldn't have kissed Darius in the first place. The thought of Max gave me butterflies, the potent mix of lust and regret fizzing like a soluble vitamin tablet in a glass of water. Then Summer's angelic face took over, and the way Darius's kiss had brought back memories of the good times, and I was left as confused as ever.

"Maybe Eve will find a wealthy American over here." Tawna grinned. It was the same as when the two of them discussed my love life in my presence as though I couldn't hear what they were saying. "I should have got that businessman's number for you. He was all right looking, if you go in for the briefcase and braces type."

"Let's join the queue," I said in an attempt to kill the conversation. I sensed Eve's discomfort from the way she shifted from one foot to the other. "We don't know how long we might be waiting for a lift."

We stepped into the lobby, cooing over the gleaming walls. The air conditioning was a welcome contrast to the claustrophobic heat of the city on the street.

Conversations of love were long forgotten as we joined the queue, chattering about the iconic building's place in film history in movies such as *King Kong* and *Sleepless in Seattle*. However, Max remained very much at the forefront of my mind.

I checked my phone.

We were flagging by the time we made our way back to the hotel, adrenaline only able to keep us awake for so long. Our trip to the top of the Empire State Building had taken up more of the day than we'd anticipated, the winding queue inside slow-moving; but it had been worth it for the views out over Manhattan and beyond, the cloudless aquamarine skies the perfect backdrop for the cityscape below. We'd posed for photos on the deck, laughing and smiling despite our exhaustion, because that's what three Geordie girls in New York City do.

When our feet were back on solid ground, we found a bar which served extortionately priced fruity cocktails in sugar-rimmed glasses, glad of the alcohol soaking into our weary bodies. Tawna was still on the lookout for a man for Eve, eyeing up every male who walked through the door as a possible future husband for our friend. Unfortunately for Tawna (but fortunately for Eve) most of them came in with girlfriends, or didn't pass Tawna's stringent quality testing, so it remained just us three, laughing and chatting and reminiscing like in the old days, as we enjoyed our cocktails.

By the time we made our way back through the crowds in Times Square we were tipsy, and tipsy and tired wasn't a good combination for me. In fact, it was right up there on a par with hungry and tired for making me short-tempered and foul-mouthed, which was how the argument started.

Tawna's opening gambit was probably innocuous in her mind, a "joke" about how me and Eve were lightweights for needing to go back to the hotel after a few cocktails.

"You never used to be like this, Sophie," she slurred, teetering on her heels like a toddler taking her first steps. "You used to party as hard as the rest of us."

"Pacing myself," I mumbled back.

"It's my hen do." Her lips protruded. "Stop being so boring. You've been checking your phone all night long and your face is like a slapped backside. We're supposed to be having fun."

"We are having fun," Eve replied, ever the mediator, "but it's been a long day. If we go back to the hotel, we can have a cheeky disco nap and a freshen up and then go out again later."

None of the crowds were walking in a straight line, they darted in and out of the oncoming human traffic, zigzagging across the wide pavements and clashing shoulders without so much as a glance back to check the person they'd bumped into was okay. The enormous neon signs flashing up colourful advertisements caused me to blink until I could barely focus.

"It's you two who don't have the stamina. I'm doing fine," Tawna retorted. To prove her point she grabbed the arm of a tourist wielding a long-lens camera. He jumped back, probably fearing attack. "I don't look drunk, do I?" she screamed in his face. "I look like I could party all night."

The man shook his head, then nodded, unsure of the correct response.

"See!" she exclaimed, turning back to us. "Maybe I should find another bar and go there on my own, as my two best friends, my two *bridesmaids*, aren't up for making a proper night of it." Her pout was so furious that she looked like Donald Duck.

"Don't be like that, Tawna." Eve sighed, as the man Tawna

had approached looked warily in our direction as he backed away. "How about we have a drink in the hotel bar? It'll be more chilled out in there."

"I don't want chilled out," she flounced, but she still turned left into the bar rather than right towards the elevators as we stumbled into the hotel lobby.

"Go on then. I'm sure I can manage another one or two." It was an attempt to show willing, even though my whole body ached with utter exhaustion. What I really wanted was a long soak in the bath and a good night's sleep, but my boundless loyalty to Tawna wouldn't let me retreat to my room. "It is your hen do, after all."

"My first hen do," Tawna corrected, grabbing a cocktail menu from the bar. "There's the '*Dirty Dancing*' night, of course. I've not forgotten you sorted that, the date's in my phone." The comment came across as patronising and her sickly-sweet smile grated on me. She was making out we should be grateful she'd remembered our efforts. "And then I'm arranging a bigger event, so everyone who wants to can join."

Eve and I shared a look as she studied the drinks list. A "what the fuck is she on about" look.

"I've hired out one of the bars back in Newcastle," Tawna continued after she'd ordered the drinks, as though Eve and I were the weird ones. "The one you had your birthday party at actually, Soph. So many people were asking what I was doing for a hen do, and I couldn't expect everyone to fly out to New York at the drop of a hat, could I?" She laughed at the absurdity, totally missing how she'd expected exactly that of me and Eve.

I was so tired, so achy, and a little bit drunk, and these three factors combined caused me to snap. Biting my tongue was no longer on the agenda, I was well and truly riled. "Why would you do that? What kind of megalomaniac needs three hen dos?"

Tawna looked at me as though she'd been slapped, before

angrily slamming the menu down against the wooden bar. "I don't think it's being a mema... megla... melogamaniac." The long word foiled her in her tipsy state. "I thought my friends would want to celebrate my last days as a free woman."

I threw back my head and a cruel laugh escaped my lips. "It's hardly like you're going to be a slave in a third world country. You're going to be living in your flawless house with your flawless husband who earns enough money that you don't have to work in a dead-end job. You haven't got a clue what it's like in the real world. You'd be nothing without Johnny and his money. It wouldn't surprise me if that's the only reason you're marrying him."

I knew I'd taken it too far when Eve shook her head at me, but even so I couldn't bring myself to apologise. Tawna was so detached from reality, and she needed to know it. Everything spilled out in anger. My debts. Eve's mum's decline. I condensed a no-holds-barred account of the past six months into five emotion-riddled minutes, and I was on such a roll, such a cathartic roll, there was no chance of either of my friends breaking my stride.

By the time I'd finished ranting, calling Tawna selfish, oblivious, and self-centred, my throat hurt and my cheeks were soaked from my tears. I'd let everything loose, from the huge things like the red letters from the credit card company right through to the smaller things like how her obsession with whether using real crystals as table confetti was old-hat is a first-world privilege. (I'd also told her I had no idea whether or not it was old-hat, but that if she put semi-precious jewels on the tables, I'd be collecting them up and selling them to pay off my debts.)

Eve stared at the polished table, as though examining the grain of the wood for flaws. Tawna, unusually for her, was stunned into silence, and when I finally came to a halt, flat out of both breath and home truths to reveal, her lips remained clamped together.

The kindly barman subtly placed what I presumed to be a glass of water in front of me, which I guessed was to help me calm down and cool down. I winced as I took a sip. It was vodka, neat and without even a solitary cube of ice. The element of surprise brought everything into sharper focus, and I noticed I wasn't the only one with a tear-stained face. Eve had been crying too.

"If I'd known how much you were struggling I would have helped," Tawna said, which was just so like her to think she'd have all the solutions.

"As if," I said derisively, inelegantly rubbing the back of my hand underneath my snotty nose. "You don't give a damn about us anymore. All you care about is your wedding."

"That's not true!" Tawna's mouth gaped.

"Really?" A drunken laugh escaped my lips, a twisted sarcastic cough of disbelief. "Every time we see you it's because you want us to get fitted for dresses or show us the shoes you're wearing. It's always got to be about you and your 'big day'." I punctuated the final two words with air quotes and an eye-roll.

"When I did invite you over you blew me off for Max." Tawna's tone was indignant and defensive, "So don't you tell me that I've not tried."

"You were interfering!" I bellowed, pushing myself up from the stool I'd been sitting on. I obviously used more force than I'd intended to as the stool crashed, with a sharp ear-splitting clatter, against the dark-wood floor of the bar. "You weren't bothered about seeing me, all you were bothered about was trying to get me and Darius back together so there'd be no bad feeling on your wedding day! If it wasn't for you being so hell-bent on pushing us together I might be with Max now."

People stared, watching cautiously over the salted rims of

their margarita glasses, but I was too angry and too drunk to care that I was causing a scene.

"You've got it all wrong," Tawna replied, her eyes glistening with tears which threatened to fall. "I was doing it for you. I want you to be happy."

"Really, Tawna? Really?" I stared her down, or at least, I attempted to. It's hard to eyeball someone when you can see two of them. "Because lately it seems like you're not interested in me or Eve unless there's something you can get out of it."

Tawna picked up her cocktail, removed the straw and, drinking straight from the glass, knocked back the drink, including the sprig of mint which I'm sure she'd forgotten had been used as a garnish.

"If that's what you really think, then I don't know why you're here," she replied, before deliberately turning her back on me and clicking her fingers to get the attention of the barman.

I faced Eve, who was examining her nail varnish in a bid to remain impartial. That annoyed me too, because I knew she'd been as pissed off by Tawna's behaviour as I had. Surely she could back me up, rather than sitting so firmly on the fence that she might as well be nailed on?

"I'm going to bed," I said, nodding in the direction of the lobby. Shooting stars flashed before my eyes at the sudden movement. "Come on, Eve."

I strode out of the bar, head held high even though I was fully aware of the punters cautiously watching me, the reason for the commotion. I tried to sashay like a catwalk queen, but my heel skidded on the slippery surface of the floor, and I went over on my ankle. It hurt.

Only when I limped to the lifts, pressing the "call elevator" button so hard that I almost snapped my finger in two, did I realise I was still alone. So much for Eve not taking sides.

Five minutes later as I climbed into bed, the Times Square

billboards shining brightly through the crack in the curtains, my chest tightened with dread. What would happen next? Tawna and Eve were the only people I knew in the whole of America, and they hated me. As I sobbed into my super-plump pillow all I could think was that there really was nowhere to run.

CHAPTER 24

Eve and Tawna came to bed not long after I'd stormed out of the bar, and although I wasn't asleep I screwed my eyes shut and pretended to be dead to the world. I lay still as the pair of them pottered around me talking nonsense as Eve took out her contact lenses and Tawna followed her nightly skin care rituals.

They carried on chatting long after they switched out the light, reminding me of summer sleepovers where the three of us would share our deepest secrets in the safety of the darkness. This time though, I remained silent, holding my breath as I waited for them to discuss the night's events. They didn't, instead making up daft lyrics to an Ed Sheeran song and debating whether orange Smarties tasted different to the other colours since they replaced the delicious E numbers with natural flavourings.

When the telltale snoring from either side of me confirmed Tawna and Eve were asleep, I swung my legs out of the bed, slung my cardigan on over the top of my pyjamas (plain black, more loungewear than nightwear) and pulled on my trainers. I needed fresh air, but most of all I needed space to think.

Turning left out of the hotel, I headed towards downtown Manhattan. It was quieter than it had been during the day, but sunshine yellow taxis were still ferrying people about and revellers were spilling out of the bars. New York might be the city that never sleeps but, even along the main drag, it wasn't a place where I wanted to be alone at night. I felt sadness for the homeless men huddled in doorways wrapped in grubby coverless duvets; and the skyscrapers that had seemed so ambitious during the day – reaching symbolically upwards to the heavens – were now oppressive, looming over me like monsters.

I didn't stray from Broadway, well lit and well populated, and I thought and walked, thought and walked. Although I was both mentally and physically exhausted, the sensation of my feet pounding against the concrete was grounding, but as the cushioned soles of my trainers pushed me further south, I made a decision. It wasn't the one I'd set out to make, how to mend the fractured relationship with my two best friends, but as I sat on the bench on the outer edge of a large landscaped square (the open space making me feel far less oppressed), I took my phone from my pocket, logged into my PayPal account and, seeing I'd received more payments for clothes I'd sold online, transferred the balance into Darius's account.

I felt marginally better. I fired him a text to let him know I'd made the payment. It was a day late, with it being seven in the morning in Britain, and it wasn't the full amount he'd asked for, but it was all I had to give. Hopefully it would be enough to keep Nadia sweet in the short-term, so Darius and Summer could stay within easy travelling distance of each other. My phone beeped a response almost immediately, but where I'd expected a message of thanks from Darius, there were five words.

We need to talk.

Max.

There were no kisses, no "I miss you"s. Nothing to suggest anything he had to say was positive. Unsure of how to respond, I ignored the message and switched my phone off.

I sat for a while, squinting past the street lights towards the foreign, starless sky. People milled around, but I didn't feel threatened, and although my head was sore I no longer felt drunk. The rage that had consumed me had dissipated too and I wanted, more than anything, to be back in the hotel room with Tawna and Eve. But would Tawna hate me after my bitchy comments? And would Eve mind that I'd told Tawna about her own private business? I only hoped they'd be able to find it in their hearts to forgive me.

I started walking, heading north.

"Where have you been?" Tawna fired. "We've been worried sick."

She looked haggard, which was rare. Her eyes were slits, the whites a bloodshot red.

"Walking," I mumbled, sitting down on the edge of my bed to pull off my trainers.

"At this time of night? In New York City? Are you crazy?" Eve's eyes were the polar opposite of Tawna's, wide cartoon-like circles. "I woke up and you were gone. I was frantic."

"You should have phoned."

"We tried eight times," Tawna replied bluntly. "It went to answerphone every time."

"I thought you'd been mugged or worse..." Eve's voice tailed off and she lay back on her bed. "You've no idea how worried we were. I'll tell you something, that's one way to sober up sharpish."

"I went for a walk, that's all. I wanted to clear my head."

"I'd have walked with you," Eve wailed. "Don't you ever scare me like that again, Soph. Promise?"

Guilt flooded through me. "I promise. And I'm sorry for what I said earlier." My eyes connected with Tawna's zombie eyes. "I was angry, but I shouldn't have let my mouth run away with me."

"You were right," Tawna said, her voice croaky with sleep. "I haven't been a good friend to you two lately, but that's going to change, starting now. I know how lucky I am to have you both. Your friendship means the world to me, and that's not going to change when I get married. Friendship never ends."

She looked so serious, even though she'd ended her heartfelt speech by quoting the Spice Girls.

"We're all lucky," I added, "but we need to learn to be one hundred per cent honest. If we can't be ourselves with each other, then who can we be ourselves with?"

"True," Eve affirmed, having regained her composure. She raised her glass of water in a toast. "To honesty."

"To honesty," Tawna and I repeated, holding imaginary glasses aloft.

"And now," Tawna said, burying her bleary-eyed face into her pillow, "sleep."

"How are you feeling this morning, sleepyhead?" Tawna asked, placing a mug of steaming coffee on the bedside table.

"Rough as," I moaned, as she ruffled my bedhead hair.

"You've looked better," Eve said with a laugh, before clutching her head and saying, "owww." She couldn't laugh too long or too hard. Her hair was looking wild too.

"Shut up," I growled affectionately, plumping up a pillow and pulling myself into a seated position. Even that hurt.

I was amazed by how good Tawna looked, fresh as the proverbial daisy, her hair washed and blow-dried, her barely-there day make-up applied to perfection. It was as though the tired, bloodshot eyes of the previous night never existed. "Thank you for opening up to me, and I'm sorry I've been such a crap friend lately. I won't shut you out again."

"It's in the past." Eve yawned, her mouth stretching into a wide tunnel-like O. "And now we're all up to date on each other's lives so none of us need to struggle alone."

"Too right." I made myself take a sip of the coffee. It burned, but as the caffeine jolted through my bloodstream I felt fractionally more human again. Perhaps I would be able to drag my sorry arse out of bed after all. "Although there is something else I need to share with you."

I took a deep breath before telling them about Darius and the money. Eve looked horrified when I told her about my middle-of-the-night bank transfer, and even Tawna couldn't conceal her shock.

"He never mentioned any of this to me," she said, "although nothing would surprise me when it comes to Nadia. I'm surprised he hasn't told Johnny though."

"Maybe he has, but told Johnny not to tell you?" Eve suggested, stifling a yawn. "You know Darius. Typical alpha male. He wouldn't want to admit to being under Nadia's thumb."

"There are no secrets between me and Johnny!" Tawna spluttered. "He'd tell me anything. Maybe you're right though, Darius doesn't like to come across as needy. It must show that he trusts you, Sophie, to approach you. That takes guts."

"Max messaged me too," I said quietly, scrolling through my phone to look at the message.

We need to talk.
Max.

Nothing about the message filled me with hope, but I held it up for my friends to read.

"You were desperate to hear from him, Soph, and now you have. That's great!" Eve said.

"I don't know. It sounds ominous to me."

"You wanted him to reach out first and he has. Have you messaged him back?" Tawna asked.

I shook my head. "I think I'm going to leave it, at least until we get back home. This week's been traumatic enough without long-distance arguments making it worse. I think I'm going to switch my phone off for the rest of the holiday, actually."

Tawna gave me a disbelieving look. "You'd never manage without it. And how would you take photos without your phone?"

"I'll pinch yours off Instagram," I said with a shrug, and then I held my finger against my phone's power button. When the screen went black, I threw my handset into my suitcase, which was lying open at the foot of my bed.

"Do you still want to go to The Statue of Liberty today?" I knew that was the one landmark Tawna had her heart set on seeing.

She nodded, then said, "But let's get brunch first. I could do with a stack of pancakes drowned in maple syrup to set me up for the day."

I couldn't decide if that sounded amazing or awful. Pancakes would normally be my dream breakfast, but my stomach was still lurching up and down as though I was riding the Cyclone rollercoaster at Coney Island.

"I'm up for that. My stomach feels as though it's been hollowed out." Apparently the mere mention of pancakes was all that was needed to get Eve stripping off and preparing to get in the shower. "Aim to leave in half an hour?"

I groaned. Having to force myself out of my pit wasn't appealing when my head was having its own private disco.

"We're in New York!" Tawna reminded us, punching the air. "The best city in the world. Surely you don't want to waste our time here lying in bed."

"You encouraged it by getting me rollicking drunk." I smiled, but her words hit home and I swung my legs out from under the covers. It's not every day I wake up in one of the greatest cities in the world. "You said it yourself, I'm a lightweight."

"Maybe we should stick to just a few cocktails tonight," Tawna said thoughtfully. "Can't have you feeling this rough in the morning. We've got an early start tomorrow." She clamped her hand over her mouth then mumbled through her fingers, "Oops, I shouldn't have said that."

My eyebrows slid down my face into a frown, mystified by her secrecy. "What do you mean?"

She lowered her hand then jutted out her chin. "Never you mind. You'll just have to wait and see."

I knocked back what was left of my coffee. It was no longer scorching enough to make me feel like I was being burned alive from the inside. "Nothing bad though? You promise?"

"Of course it's nothing bad! It's a treat for my two best friends. You'll love it."

"Hmm."

The glimmer of a smirk on Tawna's face left me wondering, but as Eve stepped out of the bathroom wrapped in a fluffy white towel, followed by a hazy mist of lemon-scented steam, I didn't have the chance to dwell on it for long. I needed every ounce of energy I had to drag myself in the shower and sober up good and proper.

My earlier coffee sloshed in my stomach, my hands gripping the silver railing that lined the deck of the boat taking us to Liberty Island. The sensation wasn't pleasant, but it could've been worse. A boy further along the deck was throwing up into a brown paper bag. At least my pancakes had the decency to stay down.

Lady Liberty stood tall and proud on her tiny island at the southern tip of Manhattan, and it struck me how surreal it was that the monument I'd seen so many times in films and on TV was right in front of me. Her turquoise frame looked smaller in reality than it did on screen, but no less impressive. As the sun reflected off her body, she glowed.

"I can't believe we're here," Eve breathed. "Back when we were kids I used to dream about coming to New York but never imagined it would actually happen. Look at us now. Here we are." She scooped our hands, Tawna's with her right, mine with her left. "It's incredible. And there's no one I'd rather be here with than you two."

A sigh of happiness escaped Tawna's lips and as I caught Eve looking up at Liberty, her eyes full of awe, I had no regrets about this trip. Yes, it was an expensive holiday and using the money to pay off my debts would have been the more responsible thing to do, but I'd still transferred more than the minimum payment to the credit card company, even with the unexpected expense and giving Darius the money for Summer.

Being with my girls on a once-in-a-lifetime trip was worth it anyway. Who knew where we'd be in the future? Tawna and Johnny were already settled in their nest and it wouldn't surprise me if they quickly took the next step and filled it with fledglings, and Eve had mentioned she was hoping for promotion at work. Her boss was nearing retirement and when the time came for looking for his replacement Eve would be there waiting to fill his empty lab coat. And I'd started making steps towards changing my own life for the better, even if I still had a way to go.

"Besides my family there's no one who's been in my life as long as you two," I said, pensively. "Let's cherish every minute of this holiday. Squeeze every bit of magic out of our time here."

"Too right." Eve nodded, and as the boat docked, the three of us linked arms, stepping onto Liberty Island as one.

I breathed in a lungful of Liberty Island air, still heavy with sunshine but free from the pollution of the city, as I gazed across the bay to the Financial District. Freedom Tower dominated the skyline, a giant splinter of glass piercing the island of Manhattan. The neighbouring skyscrapers were comparatively unimpressive – office blocks, apartments, meeting places – but they all served their own purpose and were all important in their own right.

"Let's do this," I said, leading our human chain in the direction of the ticket and security checkpoint, but not before buying three foam crowns so we really looked the part. Like typical tourists, but like typical tourists having the times of their lives.

I hugged Tawna and Eve close, drinking in the moment, because days like these didn't come around very often, and when they did you had to savour them.

It had been a mad trip. After our jaunt to Liberty Island (where Eve threw up when we reached the plinth, her hangover combined with her longstanding phobia of heights winning out over her strong constitution), we'd treated ourselves to a hideously overpriced buggy ride around Central Park, where the horse had a severe bout of loud and pungent flatulence; followed by a guided bus tour around the key sightseeing spots, where Tawna insisted she spotted Julia Roberts walking down Fifth Avenue.

Tawna had made us get off the bus to stalk her but, four blocks later when we finally caught up with the red-headed woman, she looked nothing like the famous film star and Tawna's feet were ripped to shreds from running in her heels.

Our third day in The Big Apple had begun with Tawna's big secret – which hadn't gone down well with Eve – a helicopter ride over Manhattan for the three of us. The back of my hand would probably be permanently scarred by the crescent-moon-shaped marks Eve's nails had left as she clung on to me for dear life.

Thankfully the evening had been more enjoyable (and less painful), taking in a Broadway show. That was fabulous, actually, and we did get to have a group selfie with one of the actresses at the stage door. She wasn't Julia Roberts' level of famous, but she'd starred in a few well-known films.

There'd also been food and lots of it. We'd eaten our body weight in salted pretzels from food carts on the street and more pizza than necessary at John's Pizzeria, as well as sampling the restaurant Tawna had been so keen to try out. She'd probably eaten more carbs in the time we'd been away than she had in the previous year.

That along with the drinking – way too much drinking, even though we'd said we were going to pace ourselves after our first eventful night – was Tawna's hen do in brief. It had been emotional and exhausting and wonderful, but the time had come for us all to return to our realities back in the UK.

As we sat at the airport, waiting for our flight to be called, we enjoyed one final holiday cocktail in the bar. That was when I switched my phone back on and an influx of messages popped up on the home screen. The name that flashed up on the screen over and over again caused me to catch my breath.

Four new messages from Max.

Did you get my last message?
Max

Please, Sophie. Call me when you get this.
Max

Sophie, it's about Darius and the money.
Max

I guess you don't want to talk about it. I'll leave you alone.
Max

I read the messages three times, trying to make sense of them. How did Max know about Darius and the money?

I clicked to make the FaceTime call even though that'd enable him to see me in my post-holiday state. My skin was a sallow shade from lack of sleep and bad dietary habits and deep dark rings circled my eyes. I'd tied my hair back in one of those messy buns which look chic when celebrities wear them, but just looked downright scruffy on me. But none of it mattered. I needed to speak to Max.

"Sophie," he said, and I thought that maybe, maybe, something like longing lingered in his voice. "I wanted to talk to you."

"I wanted to talk to you too," I blurted, "but I'm still in New York with the girls. We're about to board the plane home. My phone's been off for days so I've only just picked up your messages."

"Yeah, well, there are a few things I think you need to know. I'll meet you at the airport, if you like? Drive you all back."

"We're flying into Manchester, not Newcastle," I said with regret, as a tannoy announcement let us know our flight was ready for boarding. Tawna and Eve tried chivvying me along, but I batted away their attempts to get me to hurry.

"So? I can still come and pick you up. What time do you land?"

We'd reached the gate, a smartly-dressed flight attendant checking our boarding passes and passports.

"Three thirty-five in the morning. Honestly, it's the middle of the night. Don't come, please. It's too far."

"I want to. There are things you need to know, and it'd be better talking about it in person rather than over the phone. I'll be waiting for you at the gate."

As I settled into my seat on the plane, crammed between Tawna who'd bagsied the window and Eve who preferred the aisle so she could stretch out her long legs, I replayed the call over in my mind. Surely he wouldn't have offered to come and collect us if he hated me? In fact, would he have messaged at all if he was that upset?

Seeing Max on screen made me realise how much I liked him. He was gorgeous, and not just on the outside. When the flight took off I wrapped myself in a blanket and although I didn't sleep – my mind being too full of thoughts of Max – I allowed myself to daydream; to wonder if he'd be waiting at the arrivals gate like he'd said he would.

CHAPTER 25

He was there, looking sleepy and cute as he leant over a barrier holding a sign saying "Tawna and Hens". If anything was going to win Tawna around, it was that.

Seeing him in the flesh was like receiving a sucker punch to my stomach. Before the trip I'd been aware of the attraction between us, but now the thought of us not being together set off a very real pain in my chest. All I could think was please, please, please, don't let him hold the kiss with Darius against me, not when I'd finally accepted there was only one man I wanted, and he was right there in front of me, his hair mussed up like a scarecrow's and his oversized jumper drowning him.

My body ached terribly, the activities of the trip combined with the onset of jet lag wiping me out as we clambered into Max's vehicle, but as I tilted my tired head back against the headrest, I couldn't tear my eyes away from Max.

His hands were firmly wrapped around the steering wheel as he drove, his eyes focused on the road.

Tawna snored away on the back seat, her animalistic snorts drowning out the low hum of the Motown classics playing on the radio. Eve had her headphones on, most likely listening to the science podcast she was devoted to.

"How does it feel to be back?" Max asked, eyes still fixated on the motorway.

"America was incredible, but it's good to be home," I said, before softly adding, "It's good to see you, Max. I'd been wanting to phone you, but I was scared. I thought you might not want to see me again."

I longed to reach out and touch him but was afraid of distracting him when he was driving. The hug he'd given me at the airport had been so tight I'd felt the air being squeezed from my lungs.

"I saw you and your ex at the festival."

I could feel my cheeks heating up, and I was glad it was still dark outside so I could hide behind the night's veil.

Max looked over his shoulder to the back seat of the car. When he was happy my friends weren't eavesdropping on our conversation he added, "I was jealous, and angry. So fucking angry! Do you know how much it takes for me to trust people?" He laughed bitterly. "Of course you don't."

A fire I'd not seen before burnt in his eyes and there was tension in the way his fingers coiled around the steering wheel and the rigidity of his jawline.

I spouted my pre-prepared lines about how the kiss with Darius hadn't been planned and how it had only happened because I'd been vulnerable and upset about Fred, but even to my ears they sounded like something from a low-budget soap opera.

"And it had to be him, of all people," Max continued, all but spitting the words. "My brother, Chris, knows him. They've got some friends in common, what with them working in the same field. In fact, Chris's business partner is with Darius right now. In Vegas. They flew out yesterday for Johnny's stag."

He turned to look at me and the harsh motorway lights reflected his eyes. They looked steely and cold.

"Darius isn't going on the stag do." I was talking slowly, but still tripping up over the words. My mouth was bone dry. "He told me at the festival. He's giving the money he was planning to use to pay for the trip to his ex, instead – for his daughter."

"He's in Vegas now," Max insisted. "The photos are all over Facebook."

I instinctively reached for my phone before remembering Darius and I were no longer connected on social media. But me and Johnny were...

I clicked on Johnny's account, scrolling past his profile picture and personal information. And sure enough, group photos from the stag do confronted me, eight inebriated men standing in front of the iconic "Welcome to Las Vegas" sign. And right at the centre of the group, posing next to the groom-to-be, was Darius.

Bile rose in my throat as the penny dropped. For the second time in less than a week I felt trapped in an excruciating situation. I wanted to jump out of the car. I would have, if we hadn't been doing seventy miles an hour on the motorway.

"Seen it for yourself, have you?"

"He told me he had no money," I said, my voice barely audible. "I gave him some. It was supposed to be for Summer."

"I know. Everyone in Newcastle knows. He's been bragging to the lads about how he's still got you wrapped around his little finger, and you know how fast gossip spreads. Chris told me, and I messaged you straight away. I thought you had a right to know."

"He wouldn't spend money like that on the stag do," I said, as much to convince myself as Max. "His daughter's mother is blackmailing him, threatening to move Summer to the other end of the country unless he gives her more money. He's struggling, because he already gives her more than half his wages."

"He's obviously not that hard up, if he can afford to fly out to Vegas. They're going to the big fight at the MGM Grand too, apparently. Tickets for that must have cost a fortune. Not exactly the actions of someone who's trying to save every penny to keep their daughter close. I'm not saying this to be a bastard. It's not revenge." Max's voice cracked. "I just think you deserve to know what he's really like."

"I'm sure there's a reasonable explanation," I replied, although I couldn't for the life of me think of one. "There has to be."

"And you're still defending him." Max slammed the heel of his hand against the steering wheel. "I guess that kiss at the festival wasn't as meaningless as you've been trying to make out after all."

The lights of my hometown twinkled in the distance like a blanket of stars. "I'll drop Tawna and Eve off first. You'll need to give me directions." His voice dropped, quiet and throaty. "And then I'll take you home."

CHAPTER 26

Funerals are never pleasant but, although I was surrounded by people I knew, I felt more alone than ever as I sat in the crematorium. Max had been replying to my texts, but only with a few short words saying he wasn't ready to talk, and although he'd been back from America for a week Darius hadn't replied to my messages. Tawna and Eve were busy with their own lives after our New York jaunt. Scrat Cat was my closest friend, that's how sad my life was.

Mum sat beside me for the memorial service, and I knew she was fighting with her emotions from the way she was searching through her handbag for a tissue. I couldn't peel my eyes away from Norma, dressed head to toe in black, sat at the front of the room with Bri, his wife and other members of their family. She was so strong.

I was proud of myself for holding it together through the eulogy, taking long deep breaths to stave off tears. I managed not to cry as Norma shared the story of when she had met Fred, and how he'd wooed her with a bar of Fry's Turkish Delight.

What happened next caught me unawares.

"And now," said the celebrant, "at Fred's own request, we're going to play a song that meant a lot to him."

As the wine-red curtains closed around Fred's coffin, the opening bars of "Going Home" started to play. And that was when I openly sobbed my heart out for our very own local hero.

❦

"I'm sorry for taking your last tissue," I said to Mum, as we stood reading the cards on the array of floral tributes. "That song just got to me."

"I know, love. I know." She pulled me into a hug. "Your dad had a tear in his eye too."

"It won't be the same at the ground without him there," I said, as an awful thought struck me. "And who's Norma going to sit with on match days now? Who's she going to palm her sweets off onto if Fred's not there?"

"She'll have your Dad and Bez, and Finley and Joel," Mum said. "Or maybe she'll move her seat and sit with Bri."

"Maybe," I said, although I couldn't see her switching to the side stand. The Gallowgate was where Norma belonged, right at the heart of the supporters.

We went to pass on our sympathies to the family mourners, even though we'd already made our sorrow known. Norma looked exhausted, bless her, and seeing her trying to hold herself together for the sake of everyone else set me off crying again.

As I turned away I noticed a figure standing underneath the central archway on the other side of the garden of remembrance. The silhouette was familiar; the fair hair reflecting the brilliance of the sun, which seemed too joyous for such a sombre occasion.

The figure raised his hand in a wave, and I raised mine back, then we were heading toward each other, pulled by a force greater than gravity. When we were face to face Max pulled me into an embrace, an embrace he realised I needed before I even realised I needed it myself.

§

A lot of talking and a lot of tears later, we curled up together on Max's bed. Even though his mattress was hard and his bedding smelled strongly of an unfamiliar fabric softener, it had felt right snuggling up to him, fully clothed and on top of the covers. As we cuddled and talked, I felt safe.

Max told me everything he knew about Darius from his brother's business partner. Words like manipulative and controlling were used as he filled me in on how Darius had been bragging about how he was going to win me back, especially after the festival.

"He was using you, and I hate him for that," Max said, brushing a stray hair out of my face. "How could he take advantage of your love for Summer like that? Especially when you were in the depths of grief."

"I nearly didn't give him the money. But in the end I couldn't not, not when I thought it was going to keep him and Summer together. I don't understand why he'd spend so much money on going to Vegas if Nadia's threatening to take her away. I've tried texting him, ringing him, everything... but he's not replied."

"I hate to say it, but he doesn't need you now he's got what he wanted. He's a bastard, Sophie, a heartless bastard."

"I trusted him." My voice was meek, barely there. "I ignored all the warning signs and didn't listen when people tried to tell me what he was like. I was a fool."

"We're all capable of being a fool when we're in love," Max said, stroking my hair. I closed my eyes, enjoying the relaxing sensation his touch brought to me. I was halfway between wake and sleep as he added, "And I should know."

He wrapped an arm around me and I shuffled sleepily until my body was pressed against his, succumbing to the exhaustion. I fell asleep, and it was the best sleep I'd had in a long time.

"Hiya." Max's croaky voice told me that he was only just waking up – that and the dusting of sleep that nestled in the corners of his eyes.

"What time is it?" I squinted, turning to look at the small blue alarm clock on the bedside table, shocked to discover how late it was. "It's almost eight!"

"Which sounds like a good excuse to go out for tea," Max said, although he made no move to get out of bed. In fact, he pressed his lips against the spot behind my ear and proceeded to plant delicate fluttery kisses down the back of my neck. I tilted my head at the tickle of his stubble, turning to fully face him.

"You could give me the guided tour of the house before we go," I suggested.

It would have been impossible not to have noticed the sheer size and grandeur of the house. It wasn't in an area of the city I knew particularly well, but I did know it was expensive, and I wondered how Max could afford to live here on his wage.

"Ah," he said, pulling his arm away. My body cooled instantly at his release. "There's something I ought to tell you."

The sheepish expression he was wearing seemed out of place on his normally open face, and he turned away from me as he climbed off the bed, stripped off his shirt and pulled on a fresh plain black T-shirt.

Dread filled me. I knew it was too good to be true. Nothing in my life went smoothly, so why did I expect it to with Max? In one single second a million thoughts rampaged through my head.

He was a murderer.

Secretly married.

A drug addict.

He liked Status Quo.

None of them was feasible, except the Status Quo one as an outside bet, but it didn't stop me fearing the very worst.

"This isn't my house," he said finally.

"O-kaaay," I answered slowly.

I began to wonder if it was a repeat of what Tawna had gone through in one of her pre-Johnny relationships. A man she'd been seeing had borrowed the keys to his friend's penthouse apartment in the hope that it'd charm her pants off. His own abode was far less impressive – a shared house riddled with damp.

"I do live here," he explained, "but it's my parents' house." He was still facing away from me. "They're away for the weekend visiting my grandad."

"You still live at home?" I did a poor job of disguising my surprise.

"Yep," he admitted, embarrassment in his eyes. "I know it's not exactly a turn-on. You probably think I'm a real mummy's boy."

"I don't think that at all. I just don't get why you'd keep it a secret."

He paused to pull a hoodie out of his wardrobe. "I did move out once. I had a place of my own, but two years ago my dad was diagnosed with MS. He's doing well at the moment, but when he has a flare he can hardly move. He was reliant on a wheelchair for a while and he was too heavy for my mum to lift or push in the chair. I moved back to help."

"I'm so sorry." I knew through Eve how hard it was caring for a parent, the emotional and physical burden. "That must be tough."

"It is what it is. Thankfully he's doing well at the moment, although he has to use a stick to walk. He used to love running, even did the Great North Run a few times. It's hard to believe that, looking at him now."

I got the impression from the sadness in his eyes that he didn't want to talk about it anymore.

"Can we get going for that food?" I was suddenly famished. "I really fancy an all-day breakfast."

"I'm sure we can find a pub that can stretch to that. Do you still want the tour of the house first though?"

I nodded, keen to see the place he called home.

Max gave me the grand tour, and it actually was pretty grand – five bedrooms (three with en suites), two living rooms, a dining room, an office and a large kitchen diner. That was without mentioning the garage, the summer house, the large garden complete with pond and water feature... It was a beautiful home.

When I'd finished admiring everything about the house, from its convenient location to the tasteful yet individual décor (which Max told me was all his mum's doing) we made our way to a pub Max insisted served the best pick-me-ups in the city.

We'd only just sat down when my mobile rang.

"Hello?"

"Sophie? It's Mum," she said through strangled sobs. "I'm afraid I have some awful news."

CHAPTER 27

"What is it, Mum? What's the matter? Is it Norma?"

You heard about couples who literally couldn't live without each other. What if Fred's funeral had hit her so hard that she realised she couldn't physically live without him?

"No, no, Norma's fine." Mum's voice wavered as she continued. "I've just been on the phone to Nick. There's something wrong with the twins." She gulped loudly, then sniffed.

I clenched my fist so fiercely that I feared my thumb might break as I scrabbled around my brain for something – anything – I could say that might make the situation better. I failed to come up with anything.

"Are you sure? Everything was fine at the last scan, Chantel told me. They're checking her regularly to make sure her and the babies are okay."

"After you left the funeral Chantel called the midwife because she'd had some pains." Mum was trying to be matter-of-fact, but she couldn't conceal the trembling in her voice. "They sent her straight to the hospital for another scan and it showed that one baby is significantly bigger than the other."

I swallowed. It hurt.

"They said it can happen when twins share a placenta, the bigger one is taking more blood. Normally it's picked up earlier than this, but it's serious, Sophie. They said there's a possibility she could lose one or both of the babies."

My stomach knotted at the thought of my poor sister-in-law coming to terms with the fact the babies she'd been so excited for, buying tiny packs of pure white cotton Babygros that she "just couldn't resist" along with her Waitrose shop, might not make it. When was our family going to get a break?

"What happens now?"

Mum exhaled. Even her sigh sounded wobbly. "They're monitoring her closely, but they've warned them that if it gets worse they may have to deliver the twins early. Obviously the longer they can stay where they are, the better, and Nick did say there were other treatments available, but there are no guarantees. They've told Chantel to rest as much as possible in the meantime." Mum sobbed audibly. "I can't imagine what they're going through."

"Is there anything I can do? Maybe look after Noah for them?"

"Chantel's parents have still got Noah," Mum said. "Chantel hadn't collected him because she went straight to the hospital from the funeral. She wanted him with her, bless her, but she's exhausted and tearful, and Noah would only pick up on her stress, so she agreed he'll stay at her mum and dad's tonight."

"Well, if they need me to have him in the future, I will. Family comes first."

"You're a kind and thoughtful soul. You always have been." My heart clenched. "I hope you know how much I love you."

"I love you too, Mum."

And then my mum broke down in tears, and I broke down in tears, and we didn't say another word. We just cried our hearts out, companionably, down the phone line for a very long time, until Max took me back to my house, because as grateful as I was for his support, I wanted some time alone to think.

I never even had chance to order the food I'd so been looking forward to.

❧

When I woke the next morning, my neck hurting from where I'd been lying at a funny angle, my spine was stiff, as though it needed to be cracked back into shape. The sun streamed in through the window where I'd not had the foresight to draw the curtains, and for one bliss-filled second I believed in the beauty of the day.

Then I remembered. Nick and Chantel's babies were in danger.

I'd contemplated phoning them in a show of support, but hadn't wanted to be a bother, plus it had been late by the time Max had finally thought me calm enough to be left alone, so I'd settled on sending a text instead. When I'd tried to package my concern into a measly amount of words it came out sounding insincere, so after deleting my message numerous times I'd settled on a simple, *Mum told me your news. Call me if I can do ANYTHING. Love you, Xxx.*

I padded my way to the bathroom, pushing my shoulders back to wake myself and my body up. The image that greeted me in the mirror shocked me. Hair full of static stuck out at all angles, and I looked exhausted. Streaks of black mascara under my eyes highlighted the puffy dark bags, a combination of jet lag and stress, but I didn't care about my appearance. I didn't even care that Darius still hadn't had the decency to reply to my messages asking for answers. It wasn't life or death.

Pushing the plug into the plughole, I turned on the cold tap and filled the sink with icy water. It spurted and spluttered the way the cold tap always did, but the relief as I splashed the water over my face was exactly what I needed. It felt brutal, but as well as washing away my smeared make-up, it cleared my head.

For so long I'd convinced myself I was the only person whose life wasn't going to plan. When my relationship with Darius ended, I'd felt hard done by. My plans for the future – a lavish wedding day, building a home to fill with a family, playing the part of the dutiful wife – had blown up in my face. Looking back, that mindset was laughable. As my life was spiralling out of control, everyone else's was too to varying degrees. Some were doing a better job of hiding it than others, that's all. Eve with her mum's Alzheimer's. Max helping care for his dad. Tawna bickering with her mum over sugared almonds. Nick and Chantel facing an uncertain future. Everyone had problems.

I splashed the water against my face again, before studying myself in the mirror. Still a mess, but at least I was more awake. Smoothing the damp palms of my hands against my hair, I closed my eyes and inhaled. It was time to face the day, and the world had better watch out, because I wasn't going to be a fool anymore, nor was I wasting my precious and beautiful life worrying about things I could no longer change. It reminded me of that prayer, the one about having serenity to accept what can't be changed, courage to change what can and wisdom to know the difference. That was what I was striving for. Serenity, courage, wisdom.

My latest statement had the audacity to arrive, testing my resolve. Although I'd expected it, I was disappointed to see the amount I'd paid the previous month was the smallest yet, having used money meant for cancelling out my debts on the hen do and paying Darius.

Courage to change the things I can.

I was running out of clothes that had any monetary value, but for my own sanity I needed to make a significant payment. There had to be something else I could part with.

There was the Le Creuset kitchenware, but I used that regularly. I considered selling my laptop, but I didn't have a separate TV and was reluctant to give up instant access to any box set I felt in the mood to watch. Anyway, I knew neither of those would make enough money, not in their well-used states.

I looked around my bedroom for inspiration and when my gaze lingered on my jewellery box it seemed so obvious. I knew exactly what I could sell – the diamond-encrusted choker Darius had bought me for my birthday the year before last. When he'd handed me the red velvet box, I'd expected an engagement ring, and although it was a beautiful piece of jewellery I'd known immediately that I'd never be able to wear it without feeling cheated. That's why its one and only outing had been on my thirtieth birthday, and my life had been spun on its axis since then. Selling the choker made perfect sense, and there was a pawn shop on the same street as my office. I should have thought of it sooner; I knew it was valuable because Darius had ensured I'd added it to the contents insurance.

I picked up my knitting, glad to have found a solution. If only everything else in life was as easy to fix.

The morning had passed in a tangle of wools and threads and buttons, as I'd finished knitting the tiny cream booties I'd been making for Nick and Chantel's babies. I'd considered unravelling the wool, wondering if it was insensitive to make booties that might never be worn, but I needed to finish the project that had been started when we'd all been so full of excitement.

My stitches were too taut, the tension all wrong as my teardrops soaked into the palm-sized object I'd made, but as I said a quiet prayer as I threaded the satin ribbon through the loopholes I'd made, I was pleased I'd opted to finish them. We had to remain hopeful, for what is a world without hope?

When my phone rang, I was relieved it was Max rather than my mum. No news was most definitely good news.

"Max," I said, as I accepted the call.

"Sophie. I was going to ring you when I got back last night, but I knew you'd worry if the phone rang in case it was your mum. Are you okay?"

"I'm okay." I looked at the two pairs of little booties on the mantelpiece. "Worried, obviously. So many people I love are having a tough time at the moment." I didn't want the conversation to be a total downer, so I said, "What about you? What are you up to?"

"I wondered if you wanted to come to the fete at the hospital this afternoon? I understand if you'd rather be at home, but there's usually a load of craft stalls there, the sort of thing you love."

"Sounds great." I smiled, my first proper smile all day. "But will there be a tombola too? I love a good tombola."

"I expect so. I bet there'll be all the old favourites: coconut shies, plate smashing, that kind of thing. And I've heard the cake stall is legendary."

"Legendary cake sounds good."

Max suggested we met at a coffee shop opposite the hospital. I was about to end the call, thinking we'd organised everything we needed to, but Max had one final message to give.

"Sophie?"

"Yeah?"

"If you change your mind and decide it's too much, I'll understand. Family comes first."

"There's nothing I can do that'll change anything," I said, my voice far more calm than I felt. "Better to be out and distracted rather than moping at home. I'll see you soon."

"See you soon," he echoed.

When our call ended I headed back to the bathroom to look at my reflection. The water I'd dampened my hair with earlier had encouraged loose messy waves, and although the bags under my eyes were still there, they no longer looked as puffy. My skin was far from flawless, but instead of reaching for my foundation I applied a thin layer of day cream and a slick of tinted lip balm, forgoing all eye make-up.

I expected a downtrodden version of myself to be looking back at me, but my reflection didn't look downtrodden. She looked like a woman who persevered.

I didn't even change out of my comfy clothes, black yoga pants and a loose-fitted cerise T-shirt. They were clean enough, and Max wouldn't care what I was wearing. Most importantly, I was happy wearing them. When you're not feeling on top of your game you need to do whatever you can to make yourself feel better, and comfortable clothes were a form of self-care for me. If other people didn't like it, then bully for them. Plus, Sundays were supposed to be lazy days. No one can be arsed on a Sunday.

A small flicker of pride sparked in my chest. Maybe I was growing up, after all, because I realised that while being loved by other people is special, loving yourself is the best love of all.

❧

Fuelled by takeout coffee (without my usual blueberry muffin accompaniment because I was saving myself for the cakes Max had promised) the two of us hit the hospital fete. The warm weather had encouraged people to come out and support the event, with the sideshow stalls doing a roaring trade. Lucky dip barrels entertained easily-impressed children and swarms of people hovered around the WI stand of home-made preserves. Were there really so many jam fanatics in the North East?

"How are you really doing?" Max asked, as we passed the hook a duck stall. The paddling pool hadn't even got any water in it, the rubber ducks sitting on the dry plastic base of the pool. A sign stated the lack of water was for health and safety reasons. "I couldn't stop thinking about you last night."

Max's worried face was at odds with the pretty floral bunting strung out across the hospital grounds and the jaunty music being played by a band of steel drummers (who knew there were steel drummers in Newcastle? Not me, and I'd only lived here all my life), and smiled weakly. "I feel dreadful for my brother and his wife. I wish I could wave a magic wand and make everything okay."

"Just be there for them. That's all you can do."

"I know."

I sipped at my caramel latte. The sweetness of the syrup pricked my taste buds, but the bitter tang lingered.

"They'll reach out if they need you, I'm sure. They know you're thinking of them."

Max slid his arm around my waist and it was as though his hand was on fire, burning my skin through my slobby clothes. I sizzled at his touch.

We continued to stroll, wordless, around the fete.

Max pointed out the tombola stall. The thing I love most about it is how there's no skill required. A lot of it's luck. You might win a bottle of Baileys, you might win a tin of soup, you might not even win at all. Tombolas are a metaphor for life, when you think about it.

"I'll treat you," he said, reaching for his wallet out of the back pocket of his jeans. "I did promise."

I picked six raffle tickets out of a cardboard box covered in stripy wrapping paper, desperately hoping that at least one of the tickets would end in a five or zero. We had no luck with the first five numbers. I felt like Charlie Bucket when his birthday Wonka bar didn't contain a golden ticket. Unfolding the sixth and final ticket, I let out a squeal of delight.

"670! We've won!"

My eyes scanned the tables of arbitrary objects. It looked like they'd once been in numerical order, but had ended up higgledy-piggledy as the event had gone on. I couldn't spot 670 anywhere.

"Can I help you, pet?" asked the older woman who was running the stall. She reminded me of my auntie Lynne; her foundation was too orange for her skin tone and the bright pink lipstick she was sporting had made its way onto her front tooth.

"I'm looking to see what I've won," I said, showing her the winning ticket, "but I can't see it on the table."

The lady made her way to the section of the table that was home to the prizes labelled with tickets in the six hundreds, a puzzled look crossing her face when she realised nothing had a green 670 stuck to it.

"How strange," she muttered, flashing the pink smudge on her teeth. "I could have sworn I saw that just five minutes ago." She moved along the table, picking up items and turning them to examine the numbers on the tickets sellotaped to their front. "A-ha!" she said finally, with a triumphant smile as she held a candle in a jar aloft like a champion boxer holding a title belt above their head. "I knew I'd seen this somewhere. It was just hiding."

She handed it over, and I instinctively pulled off the lid, sniffing the pink wax. It smelled of raspberry ripple ice cream.

"Thank you," Max said.

"Yes, thank you," I repeated, replacing the stopper.

We browsed the other nearby stalls – bric-a-brac (nothing appealing on offer), a second-hand book stall, a roll-the-penny sideshow that brought to mind church fetes from when I was a girl guide.

That's when I noticed two tables next to each other displaying handicrafts. "Let's go and look at the jewellery," I said, although that did the crafter a disservice – there were a diverse mix of crafts on show.

The lady smiled as we approached, matching dimples appearing in each of her doughy cheeks as though she'd poked herself in the face with the knitting needles that didn't stop moving even when her focus shifted onto us.

The jewellery she was selling was cute – drop earrings with shimmering beads, adjustable rings with Scrabble tile letters attached to the band, old-fashioned friendship bracelets of knotted embroidery threads like Eve, Tawna and I used to make back in primary school. The decoupage photo frames were nice too, and the sets of doll's clothes made with pretty printed fabric.

"You make some lovely things."

"Thank you," the lady said, flashing her dimples once more. My praise was enough to encourage her to put down her needles, the squarish white knitting hanging like a flag on a pole. Probably a back-piece of a cardigan, I thought.

"Anything you've particularly got your eye on?" she asked, and I was drawn to the Scrabble tile rings, the large black S bold against the creamy tile, the small "1" in the corner less dominant, but still there.

"I love the rings."

"They're always popular," the woman said with a nod. "Kids and adults all love them."

"How much are they?" Max enquired, picking up the S ring I'd been looking at.

The lady told us the price, and before I had time to argue, Max paid for the item and slipped it onto my finger. Third finger of my left hand, although I'm sure that was pure coincidence.

"You shouldn't have." I was mildly embarrassed at the attention – maybe even a show of affection – in front of a stranger. "I do love it though, thank you."

I fully extended my fingers to get a better look at the ring, and the lady placed her palm across her heart and aahed. I felt my cheeks getting hot. I was probably as pink as my hoodie.

"Aren't you two the sweetest couple." She beamed, picking up her needles once more. "Enjoy the rest of your Sunday, won't you?"

We both smiled and nodded, and I mumbled a thank you as we moved to the next table. The crafts weren't as high-quality, and although the bookmarks and keyrings on display were eye-catching, closer inspection showed they'd been hurried. There were a few loose ends and unsightly blobs of glue where the maker had been heavy-handed.

"Anything you like the look of?" Max asked.

"I don't think so." I could make better myself, and the woman behind the table looked miserable as sin as she hid behind a pinboard covered in home-made badges to take a puff of her e-cigarette. She wasn't subtle, but even if she had been, the sickly-sweet smell would have given her away.

As we moved from the smoking woman, fighting against the tickle of a cough building in my throat, I thought of my craft stash. The pleasure crafting brought me, the joy of sourcing perfect resources for a project... I wanted more of that in my life.

"Do you remember I told you I love making things?" I

blurted, then blushed again as Max stopped walking. "Like the things on those stalls," I added.

"I know what *making things* means," he teased. "And yes, I remember. Are you any good?"

I looked down at the ring on my finger, where the tile skimmed my knuckle. "Yeah. I'm really good, actually. I've been thinking about what you said about doing it professionally."

If he found my comment big-headed he didn't show it.

"Brilliant. You should. Maybe you could show me some of the things you've made sometime." His eyes shone as they connected with mine.

"Maybe," I replied coyly, although I'd need to give the house a deep-clean if Max was going to pay a visit. No one ever came to my place except Tawna and Eve, and they didn't count. Over the years they'd become blind to my borderline hoarding, and although my selling sprees had cleared some clutter my house would never be considered tidy.

We pottered around for a while, bumping into Oz and Isla who encouraged me to guess the name of the teddy (I plumped for Keegan. The teddy was a panda, and everyone knows black and white means the Magpies, the mighty Newcastle United. The other option was Alan, as in Shearer, but someone else had already nabbed that).

"Feeling lucky?" asked a suited man with a clipboard. He looked way too formal for a fete. I must have given him a bemused look, because he said, "Because you were having a go on 'guess the name of the bear'. We're an international company specialising in medical training. Our UK headquarters is moving from London and we're going to be based right here in Newcastle. We're already establishing links with the hospital, including pledging to donate a percentage of our annual profits to the hospital charity funds. All we're asking is for people to sign up to our newsletter, and for each person that signs up we're donating a pound to the hospital charity. We promise not to flood your inbox, but we will keep you up to date with company news and the overall total we have donated to the cause. Also, one lucky winner will be selected at random to win five thousand pounds."

"Just for signing up?"

"Just for signing up," the man confirmed.

"Go on then." Max took the Biro from the man and wrote down his email address. I nosily tried to read it, but struggled, because not only was it upside down, but he was left-handed, so as he moved the pen across the page he hid what he'd written. I'd always had a thing for left-handers. I don't know why.

"I will too. It is for charity, after all." My writing looked loopy and childlike under Max's jagged scrawl.

The event was drawing to a close, the crowd thinning out, but I wasn't ready for my time with Max to be over. He'd been a wonderful distraction from worrying about Chantel and the twins, exactly what I'd needed, so when he suggested going for a drink at a nearby pub, I jumped at the chance.

"Have you been here before?" he asked.

I shook my head.

"It's nothing special," he said, almost apologetically, "just a chain pub that does cheap food, but the beer garden's nice."

The garden at the back was a large expanse of grass surrounded by a stone wall covered in pretty yellow roses. There was a bouncy castle, popular with the children who jumped enthusiastically as their parents enjoyed a drink and a chat in the sunshine, and a group of kids were kicking a ball around, using jumpers for goalposts.

"It's fine," I assured him. "It's nice."

We bought our drinks – I paid, it was the least I could do – and found a vacant bench outside. The beer garden was busy enough to have a buzz of life, but not busy enough to be loud, exactly what's needed for escapist Sunday evening drinking.

"Let me give you some money for the drinks." Max flipped open his wallet and offered me a note. "I'm the one who invited you out, remember."

"You don't have to do that. I can stretch to a round of drinks."

I sipped at my wine. It was drier than I'd normally go for, but not unpleasant.

"That's not the point. Coming to the pub was my suggestion, and I want to treat you." He pressed the note into the palm of my hand. "Please?"

"Okay." I folded it into my purse. "Thank you."

"There was a time I wouldn't have been able to have done that. I racked up some pretty crazy debts in my early twenties. All that freedom and no concept of money, and the bank extended my overdraft without question, gave me credit cards and loans when I had no way of paying them back other than a part-time job in a twenty-four-hour supermarket two nights a week."

My head whirred at the familiarity of the situation and it took me a few seconds to realise I was holding my breath. "But you've paid them all off now?"

"I made the final payment in January," he said, a smile of pride playing out on his lips. "I didn't think the day would ever come, but when it did it was the best feeling. I'd never have been able to do it if I hadn't moved back home though. It's one good thing that's come out of Dad being ill."

"It goes to show things do work out for the best in the end." I took another sip of my drink. "There was a time when I was living beyond my means too. I've changed though. I'm paying back what I owe."

There was no judgement on his face, and at first I wondered if he'd heard me at all, but then he said, "How are you finding it?"

"Some days it's fine, but other days I feel like it's unfair. There are celebrities in magazines on exotic holidays saying they've earned a week in paradise because they work hard, but so do I. My wages aren't great." I smiled wryly. "I'm bottom of the food chain at my work."

"You've taken the first step though, and that's the hardest bit. It took me a long time to realise how out of control my spending was."

"Tell me about it." I inwardly cringed remembering how much importance I used to put on wearing designer labels, colouring my hair and changing the three "c"s in my living room seasonally to fit in with the current trends. Curtains, cushions and candles don't sound like enormous expenses, but replacing them as frequently as I had been was unnecessary. "It's surprising what a difference little changes make."

"Have you started shopping at Aldi?"

"Yes!"

"Their chocolate changed my life," he said seriously. "A quarter of the price of the brand I used to buy, but just as nice."

"I used to be really snobby about where I shopped," I confessed. "I don't know why, because no one would have known where I'd bought things from."

"I bet you're one of those people who takes a Waitrose bag with you even when you're shopping elsewhere," he kidded.

I blushed. There were times I'd done exactly that.

"Very funny."

I adjusted my new ring on my finger. "Thanks again for this."

"I know it's not worth much, but I saw the way you were looking at them. When the lady selling them asked what you liked and you said the ring there was no way I was going to let you walk away without it on your finger."

"I'm grateful."

I thought of the diamond choker Darius had given me, which the pawn shop gave me decent money for. They wouldn't see the value in the handcrafted Scrabble ring, but it already meant more to me than the precious jewels, because it had been given with genuine affection.

"You can think of me every time you wear it," he said.

I looked up at him through my lashes. "I'll wear it all the time."

The look we shared was as heavy as the summer evening air around us, loaded, and when his lips connected with mine it was as though the rest of the world fell away.

JULY

CHAPTER 28

Four weeks had passed.

Four weeks since the fete.

Four weeks since I gave Darius the money.

Four weeks of near-constant worry about Chantel and the babies.

In some ways it felt like no time at all. It could be measured in one box of tampons, one measly pay cheque, one cycle of the moon. In other ways it felt like forever.

Max and I had been spending more time together, and were officially a couple. There was no more game-playing, no more coyness from either side. We'd had a night out at the pictures and a day trip to Edinburgh where we'd climbed Arthur's Seat, rewarding ourselves with a picnic when we reached the summit. We'd borrowed his brother Grant's golden retriever and gone for a six-mile walk (she was far more obedient than Spot).

Max had even come to the house a couple of times (after I tidied up. I didn't want to sabotage our relationship before we even got started). We weren't rushing into anything, but when I was with him it felt so overwhelmingly right. That was nothing compared to the feeling when I wasn't with him though. That was the worst of all, and I'd find myself reaching for my phone to share a joke I knew he'd find amusing or tell him a song we both loved was on the radio.

In the past, Eve had been my first port of call when I had news to share, knowing she'd gladly listen to me going on about whatever was causing me heartache or hurt, but the support Max had shown me had been so sincere, so wholehearted, that he'd become my default contact when I was wobbly; and there'd been quite a bit to wobble about. My nieces (recent scans confirming the gender, which my brother and his wife hadn't originally wanted to know) were both still growing, but the doctors had confirmed Twin-to-Twin Transfusion Syndrome, which could lead to the girls needing to be delivered before their October due date. We were quietly hoping things would stay stable enough for them to stay in utero until at least thirty-five weeks, but the specialists were also realists, telling us to prepare for all eventualities.

I'd not seen Eve in a while. The last time I'd spoken to her she'd had concerns of her own, with her mum taking a turn for the worse and wandering out of the care home and onto the busy main road. Tawna had been in touch, and I'd asked her if she'd seen Darius, but he was remaining very elusive, not visiting the house as he normally did. I hadn't mentioned to Tawna how Darius had been bragging about how he could get back with me if he wanted to. It would only cause her to worry about tensions riding high on her wedding day, plus I hadn't seen her because she was spending all her free time at the gym, doing torturous classes to get wedding-ready.

My own long summer nights had been spent crafting. With Max's encouragement I'd not been able to shake the idea of starting up a small business out of my system. I wasn't deluded enough to believe it could ever be my main source of income, but the pleasure I got from creating meant any money made would be a bonus. I'd slowly but surely built up my stock and had set up an Etsy page. I'd even made plans to rent a table at some of the local Christmas fayres that year. There were always loads of them in church halls and schools and people love Christmas decorations. Glittery stars, crocheted angels... I was already full of ideas.

As I approached the charity shop, squinting into the sun as it started to dip in the powder-blue sky, nervous butterflies fluttered in my stomach. I was meeting Max's family – the whole clan – for the first time. He'd assured me they'd love me, but knowing how much his family meant to him made their approval all the more important.

Max was standing outside waiting for me, one foot casually tapping against the brick wall he was leaning against. Seeing him there calmed my nerves.

"How are you doing?" He took my hand in his, giving it a firm squeeze.

"Oh, you know. Pretty petrified about meeting the whole Oakley family."

"You have nothing to worry about," he promised, giving my hand another pulse of reassurance. "Grant and Chris thought you were lovely, and the rest will too. They're all very laid back and really friendly, I promise. I can't guarantee Dylan won't fire questions at you though."

"Nothing quite like being grilled by a child."

"Piers Morgan has nothing on him. He's so damn nosy."

I pulled a face that probably doubled as a frown. "Oh no. What's he going to ask me? I'm not used to being around kids that age. Noah doesn't say much at all yet, only a few odd words."

"Nothing too probing, don't panic. More 'what's your favourite colour?' and 'who's your favourite Pokémon?' than politics or the economy."

"Phew. I think I can manage that. Although the Pokémon one might have to be Pikachu by default. I don't know any others."

"You will by the end of the night, I can assure you. Dylan's obsessed. He'll have his cards and sticker book out ready to show you. You're his idea of a dream, the rest of us have heard it all so many times that we're nodding blankly whenever he starts talking about it."

"Well, I'll be the perfect audience for him, even if I do have to fake it a bit."

"You might end up loving it. There are adults obsessed with Pokémon. I'm not one of them though," he clarified, pointing his key towards the car and setting the headlights flashing with one press of the button.

"Maybe," I gamely replied, opening the door and buckling myself in.

I'd already made my mind up that if it all got to be too much I'd hide in a corner with Dylan and learn all there was to know about Pokémon. His questions, however incessant, were likely to be easier to answer than anything the adults would ask.

Max's parents' house was as I remembered it from the day of Fred's funeral – large and smart and set back from the road. The short driveway leading up to the double-fronted house looked like a car park, there were that many vehicles on it. The front garden was beautifully in bloom – someone with green fingers must have been tackling it – and as I got out of the car I heard laughter coming from the back of the house.

"Sounds like everyone else is here," Max said cheerily. "Ready to meet them?"

"Ready." I smiled bravely. I wasn't normally one of those

people who got nervous walking into a room but I wanted this over and done with.

We followed a path around the outside of the house until we came to a tall wooden gate. Max reached over to undo the latch and the scene that greeted us looked like it belonged in an advert. Wisps of smoke curled from a white-hot barbecue and rows of pretty garden lights were strung out between the summer house and the shed. A group were playing cards at a table on the decking, and a young boy, who had to be Dylan was playing croquet (croquet!) with a man who, by default, I knew was Dale. The genetics were strong enough to make me look twice to ensure Max was still by my side.

"Okay?" he asked, with gentle reassurance. "Not regretting saying you'd come?"

"Not at all."

"Maxwell!" Dale came over and patted Max forcibly on the back. His skin was a shade darker, his hair slightly darker too, but other than that they were incredibly alike. "Good to see you. And good to meet you, Sophie. I was beginning to wonder if Max had made up this stunning girlfriend he's been talking about," he added, teasingly jabbing Max in the ribs.

"I'm real," I replied with a modest laugh, immediately feeling comfortable in this company.

"Welcome to the madhouse." He smiled, extending a hand. "I'm Dale, Max's youngest brother. The most handsome and debonair of the Oakley brothers." He chuckled.

"Yeah, whatever you say." Max pointed his index finger to his ear and spun it in a circle, before bending down, cupping his hand in front of his mouth. "He's deluded," he said to me in a stage whisper.

"Now now, don't get competitive," said a woman who looked strangely familiar. "I don't know, Sophie. I thought it would get easier with time, but it turns out being the mum of four boys is hard work whatever stage of life they're at. They might be getting older, but they've never really grown up."

Max leant over, kissing her cheek. "You don't need to pretend just because we've got a guest. Everyone knows I'm your favourite."

Mrs Oakley smiled. "All four of you say that. I suppose it's a good thing. Better than any of you feeling unloved."

Her words scratched against my heart, reminding me how I'd felt like the inferior member of my own family for so long. The events of the past few months had brought us closer together than ever before, and I no longer felt less loved. Nick and Anna had a tight bond, but that was independent of my relationships with both of them and I knew my parents loved all three of us, the same way Mrs Oakley loved her boys.

"None of us could ever feel unloved, Mum," Dale said. "Right, I'd better go and help Dad with the barbecue. You know how overexcited he gets, you'll be eating cold sausages for weeks if I don't rein him in."

Mrs Oakley smiled. "True, in fact, why don't both you boys go and give him a hand. I'll stay here and chat to Sophie. Give us a chance to get to know each other."

She all but shooed them away, before guiding me to a swinging love seat and encouraging me to sit. "I'll get us a drink. What would you like? White or red wine, gin and tonic, fruit juice, beer? I can't drink beer these days, it makes me terribly bloated."

"A glass of white wine would be lovely, thank you."

I rocked on the seat as she fetched the drinks. Chris had taken over playing croquet with Dylan, and I recognised the man playing cards as Grant. I wondered if the woman with him was his wife, as she had a toddler on her lap and I knew Max had another nephew besides Dylan so assumed the toddler to be Isaac. The family resemblance was strong with all of the Oakley brothers.

"Here you go, Sophie." Mrs Oakley handed me a large glass of wine and I steadied the swing to accept it, not wanting to lose a drop. She sat next to me and smiled. "So, tell me about yourself."

"There's not much to tell," I replied, wishing I had something exciting I could share. "I work as a secretary for a legal firm in town."

"And how do you enjoy that?"

"Not much, most of the time," I said with a laugh, surprising myself by how honest I was being with someone I'd only just met. "It's not awful, but it's not what I thought I'd be doing at my age."

"And what did you think you'd be doing?"

"Something creative, I suppose. I wanted to be a fashion designer or an artist. In the end I played it safe."

"I used to be an artist," Mrs Oakley revealed, "before I had the boys. I was pretty good. Gave up when I found out I was pregnant though because I didn't have the capacity to focus. Baby brain, I suppose. I never really got back into it, life got in the way, but I still think about trying my hand at it again sometimes."

"You should. I've started making things again recently and it's so relaxing. Time seems to slow down and I lose myself in whatever I'm doing and forget about everything else."

"That's exactly what I used to find, nothing else mattered but the project I was working on. That's why I couldn't do it when the boys were small, because I had to stay alert for them. Even when they got older they still took up a lot of my time because I spoiled them. I should have let them do more for themselves, but I enjoyed taking care of them, and although I'd complain on a Sunday night when I had a pile of school shirts to iron, I wouldn't have changed a thing. Doing things for them was how I showed my love."

"Well, whatever you did, it worked. Not many families come together every week like this."

"I'm very lucky," she agreed, taking a sip of her wine. "Friends of mine never see their grown-up children, but mine can't stay away."

As we sat in comfortable silence, the love seat rocking gently, I wanted to inspire Mrs Oakley the way Max inspired me. "You should definitely start painting again. You must have so many ideas stored away after all these years."

"Hundreds." She grinned, and the way her eyes twinkled reminded me of Max. They were more tired, admittedly, more world-weary and the faded blue of washed-out denim rather than the misty shade of Max's, but the shape was identical, the glimmer in them as warm. "Thank you for the encouragement."

"I wanted to pay it forward. It was Max who made me believe people might actually want to buy some of the things I make."

She reached over and placed a hand on my knee. It was familiar but not necessarily uncomfortable. "He's really taken with you. We knew it was serious when he said he was bringing you here – it's a long time since he brought a girl home. After what happened with Gina–"

We were interrupted by Max's dad, shuffling towards us aided by a black curved-handled walking stick. "Andrea, have you seen that large bowl my mother gave us? I thought it would be perfect for the pasta salad."

It suddenly clicked why Mrs Oakley looked so familiar – she'd been the lady at the car boot sale, the one who'd given Eve the bowl.

"I think it got smashed," she replied, a sad smile on her face. "Bunty knocked it off the draining board last time we used it," she added, very believably. "You know how clumsy that precious cat of yours is."

"Oh. Oh, that's a shame." Max's dad rubbed his hand over his beard.

"I bought a new large bowl though, if you look in the cupboard with the Pyrex," she said, all wide-eyed innocence.

"I'll use that then," he said, before heading towards the house. On his way he made a fuss of the tortoiseshell cat who was perched on a chair, stroking its head affectionately.

"I knew he'd not hold a grudge if he thought it was the cat," she said mischievously. "He thinks the world of her."

"Did you remember it was my friend who had the bowl at the boot sale? I thought I recognised you from somewhere, but couldn't think where."

"Of course I remembered you." She scoffed. "I recognised you the minute I saw you. Faces have always been my strong point. Never forget one."

She pushed herself up from the seat. "Come on. Let me introduce you to everyone else. Do you play cards?"

"Only snap." I shrugged. "And pontoon. That's about my limit."

"We'll have to teach you then, won't we? If you're going to be a regular guest, learning cards is a must. Whist, gin rummy, that kind of thing. Nothing tricky."

I glanced across to Max, who was playing croquet. His mallet-wielding wasn't going well if the groans he was making and Dylan's hysterical laughter was anything to go by. I liked the thought that I might be a regular guest, that this family had made me so welcome so quickly.

"I'll give it a whirl," I smiled, pushing myself up from the seat, "although I can't promise I'll be any good."

"If it's not going well, you can always cheat," she said with a wink.

I pretended to be shocked, but after how coolly she'd told the story about the bowl, I wasn't. I wasn't shocked at all.

By the time Max drove me back home it was late, the evening summer skies an inky blue wash over our heads.

"I hope you didn't find that too painful. And sorry for leaving you with Mum pretty much as soon as we got there. I know she can be overbearing at times. It comes from a good place though, she's only like it because she can't bear the thought that anyone might hurt her little boys."

"I like her," I said, because I did. Andrea Oakley had been the perfect hostess, ensuring I was comfortable, always had a topped-up glass and explaining the little in-jokes so I didn't have to plaster on a smile and pretend to understand what was so funny.

"She said it's been a while since you've taken anyone back." I kept my voice nonchalant, although I was fishing for information.

"It has."

His voice was clipped, but I kept pushing. "She mentioned an ex of yours. Gina?"

Max groaned uncomfortably. "Trust Mum to bring that up."

"Messy break-up?"

"I don't like talking about it, but I suppose I know about your significant ex so I'll tell you about mine. I met Gina through a friend – Iain, actually. He'd met her through Tinder and nothing had come of it, but he thought we'd get along, so we had a blind date." Max paused momentarily, looking at me to gauge my reaction. "We really clicked and things were going great, we were together for eight months. We'd spoken about moving in together, even went to look at a few places. But then she disappeared."

I gasped. "What do you mean? Is she still missing?"

He let out a half laugh. "She was never missing, Sophie. It wasn't like she'd been kidnapped. She ghosted me."

I looked blank. "I don't know what that means."

"She stopped answering my texts, she wouldn't answer the door when I went to her house even though I knew she was in because I could hear the telly and she lived alone... basically she might as well have been a ghost because it felt like I'd imagined the whole thing. I thought I was going crazy."

"So what happened?"

"In the end one of her friends sent me a message telling me to leave Gina alone, saying I should have taken the hint. I probably should have, to be fair, but what kind of adult just breaks all contact rather than having the 'it's not you, it's me' conversation?"

"That's terrible."

"It was. It made me really wary of getting into another relationship, and it wasn't until I met you that I felt it was worth taking the risk of going through that heartache again."

"So that's why you said you weren't confident." I remembered the first night in the pub, where he'd said things weren't always what they seemed. He might have had women interested in him, but he'd never acted on it because of his own Gina-induced fears. "And it explains why you were so wary about texting me when I was on Tawna's hen do."

"I didn't want to be overbearing, and after what happened at the festival..."

I blushed with embarrassment at the memory.

"I don't give out my number very often these days either. I guess my experience has made me wary."

"I'm honoured you gave it to me."

"I should have done it sooner, but better late than never. So, that's that. Now you know. What other embarrassing stuff did Mum tell you? She didn't dig out the photos of me in the bath as a baby, did she? Because as you know, everything has grown a lot since then."

"Haha," I said, poking out my tongue. We'd become increasingly intimate lately, and I certainly had no complaints. "No baby photos. Mostly she was telling me about how she used to enjoy painting."

Max nodded. "She was really good. We were up in the loft one Christmas, getting down the box of decorations, and I saw these canvases stacked up against the wall. I'd never seen them before, because they'd never been on the wall, but they looked way too professional to be hidden out of sight. Turns out they'd been pieces Mum had done for her foundation degree."

"Wow."

"Yeah, made me feel a bit guilty, to be honest, that part of the reason she stopped was me. Not just me, my brothers too, but she gave up her dreams to be a mum."

He smiled a sad smile.

"I don't think she gave up her dreams. I think her dreams changed. You four are her world, and Dylan and Isaac. Being there tonight showed me that. You're such a tight-knit unit."

"You should have been around when we were kids." Max laughed. "It was mayhem in our house. We'd be stealing each other's CDs, or using our parents' bed as a ring so we could play wrestling. Grant broke my arm once, pretending to be Hulk Hogan. They rushed me to the hospital and I was in tears, not because of the pain, but because they made me take off the Ultimate Warrior ribbons I'd tied to my arms so they could set the cast. There were times I hated being an Oakley, like at school when teachers would assume we had the same personality because we share the same parents. I like it now though. I never have to be alone, because one of my brothers will be there for me whenever I need them. It's like a team."

"Do you want a big family?"

"Definitely. At least three. Do you?"

I bit my tongue, took a breath. Darius had said my pushiness, my neediness, was unattractive. I didn't think I'd been pushy or needy, but I wasn't going to lie to Max about how important having a family was to me. It had been different for Darius, he'd already got Summer.

I downplayed it though, not wanting to scare him off. "Sure, one day. With the right person, at the right time."

"That's how I feel. I'd want everything to be right before bringing a new little person into the world. I'd want to offer my children the stable and loving home I had growing up."

"Then they'll be very lucky."

When Max didn't speak I looked up at him. He was looking at me intently, and that's when he said it. I was so surprised I couldn't process it properly. It just rang in my ears.

I didn't say it back, but only because I was too stunned to speak. In my mind I was shouting it from the rooftops. I love you, I love you, I love you.

AUGUST

"Look at how many people are here!" I squeaked, as a jovial librarian escorted us into a back room set up with a large projector, rows of uncomfortable-looking plastic seating and an entirely female crowd whose giddiness suggested they'd already drunk their body weight in Prosecco.

"We should have had a drink before we came," Tawna whispered. "This lot are hammered."

"But they won't be able to focus on Patrick," Eve reasoned. "I doubt the clarity is going to be IMAX standard anyway, looking at the equipment. It's on a par with the overhead projector they used to use back in primary school."

She wasn't far off the mark. The projector did look like it had seen better days.

"Let's find a seat. It's already filling up," Tawna said, shuffling past two tipsy-looking women with actual watermelons on their laps.

Our seats were central, and I was next to Eve. Tawna sat on her other side, looking uncomfortable in her surroundings. She wasn't used to slumming it.

"Gummy sweet?" Eve asked, waving a packet of veggie Percy Pigs under my nose.

I reached in and grabbed a handful. She turned her back on me to offer the sweets to Tawna, who shook her head, making an excuse that she was cutting out sugar until her final wedding dress fitting, and suggesting we should be careful too, now the wedding was just two weeks away. I stuffed three Percys in my mouth in a minor act of rebellion.

The library worker – a total stereotype in large round glasses, a sensible knee-length tweed skirt and a twinset cardi and blouse – stepped up to thank us all for supporting the event and ran through a generic list of safety issues. Once she'd pointed out where the loos were, that it was a non-smoking venue and that in the event of the fire alarm going off we were to leave quickly and calmly through the door we came in through, the lights dimmed and the familiar opening of *Dirty Dancing* started to play, with Baby and her family arriving at Kellerman's holiday camp as "Big Girls Don't Cry" played out in the background.

My spirits lifted at the oh-so-familiar script, and I soon found myself mouthing along to the words. I snuck a look at my two oldest friends. Tawna caught me looking and smiled softly at me, her eyes misting over. She reached her hand across Eve's lap, and I found myself extending my hand towards Tawna. She squeezed, the motion pushing my Scrabble ring so the large tile pressed uncomfortably against my finger, but I didn't pull back. Instead I reciprocated the pulse, before turning my attention back to the screen, ready for Baby to fall for Johnny as hard as the three of us had, many moons ago.

The music faded out and the lights flickered on, everyone filtering out of the library once the main attraction was over.

"That film will never get old," Eve enthused. "It's glorious."

"It really is," I agreed.

"And Patrick..." Tawna left her sentence hanging, but her voice was laced with dreams.

"I still can't believe he died," I said sadly. The day we'd heard the news, the three of us had sat in a stunned silence as we processed it. He might have been much older than us – older than our parents even – but he'd been the object of our affections for many years. That dangerous yet caring juxtaposition was impossible to resist, and those hip thrusts... well, they spoke for themselves.

"Nor me," Tawna said, tears in her eyes. "All those hours we spent drooling over him as we watched that film over and over. We must have seen it dozens of times."

"Hundreds," Eve corrected. "And that scene where he's tapping his hands against his shoes as Baby and Penny are dancing to "Hungry Eyes" – we used to rewind that every time."

"And the sweat on his arms..." Tawna swooned.

I couldn't hold back my sigh. There was something about that scene, some quiet intensity along with the way he moved to the music that had got our hormonal teenage selves all flustered. Who was I kidding? I was equally as flustered by it now.

The night was starting to fall, a blanket of violet velvet hovering over the pinky-orange glow on the horizon, and the three of us screamed out "I've Had the Time of my Life" as though our lives depended on it as we ordered an Uber to take us into town to meet everyone who was joining us for Tawna's third and final hen do.

CHAPTER 30

Eve, Tawna and Tawna's mum and I were preparing for the wedding rehearsal.

"You look lovely with your hair up like that, Tawna," Mrs Maguire said. "Maybe you girls should have gone for up-dos for the wedding."

"The whole point is it's laid back and natural, not Hollywood glamour, Mum," Tawna replied, while sharing her annoyance with Eve and I via a silent glare. "It's too late now anyway. The wedding's in less than twenty-four hours."

"Keep still," I instructed. "Unless you're going for the wonky eyeliner look."

Tawna sat up straighter and didn't budge an inch. Even when her mum made more little jibes about her choices, Tawna was nothing but sweetness.

The wedding had come around quickly. In twenty-four hours, Tawna wouldn't be Miss Maguire anymore, she'd be a married woman. And in just one hour's time we'd be at the rehearsal.

The concept of a rehearsal amused me, but when I'd made

light of it to Tawna she'd pointed out there were a lot of people involved and plenty that could go wrong.

"The ushers need to know their role, and Johnny's brother needs telling where to go to do the readings. Paul will need showing ten times, you know what he's like. You and Eve have to be aware of when to take my flowers and help with my train. Summer hasn't even seen the church yet and I know she'll be excited. It's better that she gets it out of her system tonight rather than tomorrow."

Tawna had made a last-minute decision to ask Summer to be her flower girl. As Johnny's goddaughter, she'd love the chance to swan around in a princess dress for the day. I got a lump in my throat just thinking about it.

"I can't wait to see her again." I was less excited about seeing her father though. He'd still not replied to any of my messages, effectively ghosting me as Gina had Max.

"When we went dress shopping last weekend I was astonished by how grown up Summer is now, she's shot up again," Tawna said. "The chubbiness has completely gone from her cheeks. She's a real skinny-malinkey."

I stood back to admire my handiwork, Tawna's dramatic smoky-brown eyelids and bright red lips. The look was totally different to the one I'd be helping create for the wedding itself, but that was what she wanted.

"That'll do." I nodded.

"You're beautiful, Tawna," Eve said. "Really beautiful."

I handed Tawna a mirror and as she caught sight of her reflection she beamed with delight.

"Thanks, Soph. This is exactly the look I was aiming for."

"You're welcome." I smiled, as Tawna smoothed her index finger along her eyebrows. "It's good practice for tomorrow. I've never done wedding make-up before."

"It could be your next new career," she replied. "Sophie Drew, make-up artist."

"I don't think so." I laughed, although I was pleasantly surprised by how neat Tawna's make-up was. The eyeliner in particular. I usually found it hard enough doing my own, let alone someone else's.

"You know, I'm not sure about that shade of eyeshadow, Tawna." Frown lines appeared around Tawna's mum's eyes. "It's too dark. You look like you've been in a fight and the other person won."

"It's the fashion," Eve explained. "Smoky, sultry."

Mrs Maguire, who had always liked Eve, disagreed. "Just because it's fashionable doesn't mean it looks good. I remember the eighties. I thought I was the bee's knees with my back-combed bleached-white hair. Had delusions that Bananarama would want me to join them. When I go through the photos I can't believe how silly I looked."

"I'm sure you'll love Tawna's style tomorrow," I placated. "It's less showy and makes the most of her naturally beautiful features."

Tawna's mum softened. "She is beautiful, isn't she?"

Eve and I nodded, and Tawna looked pleased at the positive attention.

"She takes after me," Mrs Maguire added, without irony, before looking at the gold watch around her wrist. "Are we going then? We don't want to be late. There's no tradition of the bride being late for the rehearsal, is there?"

"I don't think so, Mum," Tawna said patiently, and I wondered how long it'd be before the two of them had a serious falling out. Rubbing each other up the wrong way was their speciality. There had been many times when Tawna's dad was alive that he'd had to act as referee between their spats. "We won't be late though. It's only a five-minute drive. We've got ages."

"You don't want Johnny thinking you're standing him up. He's a good catch. He might start having doubts if you don't turn up on time."

"That's hardly likely." Tawna chuckled, but the comment was still enough to make her move towards the door. "Johnny loves me. That's why he's marrying me tomorrow."

Tomorrow was going to be a big day. Bye-bye Tawna Maguire, hello Tawna Hamilton. Tomorrow, everything was going to change.

When Nadia was the first person I saw when we walked in, my heart sank. My gut reaction was to tell her to get out, that this was the wedding rehearsal for one of my oldest and best friends, but I didn't do that. Of course I didn't. What I actually did was smile as broadly as I possibly could and attempted to kill her with kindness.

"I didn't realise you'd be here." My voice sounded syrupy sweet. "It's good to see you."

"I had to be here, Summer's the flower girl." Nadia nodded in the direction of Summer and Darius, who were playing a complicated hand-clapping game. My body tensed at the sight of him. "Darius has enough on his mind with the best man duties so I booked us into a hotel for a couple of nights."

"How lovely. A few nights away is as good as a little holiday." The corners of my lips were tearing apart, I was smiling so hard.

"You're right, it's good to be away from it all. Newcastle wouldn't have been my first choice though, I'd have loved to have taken Summer to the seaside."

"There are some lovely beaches up here, but I guess you

don't need them. When you're in Devon you'll be able to spend as much time as you like at the beach."

Nadia's face contorted. "What do you mean?"

"Darius told me about how you and Summer might be moving to the coast."

Nadia recoiled. "What? Why would we be moving to the coast?"

"To be with Rob," I said. My mouth dried up, as did my courage, but I'd come so far that I kept going. "Darius said you'd only be willing to stay up north if he paid you."

"Rob's moving to Liverpool," she said, looking confused. "Me and Summer going down there was never on the cards. I wouldn't pull her out of school, not when she's happy and settled. Rob was always coming to Liverpool. He'll be away with work, obviously, but when he's got leave he'll spend it with us."

"Let me get this straight; you were never going to move?"

"Never." She looked so honest that I had to believe her.

"Darius told me you'd only stay in Liverpool if he gave you money. He asked me for a loan."

Nadia gasped at the revelation. "You didn't give it to him, did you?"

I nodded woefully, overcome by a sensation of nausea. "I gave him over a grand."

"I know the two of us haven't always seen eye to eye, but do you really think I'm vicious enough to take Summer to the other end of the country? Darius is her dad. I'd never tell him he couldn't see her."

"So why did Darius say that?"

"Because he's desperate for money, most likely. He's up to his eyeballs in debt, always has been. Surely you've noticed he's got no control over his spending, as soon as he gets money it's as though it's burning a hole in his pocket and it's gone. He barely pays his child maintenance, and he doesn't give Summer the full amount." Nadia scraped her hair back off her face, using her fingers as a comb. "I couldn't live like that, not knowing if we were going to have enough money in the bank to buy a loaf of bread at the end of the month, that's why I sent him packing in the first place. It was bad enough when it was just the two of us, but when Summer came along things had to change. She deserved more."

"He told me half his wage came to you for Summer," I mumbled. My mouth felt as though it was stuffed with cotton wool. Maybe my whole head was stuffed with cotton wool.

"Yeah, right," Nadia said drily. "He loves her, and I know that – it's the only reason I don't drag him through the courts to make him pay his fair share – but what he gives Summer would barely keep her in shoes let alone everything else."

Suddenly it all made sense, how there'd be times Darius would expect me to pay for things and other moments of extreme generosity. He'd spend until he had nothing, then get me to fund his lifestyle. How could I have been so stupid?

"I did try to warn you," she said, pity etched on her face. "The thing is, you were so taken with him there was no way you were ever going to believe me."

I thought back to our conversations, the ones where she'd told me to watch myself or to take care. I'd always thought her comments were deliberately patronising, but the truth was very different. She had been trying to teach me, pass on the lessons she'd learned from being with Darius.

"You thought I was a bitch, I know," she continued, "but I'm not a bad person. I've made my fair share of mistakes but I'm no worse than anyone else. And if you ever want to spend time with Summer, you can. She'd love that, she really misses you."

My heart burst. "I miss her too. Thank you, Nadia. And I'm sorry for believing Darius's lies."

"He knows how to pull strings to get what he wants," she said with a scowl. "I found that out the hard way."

"I can't wait to have it out with him." I was aware of my blood pumping around my body, my racing heart working overtime. "He must have thought he was so clever playing me like that."

"You'll have to wait. The rehearsal is about to start." Her teeth gleamed as she smiled, her pearly-whites shimmering as much as her coffee-tint lip gloss. "See you later, Sophie, yeah?"

"Yeah." I smiled, walking to where Eve and Tawna were waiting for me. I threw imaginary daggers at Darius, who looked decidedly uncomfortable after seeing me talking with Nadia. If looks could kill...

❧

"So-So!" Summer bundled into me at such a pace that I feared I might be bowled over like a bowling pin. A human strike. "I've got something to tell you." She cupped her mouth and, in the loudest whisper ever, said, "I've got a boyfriend at school."

I laughed. "Aren't you a bit young for that?"

"Lots of my class have boyfriends or girlfriends. Melody Jones kissed her boyfriend at the end of term disco. On the lips!"

"You're definitely too young to be kissing," I said seriously. "There's plenty of time for that when you're older."

"Are you going to get back together with Daddy?" The question came out of the blue and her face was so hopeful, so earnest, that part of me wished I could give her the answer she wanted to hear.

"No," I replied gently, reaching out and touching her arm. "I've got a new boyfriend now. He's called Max and he's really lovely."

"Can I meet him?"

"Of course you can. He'll be at the wedding tomorrow and I know he'd like to meet you too. He's heard all about you."

"What have you told him? Did you tell him I'm really clever? Because I got ten out of ten in every maths test last term," she said, proudly puffing out her chest. "I was the only person in the class to get them all right."

"Well done. And yes, I have told him you're clever. And that you're funny and kind and generous..."

"And really good at hula-hooping?"

"I don't know if I did tell him that, but I can. I'll make sure to mention it when I speak to him, in case there are any hula hoops at the wedding. Wouldn't want you to show him up."

"There won't be any hula hoops at the wedding!" Summer laughed, a loud belly laugh of complete joy and amusement.

"You never know. There might be."

"You're so silly, So-So," she said through her giggles, "but I love you."

"I love you too." I planted a kiss on top of her fine dark hair. "I love you too."

The rehearsal had all gone smoothly, with the "I will"s coming in the right places. Everyone left feeling clearer about the parts they had to play in proceedings, which was the whole purpose of it, after all.

I'd been determined not to cause a scene despite having to walk down the aisle alongside Darius. The fire in my belly following my conversation with Nadia hadn't subsided though, and it took a lot of effort not to erupt when I found myself directly opposite him when we sat down to eat. I was biding my time, waiting for the right moment.

As I studied him, his features seemed to have shifted, as

though he was a different person to the one he was when we were together. Whatever spark had once been between us was gone, stamped out for good, only the smouldering embers of our relationship left behind.

"You're looking good, Sophie." He slurped at his tomato and basil soup. It was annoying. "Have you lost weight?"

"No."

"Maybe it's your hair. It suits you longer."

"Thanks." My voice came out curt and clipped, especially annoyed that one of the reasons I'd not grown it before was because he had always said long hair was for slappers. When we were together I'd changed my image to fit with his ideals because I was petrified he'd leave me for a more glamorous model. It hadn't just been hair dyes and a wardrobe full of designer clothes I'd splashed the cash on either: I'd gone as far as having Botox because he'd suggested it might help me "look my best". Eve had been horrified when I'd told her I'd let someone pump my face full of poison to keep a man.

"Is everything all right between us, Sophie?"

"Don't push me," I spat, fighting to keep my voice low. "I know what you did. You asked me for money to fund your lifestyle and made out it was for Summer. What kind of sicko does that?"

He didn't try to deny it. He didn't even look ashamed. "You'd never have even considered it if I hadn't mentioned Summer," he said, glancing across the table to where his daughter was sitting next to Johnny.

"And making out that Nadia was bribing you, what the hell was all that about? She's not moving to Devon at all, she told me earlier that she would never move Summer away from her friends and her routine."

His jaw twitched. "My credit cards are constantly up to their limit. I've got a bank loan that I'm struggling to pay back and I owe money left, right and centre. I had to get Johnny the final payment for the stag do before we flew out to Vegas, I was desperate."

"My heart bleeds for you."

"I'm in a real mess, robbing Peter to pay Paul each month."

"If things are that bad, you need to get some professional help... counselling or financial advice."

"I can't do it," he said, resting his spoon on the cream tablecloth. The orange of the soup spread through the fibres like ink on blotting paper. "It's an addiction. As soon as there's money in my bank I see it as a licence to spend."

"Even more reason for you to get help." My voice was hard; still quiet, but firm. I'd pulled myself up by my bootstraps, he should be big enough to do the same. "Especially if it's making you callous enough to take advantage of people who cared for you. I bailed you out so many times, Darius. So many times. I got myself into debt, and I'm only just getting back on my feet. But I made a decision, I made changes, and finally my life's on track. You could sort yours too, if you wanted to."

"You're strong, Sophie. I'm not as strong as you. I don't think I'm brave enough to ask for help."

I almost laughed at that. Strong? Brave? They're not words I'd ever use to describe myself, and for Darius, who only ever cared about how I looked on his arm, to praise these personality traits was surreal to say the least. Image and other people's opinions had been his primary concerns in the past.

"It's your choice. Your life. You have to live it how you see fit, but I'm telling you, if I hear of you using Summer as a bargaining tool again, I'll kick you in the bollocks so hard your balls will fly out of your mouth." I glowered, determined to show I meant it. "Nadia's said I can see Summer whenever I want, and I will. She's a special little girl."

"She is, isn't she."

"She deserves better than a dad who won't face up to his problems, that's for sure," I replied harshly, removing my napkin from my lap and neatly placing it alongside my empty bowl. "You're a parent. You need to act like one."

The blood pumped through my veins as I strode to the bathroom. I wasn't strong, I wasn't brave. I was just a thirty-year-old woman trying to get her shit together.

I shut myself in a cubicle, grateful for the privacy.

The inane pan pipe music that was playing out seeped into my brain, soothing me until I was numb to Darius. I felt nothing for him, good or bad. The embers were no longer smoking. It was as though a bucket of water had drowned them out, then washed them away for good.

CHAPTER 31

Emotion swelled in my core as it hit me that Tawna really was getting married. With four hours to go until the ceremony we'd already got through half a box of tissues with all our blubbing.

I was glad Eve, Tawna and I had stayed together at the hotel for Tawna's last night as an unmarried woman. There had been much reminiscing, a few tears and plenty of sharing of our hopes for the future. It reminded me how lucky I was to have these women in my life.

We were at the hairdressers, sat in a row as we each had our hair curled and set, the sides loosely pinned up off our faces with delicate wisps framing our faces. Whenever I wore my hair that way at home I used one grip for each side, then complained when it worked its way free after ten minutes. The hairdresser used about ninety, ramming the pins so sharply that I began to wonder if they were piercing through my skull.

"Do you want a glass of champagne?" the young girl who washed our hair asked us. "Complimentary, seeing as it's such a special occasion."

Tawna adamantly shook her head. "No, thank you. I want to be able to remember every minute of this day, and if I've been drinking I won't. I'd love an orange juice though, if you have it?"

"I think this is the first time I've known you refuse champagne," Eve teased affectionately. "You've changed already and you're not even married yet."

"I'll have a drink or two later," Tawna said, "but I'm not going to go mad. I don't want to spend my wedding day with my head down the toilet."

"Especially not when your hair's looking as fabulous as this," the lady doing Tawna's hair said, carefully patting her hand against Tawna's newly-curled locks. "You're every inch the blushing bride, and now your hair's sorted you just need the dress and you'll be ready to walk down that aisle."

"Oh, now my tummy's doing loop-the-loops."

"It's normal to have nerves on your wedding day," the hairdresser assured her, as the young assistant returned, placing our drinks on the counter. "So long as you're not having second thoughts, nerves are a good thing."

"No second thoughts." Tawna twisted her head to examine her new style. "I couldn't hope to find a better man than Johnny."

"He *is* Mr Perfect," I confirmed. "Imagine a male model, with his own business, who loves his mum and you're on the right track."

"Sounds like quite the catch," the woman doing my hair said with a chuckle, before jabbing one final hairpin into my scalp with such force that I bit my tongue to suppress my yelp. "My Mike was like a model when we got married. He had a beautiful head of hair and a fantastic body. Now he's bald as a coot with a beer belly. Such a shame."

"That's what your future holds, Tawna." Eve twisted one of

her curls around her index finger. "Receding hairlines and expanding waistbands."

"I don't care," Tawna replied happily. "It's not just about looks, I'd love Johnny no matter what. I'm lucky to have him."

"You're a good match, and he's lucky to have you too," I said, then took a sip of my champagne. The bubbles tickled against the underside of my nose. "Does it feel weird to think you'll be Mrs Hamilton in a few hours?"

"It feels great." Tawna's face was radiant, as though sunbeams were shining out of her pores. "I can't wait to be married. Bring it on!"

"Bring it on," Eve echoed, holding up her champagne. The three of us chinked our glasses.

"To Tawna and Johnny," I added, before taking a swig. "May their day be unforgettable."

"Are you sure it's on straight?" Tawna asked, scrutinising the position of her tiara in the mirror.

"It's straight," I confirmed.

"You look beautiful, stop panicking," Eve added. "You're the most gorgeous bride I've ever seen."

Tawna blushed. The delicate pink flush against her peachy skin reminded me of how she looked back at school.

"It's time to leave, girls," Mrs Maguire said. "There's late and then there's late," she added pointedly.

Eve and I picked up our bouquets, hand-tied arrangements of lemon and peach and pink gerberas. It was like holding springtime in my hands.

"See you at the church," I said to Tawna, the emotion of the moment causing tears to prickle against the backs of my eyes.

"Don't cry," she instructed. "If you cry, I'll cry, and if I cry then I'll look like Alice Cooper, and no one wants that on their wedding day. At least, no sane person."

I took a deep breath to compose myself and Eve rubbed her palm in calming clockwork circles against my back.

"You're supposed to be looking after me, not making me emotional," Tawna scolded, but there was a tenderness in her face.

"I'm going, I'm going." I turned away before she caught sight of the teardrops welling in my eyes.

A suited and booted man who could have doubled as the fat controller in the Thomas the Tank Engine books ushered Eve and me into the vintage car that was taking us to the church, and only when we were safely in the back of the vehicle and out of Tawna's view did the pair of us allow the tears to freely flow, tears of happiness for the friend we'd known almost our whole lives who was about to start her most exciting chapter yet.

"You look stunning." Max eyed me appreciatively. "Honestly, I think you might outshine the bride."

"Don't let Tawna hear you say that when she arrives," I said, my voice hushed. "She's the main attraction today, and rightly so. She's been dreaming of her wedding day her whole life. When we were younger she used to say she wanted an enormous wedding with a princess dress, a horse and carriage, the works. I think she'd seen Cinderella one too many times."

"This is nice though," Max said, gazing up at the church spire. "Nothing beats a traditional wedding. Except a good party, maybe."

"Tawna and Johnny have that covered. Parties are their forte. I can't wait to take off these uncomfortable heels and dance the night away."

"Save one of the smoochy slow dances for me." He winked.

"I will."

Johnny's brother, Paul, interrupted, ushering everyone through the ornate doorway to take their seats ready for the service. It was reassuring to see he was taking his duties seriously.

Just me, Eve and Summer remained in the churchyard as the vintage Bentley carrying Tawna and her mum pulled up. A chauffeur dressed in the same formalwear as the driver who'd brought Eve and me to the church opened the car door for Mrs Maguire before moving to the other side of the car to unlock the door so Tawna could take her last steps as a single woman.

Eve and I hurried to her side to ensure the large skirt of her dress didn't get dirty. The ground was dry after a rain-free week, but the stone paving slabs leading to the church were dusty.

The photographer clicked away; the sound of the camera shutter loud against the peaceful surroundings.

"Are you ready?" I asked.

"I'm ready," Tawna replied but, as I looped my arm through hers, her arm trembled against mine.

"Do you want to take a moment?" Eve asked. "Compose yourself before you go in?"

Tawna shook her head defiantly. "No. What I want is to get in there and marry Johnny." She smiled. "I've waited so long for this moment, and I don't want to wait any longer."

The heels of my shoes sank into the carpet in the church vestibule, and I patted my friend's arm before standing aside.

"Enjoy every second," I whispered, the words melting into the flecks of dust which speckled the air as the organist played the opening bars of "Air on the G String".

Summer led the way down the aisle, leaving a trail of fresh rose petals in shades of pink in her wake.

When she reached the altar, Tawna and her mum made

their way down the aisle, Eve and I checking the train of Tawna's dress was neatly splayed out behind her before following on. The walk seemed excruciatingly slow, but I savoured the moment. It wasn't every day someone I loved got married.

Familiar faces made up the congregation and I smiled as I walked past the pews, the bunches of flowers tied to the end of each row perfectly matching those Eve and I were carrying. Everyone admired the bride and I noticed Eve's mum, sat alongside my parents, dabbing her eyes with a tissue. I wondered how much of this she understood. Either way, it was lovely that she'd been able to make it, and I was touched when my mum put a comforting arm around her quivering shoulders.

Johnny and Darius waited next to the vicar, resplendent in slate-grey suits and ties the same pale pink shade as the dresses Eve and I were wearing.

The sun streamed in through the stained-glass window, the colours turning and twisting like a kaleidoscope, as the vicar welcomed the guests.

I drank in the moment as the first hymn, "All Things Bright and Beautiful", sounded out. Johnny's loving expression was so touching, so tender, as he took in his bride. Eve's hands were wrapped around both her bouquet and Tawna's, as if to let them go would be a bad omen. Darius stared intently at the order of service, mumbling the words to the famous hymn, and Tawna's mum was on the verge of tears. It must have brought back memories of her own wedding day too, and of Tawna's dad. For all her tough exterior, she had to be particularly aware of her husband's absence on a day centred around love. Tawna had always been a daddy's girl, and he must have been in her thoughts as she'd exited the car – I wondered if that was what had made her wobbly. It was only natural that she'd wish he were here to share her happy day.

Despite my determination to take it all in, the service slipped away from me. The walk down the aisle may have been slow, but the ceremony flew by. The vicar spoke about the sanctity of marriage and Paul read that reading from Corinthians about love that's read out at every wedding. Another hymn followed, one I didn't know and that, judging by how everyone mumbled along Darius-style, other people seemed less familiar with too.

And then it was time for the vows, Johnny and Tawna looking deep into each other's eyes as though the rest of us had evaporated and they were the only two people in the place. As Johnny slid the wedding band onto the third finger of Tawna's left hand, her eyes glistened as brightly as the whopper of a diamond in her engagement ring. They looked so full of hope and as they signed their names on the register I sent the pair of them telepathic messages of support. *I will be there for you both*, I thought. *If you ever need a friend, come to me.*

The ceremony drew to a close with a harpist playing an angelic melodious tune. I was partnered with Darius as we filed down the aisle two by two, like animals heading into the ark, as we exited the church, but I kept my distance. Even on a day of love and celebration I couldn't quite bring myself to forgive his lies.

We formed a guard of honour ready to shower confetti over the new Mr and Mrs Hamilton, Summer jumping up and down excitedly next to me as she clutched a cone of deep-pink dried rose petals. As Tawna and Johnny stepped squinting into the sunshine, petals rained down on them. My friend clutched her new husband's arm, and I didn't think I'd ever seen such a wonderful advert for love before. They were besotted with each other, the bond between them so obvious and strong. By the time they passed me, petals were tangled in Tawna's hair so she looked like a gorgeous flower fairy.

"Happy wedding day!" Summer shouted, throwing a handful of petals.

Johnny held out his hand for a high five, Summer beaming as her godfather's hand connected with hers.

"That was lovely, wasn't it?" Max said.

"It was beautiful," I agreed, as the photographer instructed the guests to congregate in front of the church for one of the few structured photographs – a shot of everyone together surrounding Johnny and Tawna.

"Everybody say cheese," the photographer barked. We did as we were told.

The flash of the camera dazzled me, stars flickering in front of my eyes. I tried to blink it away but a wave of nausea washed over me. One of my legs buckled, and I was glad I was holding on to Max.

"Sophie? Are you okay?"

"I don't feel so good," I admitted, deliberately trying to keep my tones hushed. "Can I keep hold of you?"

Max put a supportive arm around my waist which made me feel more stable. "You look pale. Do you feel sick?"

"I feel a bit dizzy, that's all. It's nothing."

"Maybe you'll feel better when you've eaten. I've been thinking about that slow dance you promised me all service."

That made me smile. "I'll be fine. Probably just all the excitement."

"Well, I'm right by your side."

"Nurse Oakley," I joked. "And I know all about your bedside manner."

"I have a very good bedside manner, thank you very much. Whenever you've had too much to drink I'm on hand with fluids. And when you had that toothache I was ever so patient."

"You were. And I was a real misery. I've never known pain like it. It felt as though my whole jaw was on fire."

"You did mention it, once or twice." He laughed. "But

seriously, if you're not feeling good, let me know. I don't want you keeling over."

"I'll be fine."

An old-fashioned double-decker bus ferried us to the reception venue, Tawna's great-aunt reminiscing about how her dad used to drive the exact same buses. They wouldn't have had the dulcet tones of Ed Sheeran's "Thinking Out Loud" playing on repeat though.

The twisty country roads bended and waned, and I peered out of the window at the barren fields to try to distract myself from the pressure that was building in my temples. Max's hand, firmly placed on mine, reassured me.

I hoped Max was right and that food would sort me out. I'd not eaten all day, no wonder I was tired and emotional. A wedge of wedding cake with a thick layer of royal icing would provide me with a much-needed sugar rush. If only the cake cutting was the first thing that would happen when we got to the venue rather than the welcome line and obligatory canapes.

The bus pulled up outside the venue, a typical country house that belonged in a Jane Austen adaptation. The trees were dressed in a thousand shades of green, the flowerbeds a multicoloured blast. The scenery was, quite simply, beautiful.

"You're sure you're all right to stand?" Max checked, before we disembarked.

"Stop fussing," I said, but I was grateful his hand stayed firmly pressed against the small of my back.

A waiter with a tray of champagne-filled flutes greeted us, and I took one to be polite although I wasn't sure alcohol was a good idea when I wasn't feeling at my sparkling best.

Max, picking up on my discomfort, guided me to a table in the wonderfully ornate entrance lobby. The walls were a bright-red that would look hideous in a smaller room but managed to look majestic when contrasted with the dark-wood furniture and golden trimmings. It had an old-fashioned elegance.

"Sit down," he said, helping me onto a regency-striped chair. "Before you fall down."

"I'm not going to fall," I said, but as I lowered myself a wooziness hit. My vision was warped, a darkness closing in around me, and as I slid off the seat and to the floor, my hand sliding along the plush carpet and burning with the friction, I wondered if this was how it felt to faint.

And it was, because the next thing I knew everything was blindingly bright and people crowded around me, propping me up with silky gold cushions like I was royalty.

"Sophie? My name's June, and I'm the registered first aider on the premises. That was quite a fall you had. Does anywhere hurt?"

Nothing hurt, I just felt like a fool. "No, I'm fine. My head's throbbing though."

"She suffers from migraines," Max explained.

"Have some water." June offered me a plastic cup. "Sip at it though, in case it makes you feel sick."

I tentatively drank, as everyone watched on.

"That's the way," June encouraged. "I've sent someone to get you a biscuit too. Nothing exciting, just a plain one, but it'll give you a bit of energy."

"Thanks."

People stopped nebbing once they knew I wasn't in a critical condition, and soon just Max and June were alongside me.

"Did it come on quickly?" June asked.

"I've been a bit dizzy but I put it down to rushing about. I'm the bridesmaid," I explained. "This is my best friend's wedding."

I could see Tawna and Johnny standing in a welcome line, hugging people as they filed through for the sit-down meal.

"That's probably it," June agreed. "When I saw you go down

like that it brought back all kinds of memories. When I was pregnant with my youngest I fainted three times in a week. I didn't have a clue why I kept passing out. It was only when I went to the doctors and she asked if I could be pregnant that I realised," she chortled.

A look of panic flashed across Max's face.

"It's just a migraine," I blurted. That said, my unpredictable cycles were never easy to track. It was a pain never knowing when my period would arrive, but my hormones affected my migraines so I'd probably come on over the next few days. I'd half expected to be in full flow for the wedding, but nothing had come to fruition, thankfully.

"You don't need my whole family history," June clucked as she headed back to the reception desk, "but don't you go overdoing it. Stay sat there for a bit longer, and get your husband to help you when you go through to the main hall."

Neither of us corrected her.

"You scared me half to death there, Soph. You went down like a ton of bricks."

"I'm sorry." He did look like I'd given him a fright.

"I'm just glad you didn't hurt yourself when you fell. Your head came dangerously close to the edge of the table. You still look pale too. Do you want me to fetch you something to eat? Find the biscuits June was talking about?"

I pulled myself up, using the chair to help me, even though spots were floating in front of my eyes. "I want to go and join everyone else. I can't miss today, not after all the planning."

After an unsteady walk, Max pushed the door to the impressive hall open, the tinkle of Darius striking a fork against a glass welcoming us.

"Food will be served in five minutes," he announced. "And speeches will follow after the meal. But let's start as we mean to go on by raising a toast, to the new Mr and Mrs Hamilton, and to the future."

"To Mr and Mrs Hamilton, and to the future," everyone echoed.

I raised my glassless hand into the air. The future.

CHAPTER 32

The migraine I'd been fighting on Tawna's wedding day hung around, dizziness not only making me feel as though my head was split in two but also affecting my appetite. I couldn't keep anything down, not even water.

I spent five days in bed, my mum and Max looking after me in shifts, while I complained the room was too bright despite the curtains being permanently drawn.

Max had gone above and beyond, ensuring I had hot water bottles, ice packs and whatever else I demanded in my poorly diva state. He'd driven to the supermarket at eleven at night to fetch me lollies to suck in a bid to keep me hydrated, and literally mopped my fevered brow. He was everything an ill girlfriend would wish for in her boyfriend, which is why when he'd told me he "needed to talk" I'd been baffled as to what was on his mind.

It transpired that after the wedding reception (which I'd been forced to leave early, my willingness to be the last woman standing beaten by the worst migraine of my life) Chris had gone to a casino with a group of people, and it had been Darius leading the way. Apparently he'd been throwing chips around with abandon, and when his lucky black 13 had come up trumps on the roulette wheel, not just the once, but twice, he'd been flashing the cash, insisting on buying drinks for the whole party. Chris said that hadn't put even the slightest dent in his winnings. Put simply, Darius wasn't short of money at present, but paying me back what he owed me wasn't at the top of his agenda.

"He's never going to change," Max said. "You'll never see that money again."

"Probably not," I agreed. "But I had to give it him. What if he hadn't been lying about Nadia bribing him? She might have taken Summer to the other end of the country. He's not a good man, but he's a good dad to her, mostly. I didn't want to let her down."

"You didn't let her down," Max replied fiercely, without so much as a flicker of his usually jokey, smiley expression. "There's only one person who's done that, and that's Darius."

"We'll have to go and visit her in Liverpool one weekend when I'm better. She's the closest I've got to a daughter."

"I'll need to practise my hula-hooping." At the wedding Summer had taken great delight in telling Max exactly how long she could keep a hoop spinning for, challenging him to a duel next time they were together.

"You really want to come?"

"I'd like to. She's a great kid."

We were giggling about her enthusiastic storytelling when my phone rang. I answered with trepidation. "Nick? Is everything all right?"

I held my breath. Chantel was thirty-three weeks pregnant, and still under the watchful eye of the hospital consultants who'd told her to prepare for an early delivery. They'd felt the smaller twin would have a better chance out of the womb than in and a planned C-section had been scheduled.

"They're here," he said, through sobs of happiness. "My girls are here safe and sound."

"Oh, Nick, that's wonderful!" I said, choking back my own tears.

"Alicia and Imogen. They're so beautiful, Soph."

"And they're doing okay? And Chantel?"

"Chantel was amazing. She was so calm, even the nurses commented on how relaxed she was. And the girls are doing really well. Imogen's tiny, as expected, and they're both on the neonatal intensive care ward, but they're little fighters, even the doctors say so. I can't wait for you to meet them. You'll adore them."

"I already do."

"Anyway, I'd better go. I've got to ring Anna and Jakob to tell them the news."

"They'll be over the moon. Congratulations, Dad of Three."

"Congratulations to you too, Auntie of Three."

My smile was enormous as I shared the news with Max, my heart surging with love for the new additions to my family.

It was only when Max spooned me as we were drifting off to sleep that I realised Nick had called me before he'd called Anna. That gave me such a glow of contentment that if Max had told me I was shining luminous, I wouldn't have been surprised. It was the ultimate seal of approval from my brother.

NOVEMBER

CHAPTER 33

If March comes in like a lion and goes out like a lamb, November must be the reverse. The dip in temperature was sudden and unwelcome, a bluster of snow flurries a reminder that winter had well and truly arrived.

Most people had been grumbling about the bitter winds and frosty mornings, but I embraced the new season with a creative gusto. I'd felt rotten for so much of the autumn, a tiredness seeping through my bones that I'd put down to the change of seasons and being wiped out after recovering from the migraine from hell. It was good to feel stronger as the year came to a close, but I was starting to suspect that my symptoms hadn't just been a result of the migraine, and I wasn't yet ready to face up to what that might mean.

I'd got into the habit of coming home from work and treating myself to a hot chocolate, lighting a candle (one of my latest projects) and settling myself down to some serious crafting. Most nights Max would keep me company, often cooking up a storm in my kitchen (with Scrat Cat for company) because I'd discovered Max was a surprisingly adventurous cook. I probably wouldn't eat at all if it wasn't for him making me taste his flavoursome curries and spicy soups, because having plenty of stock for the forthcoming Christmas fayres was my priority.

Our evenings were very hygge, spending time enjoying our own hobbies before finally curling up together on the settee, Max's arm draped around my shoulder and a shared blanket wrapped around our legs. Our evenings were productive but never stressful, and although we were busy, the pace of life never got to be too much to bear.

We made time to enjoy the company of our families, going for meals at the Oakleys' each Sunday and visiting Mum and Dad, and Nick, Chantel, Noah and the twins, who were home after a six-week stint in hospital. We'd even been to Liverpool for a weekend to see Nadia and Summer, where we'd met Rob for the first time. I could see why Darius's ego would be threatened by him. He was very like my ex in looks, but with a naturally generous heart.

Everyone had warmed to Max immediately which mattered to me more than I'd realised.

With just three days left in November I was setting up my first ever craft stall in a draughty community centre.

"It looks great," Max assured me, as I moved the stock around for the hundred-millionth time. "Stop panicking."

"I can't help it. What if no one buys anything? I might have made all this for nothing."

"People will buy them, believe me. You sold all those candles online, didn't you? And that Christmas bunting. I'm sure there will be plenty of customers, and anything you don't sell today you can sell at another event. That's the great thing about it. Imagine if you were a baker." He nodded discreetly in the direction of a couple setting out trays of pastel-topped cupcakes. "They can't just shove any unsold buns in a box for another day."

"They probably eat them." I laughed, thinking it wouldn't be much of a hardship having to eat tons of cupcakes. They looked delicious.

"Maybe you should start selling cakes after all," Max joked.

"You're the one who's handy in the kitchen," I reminded him. "If anyone's going to be selling cupcakes it'll be you."

"I'll stick to buying us some, support other small businesses. Any preference on a flavour?"

"Carrot cake?" I screwed my nose up hopefully. "Or just good old vanilla."

"I'll see what I can do." He smiled, making his way towards the cake stall. The couple beamed in delight at their first customer of the day, as I straightened a pile of business cards. I'd had them printed especially for the occasion, and although I felt a bit like an imposter for having them, I was pleased with how they'd turned out. If they brought custom my way they'd be well worth the money I'd spent on them. Speculate to accumulate, and all that.

My most recent credit card statement had shown huge improvements, and it was cheering to see my efforts paying off. They'd even lowered the minimum demands, which suggested I was no longer one of their worst cases.

The money I'd made from crafting had been saved in a separate account ready for when it was time to file my tax return, but with overtime hours at the office and some hardcore eBaying, my debts no longer scared me shitless. The amount I owed had halved within the past eight months thanks predominantly to my selling sprees (my clothes acting as an investment of sorts). As my thirty-first birthday approached I was feeling confident about the future.

"We'll be opening up to the public in five minutes," called the efficient gent with a swirling grey moustache who was organising the event. "If you want to go to the loo or grab a cup of tea, now's your chance."

"Do you want a drink?" Max asked, placing a cake iced with yellow frosting and a small purple flower on top of it in front of me. "I can go and get you one?"

"No," I replied quickly. "Stay here with me for a bit, just until the doors open. I'm getting nervous now."

"Stop it," he said, kindly but firmly gripping my wrists as he looked me in the eye. "I've seen what other people are selling here and it's all right, but your stuff blows it out of the water. Believe in yourself, Sophie. You can do this, because I believe in you."

"I know you do, and I'm grateful, but–"

"Ssh," he said, placing his index finger against my lip. "No buts. You've got this, Sophie Drew. Do you hear me? You've got this."

And as the doors swung open, the chatter of potential customers filling every corner of the large hall, I started to believe him.

CHAPTER 34

"Hector! Hector!"

I battled to stifle a smile as Andrea beckoned her husband. Max's dad was carefully carrying a cardboard box filled with cakes bought for the next day's family get-together. It was heartening to see him looking good and moving, albeit slowly, without his stick. "Look at how talented Sophie is. Aren't these beautiful?" she said, fingering at a beaded bracelet that was a particular favourite of mine.

Hector nodded politely. "Very nice."

"I think Mum's hinting, Dad." Max laughed. "Christmas will be here before you know it."

"Oh, don't." Andrea pulled a face. "I've got so much to do between now and then. I don't want to think about it. I've got a list that I'm working my way down to make sure I don't forget any of the essentials. First thing tomorrow I need to call the butchers to order a bird, then I must make a start on the cards going overseas."

"It's not last posting day yet, is it?" I asked, flustered. "We've got family friends in Adelaide to send to."

"Mum always likes to make sure she gives it plenty of time,"

Max explained. "There's probably another fortnight before the actual final day."

Andrea threw Max the death stare, but it wasn't long before her face cracked into her usual warm affectionate smile.

"There's nothing wrong with being organised," she pointed out. "Speaking of which, I wondered if you were planning to come around at all on Christmas Day, Sophie? I wouldn't ask, but I'm going to do the food shopping online this year except for the meat and the fresh veg."

Hector raised his eyebrows. "She means she's ordering the booze online."

"Not just the booze, Hector," Andrea chided fondly before looking at me. "There's all the nibbles as well. Cheese and biscuits, chocolates... He seems to think they magically appear in the cupboard ready for when he's flaked out on the sofa in front of the big Christmas film on BBC One."

"I hadn't thought about Christmas Day," I admitted. I'd been so consumed with planning for fayres that the day itself hadn't even crossed my mind. "I'd love to see you at some point, but I'll be at my mum and dad's in the morning with my brother and his wife and their children."

"Well, you'll be very welcome to join us in the evening if you want drinks and board games," Andrea offered. "Although you know my boys are very competitive, so it sometimes gets a bit out of hand."

"It's you who causes the arguments with your cheating," Max said lightly.

"Nonsense!" But Andrea discreetly winked at me.

"That sounds lovely. Can I let you know for sure when I've spoken to my mum about her plans? She's coming here later, I think."

"Absolutely," Andrea nodded, "and if you can't come

Christmas Day then you're welcome Boxing Day or whenever else suits. I know Max wants you around."

"Thanks, Mum." Max rolled his eyes. "I'm sure if Sophie wants to come then she will."

"I wasn't meddling," she insisted, picking up the bracelet and folding it into his palm. "I just wanted to make sure Sophie knew you'd want her there."

"I'm sure she knows that already, Mum."

"Now, seeing as your dad isn't taking the hint, you can buy this bracelet for me for Christmas," she said to Max, nodding to the bracelet in his hand. "It'll go perfectly with the dress I'm wearing on Christmas Day. It's exactly the same shade of green."

We were interrupted by the squawky cries of two tiny babies – my nieces – who were strapped into a double pram and wrapped in matching crocheted blankets made by their loving Auntie Sophie. Nick, pushing the girls, was with Chantel, Noah and my parents.

"Hi!"

I wrapped my brother up in a hug, then my sister-in-law before ruffling Noah's hair as he started touching my wares.

"How's business?" Dad asked, bending down and kissing my cheek, after I'd introduced him to Max's family.

"She's already sold a bracelet to me because Mum was dropping endless hints," Max said.

"And I've sold a few felted Christmas decorations," I said proudly. "Hopefully it'll get busier as the day goes on."

"It will," Mum said, picking up a knitted Santa that Noah had taken a shine to. "I'm going to buy this Father Christmas toy for Noah, for starters," she said, rifling through her purse for change. "I'm really proud of you, you know."

I nodded. I knew.

❧

The fayre had been brilliant; if not a roaring success, far more than the whimper I'd anticipated. I'd sold a fair few items and my confidence had been bolstered by so many familiar faces coming to show their support. Besides mine and Max's families, Kath (who'd looked at the eye masks I'd made and actually vocalised that she thought they'd make good blindfolds for use in the bedroom) and Norma came by. She'd been looking for a present for Joel and Finley. When I explained the similarities between the rainbow I'd embroidered onto a pair of oven gloves and the Pride flag, she'd snapped them up, never mind that the boys ate out at least five times a week and rarely made anything from scratch.

As Max unlocked the front door of my house, I was unpacking the boxes of remaining stock from the back of Max's Mini, taking extra care to transport the most fragile objects even though I'd used layers of protective bubble wrap, when my phone rang.

"Aren't you going to get it?"

"Nah," I said to Max, who was carrying a black bag full of cushions I'd made and the cashbox containing my takings. First glances had suggested I'd made a decent profit and I was chuffed that it wasn't only our families who'd bought my makes. "If it's important then they'll leave a message or call back."

The ringing stopped, before immediately starting up again.

"What were you saying?" Max laughed.

"I'd better answer it." I sighed, even though it was a withheld number.

An unfamiliar voice started talking from the other end of the phone, speaking in such a chirpy tone that I was convinced the woman was trying to sell me something. I tried to interject, but she kept on talking at me, until I eventually gave up and listened.

"So," she said, "I'm delighted to announce that you're our

winner! We can't wait to make a public announcement so we were wanting to arrange a photoshoot with you. We've a big cheque with your name on it, literally."

My mind was racing, my heart was racing, but my body froze as the news sank in. Max looked at me with confusion, mouthing "Who is it?" Based on my lack of words he probably thought it was bad news.

"And you're sure it's me? There's not been a mistake?"

"Your name was selected at random and there's definitely no mistake," she confirmed. "Like I say, we just need you to come to the office to pick up the cheque and have some photos for advertising purposes, as you agreed to when you entered the competition."

"How much was the prize again?" I asked, barely able to breathe let alone speak. My chest felt as though a vice was crushing it.

"Five thousand pounds." She said it so plainly, as though it was nothing, when that would pay off the remainder of my debts and still leave me with a small amount to go in my Christmas fund.

"Thank you," I managed, my head swimming as she told me where I needed to go and when.

"What was all that about?" Max asked after I hung up.

"You're never going to believe this," I said, sinking to sit on the bottom step of the stairs. My legs were like two strands of cooked spaghetti and I didn't trust them to hold my weight. "Do you remember when we were at the hospital fayre back in the summer and we gave our email addresses for that mailing list?"

Max nodded vaguely, probably just humouring me, but I continued anyway.

"There was a prize. And I've won."

Max's eyes widened. "No way. That's fantastic!"

"It's a lot of money. Five thousand pounds."

"Wow." Max sat down. I wondered if his legs were as wobbly as my own. "You hear about people winning these kind of prizes but never think it will actually happen to someone you know."

"I know. I'm going to their offices tomorrow to have photos taken with the chief exec and one of those ridiculous giant cheques they give to lottery winners."

Max shook his head. "That's crazy."

"Tell me about it." My hands were trembling. "It's enough to clear all my debts."

"That's incredible. It's a fresh start for you. A new beginning."

He wrapped me into a hug and I gladly leant into him.

"It feels a bit like cheating my way out of debt." Voicing what I'd been feeling since the phone call was harder than I expected. It sounded kind of stupid saying it out loud. "It's not a Disney movie. I don't deserve a fairy godmother turning up and offering me the solution to all my problems out of the blue."

"You've slogged your guts out with work and craft to pay those debts off. You've sold your possessions. You deserve this as much as anyone."

Max's words were a balm and I clung to him tightly.

"Things like this don't happen to people like me," I said as a tear rolled down my cheek.

Max used the pad of his thumb to wipe it away. "This time they do."

His words only made me cry even more desperately.

It took more than a few deep breaths for me to prepare myself to share my other news.

"There's something else too," I started, my voice wobbling. "You know how my periods are irregular?"

Max nodded slowly.

"I've not had one since the start of August. At first I put it down to the stress of being ill, but now I'm not sure."

"Do you think you could be...?" Max's voice trailed off, as though scared to tempt fate.

"I don't know. I've never gone this long without one before."

"Have you got a test?" he asked quietly. "Or do you need me to go and buy one?"

Suddenly I was viewing Max differently, not just as a lover, or a partner, but as a dad. His strengths – his kindness, his gentle nature, his good humour – would make him a lovely father.

"There's one in the bathroom cabinet," I said.

We climbed the stairs without words, Max waiting outside the bathroom as I forced myself to wee on the absorbent end of the pregnancy test, trying desperately not to sprinkle on the plastic handle and all-important window.

I flushed and washed my hands as normal before joining Max on the landing to find out the result together, nervous bubbles popping in my stomach.

"Ready?" I asked, my whole body trembling.

"Ready," he confirmed.

I turned the test over in my hand, gasping as I read the one word that stared back at us – pregnant.

Max threw his arms around me as I stood, dazed.

This was it. A fresh start. A new beginning.

To be continued...
Sophie Drew will return

ACKNOWLEDGEMENTS

This book has been a long time in the making which means there are a lot of people who deserve a mention – getting a book to publication really is a team effort!

Without further ado I'd like to thank:

Everyone at Bloodhound Books for believing in Sophie's story, with special thanks to Betsy Reavley, Tara Lyons and Morgen Bailey for your input.

Julia Silk – this book wouldn't exist without you.

Philippa Ashley, Mary Jayne Baker, Brigid Coady, Miranda Dickinson, Josie Silver, Lynsey James, Keris Stainton, and all the Wordcount Warriors, A***-Kickers and Beta Buddies for your continued support and friendship.

Nicola, Jade and Caroline for answering my questions about Newcastle.

My friends and family, who've put up with me talking about this book for the past four years and haven't disowned me (yet).

And last, but by no means least, thank *you* for choosing to read *Nothing New for Sophie Drew*. It really does mean the world to me.

Katey Lovell, Sheffield, March 2021

www.ingramcontent.com/pod-product-compliance
Lightning Source LLC
Chambersburg PA
CBHW050804190726

48285CB00005B/1790